A Moveable Marfa

By C. E. Hunt

Copyright © 2020
All Rights Reserved

For Danita

1

When my cell phone buzzed, it was a pleasant surprise. I was hoping it was the new intern I'd given my number to at the office. She was from North Dakota but anxious to work in her academic specialty of anthropology for one of the republican senators. Good luck with that, I told her. The new intern, however, was also a lovely young woman. Anticipating the call, I was sitting on my usual corner barstool at Café Noir in Georgetown, DC, listening to some very relaxing Miles Davis, a specialty of the Georgetown establishment.

The moment I received that call is one of those moments I knew my mind would record all the senses—sight, smell, even the taste of the pale ale I was drinking. The entire setting would be preserved for a long time to come. Outside, the fall evening was cooling nicely. I could still visualize the trip over from the Hart Senate Office Building after taking the DC Metro to the Foggy Bottom Station. I'd heard the cicadas sing from the nearby trees as folks paraded by down the row of bars and restaurants. There was a generic murmur of chatter with an occasional laughing or loud remark. The candle lights on the tables both inside and outside were just starting to emit a warm glow. The glow illuminated a sweat droplet running down my pint. The aroma of charbroiled steaks cooking filled the air. That smell was probably making people hungry for dinner, like it most certainly did me.

It was the ideal evening in Georgetown. A great night to be alive.

Hedging my bets in case the intern didn't call or drop by, I was also waiting on an office mate to show up on this perfect Friday evening to have a few beers and purge the week from my memory. Off and on I was sneaking occasional glances at a tall brunette who from time to time gave me a fleeting but promising smile. She had a nice laugh. She kept slipping her feet from the black heels that clearly added to the shape of her legs.

The hum of my cell phone cut short one of my glances that was migrating towards a more lingering look. Had her shiny red lips almost evinced the trace of a flirtatious look at me? I imagined her smile was just for me.

"Steve...that you?"

"Hi mom."

"Steve, I've got some bad news, son. Your Uncle Clive passed away." So much for the legs, heels and red lips.

"Uncle Clive?"

"I'm afraid so."

"How is Aunt Beth taking it?"

"Oh Steve, your Aunt *Bess* passed on three years ago. That was her name, not Beth."

"Oh." That sounded sheepish. Too much time in DC, I guess. "Well mom, I'm sorry to hear that. Should I come down for the funeral?"

"Too late. They already went and buried him. Dad and I didn't even hear the news until they read the will. But, I got some big news, too. Seems he left you some money and his ranch in Marfa in West Texas. I think you remember it, don't you? Dad and I were shocked, but we're thrilled for you."

"What? No way! I haven't seen him in years. Last time I saw him was when I stayed with him and Aunt Bess for the summer. That was probably the summer before my senior year in high school. Damn, that's a long time."

"I guess...I dunno...you must'a made quite an impression those times you stayed with them. He also left you a couple a business outfits in Marfa. I'll send you the phone number for the lawyer that's handling the will and all."

"Wait! What about Clark and Amy?

"Uncle Clive disowned the both of them."

"What?"

"Clark got mixed up in drugs and Amy married a Mexican."

"Amy married a Mexican…so what?"

"Uncle Clive was a little…conservative."

"You mean racist?"

"Well sorta, maybe…but he did have some good points, you know. Dad would only see him occasionally, but he always thought Clive was a fine man and a good brother all in all. He fought in the war in Vietnam in the early years, just like Dad, you know."

"Yeah, okay Mom, thanks for the call. I'll reach out the lawyer and see what I'm supposed to do next. This is a big deal. I'll stop in Houston on the way to West Texas and visit with you and dad, too. Love you, Mom" I said as I rang off.

To my chagrin, the brunette flashed me a real smile as she left her table as I was wrapping up the call with mom. She put on some glasses and looked so smart and sexy. Well, I might have lost a new friend that evening, but mom's news was setting the stage for something even more adventurous, I realized. My young Texan ass was about to discover a whole new world. I no longer cared about the intern, the week I wanted to forget about or even the so-called excitement of DC. I didn't know it at the time, but I was done here!

2

"I think it would be perfect,"
"What about the train noise?"

About six weeks after mom's phone call in Georgetown, I found myself in Marfa at a very old and very dusty warehouse next to the railroad tracks talking to an attractive woman.

Everything had been pretty straightforward with the lawyer and Uncle Clive's will. Both Clive and the lawyer were meticulous in record-keeping and writing wills. They even knew how to minimize the effects of inheritance taxes and other legal glitches that aggravate the transfer of property. I was grateful for that!

"No big deal," my newfound Marfa business consultant said. "We'll have indigenous music in the background anyway. Customers won't even notice the trains with all the beautiful art and musical accompaniment. Perhaps we'll serve wine and hors d'oeuvres to help lighten the mood!"

"Indigenous music? Wine and hors d'oeuvres?"

Stacy put her fist on her slender hip and gave me the look I had discovered in the last few days that basically implied, "You really know nothing about the art world, do you?"

"What's indigenous music, Stacy? Wine and cheese blintzes, I understand."

"You know." She straightened up and adjusted her bra strap as she scanned the ceiling.

"You mean Native American, Mexican? What?"

"Yeah. Also, cheese blintzes wouldn't do here in Marfa. It would have to be something that combined salsa, chips, maybe chorizo, you know, more local stuff? Do you know nothing about West Texas either?"

She blew her lovely brown hair off her forehead, subtly shook her head once and twirled out the door. I was never sure what to make of Stacy and her philosophy about mixing business and art. She was my first real contact in Marfa, someone the lawyer recommended to help me orient to the business possibilities here. Stacy's initial feelings towards me seemed to be a blend of curious affection, tolerance, pity and mild annoyance. I, of course, had my own blend of feelings towards her—attraction, intrigue and bafflement laced with a trace of strained tolerance at times myself. Her behavior often suggested that she was a different species as well as gender.

As we walked outside, the sunlight was blindingly white through my squinting eyes. Marfa had the whitest sunlight I'd ever experienced. Stacy's bright neon yellow blouse made me squint even more. I'd finally located my sunglasses so I could think. The sunglasses were also important to see the cracked and uneven sidewalk in front of me; that would have to be replaced to avoid lawsuits, I thought. There was a lone mesquite tree in front of the building that added more shade than I expected in the early fall, but was welcome, nonetheless. There were only a few of these precious trees up and down the street.

"I'm so excited! This is perfect." She scanned the surrounding old buildings and I could tell she was trying to figure out how we should decorate the exterior of the old plaster building. It was vaguely shaped like a bell on the front facing the street—kind of like the Alamo. I had originally decided the faded writings on the front of the building had once announced it to be one of a variety of feed or general stores in a former live, maybe going back to the early 1900s.

"Are you sure? I mean...." It was too late. Stacy had already headed down the street—her swaying hips suggesting an air of great satisfaction with the "perfect discovery." Stacy was a formidable Texas woman to say the least.

Time to move on in my explorations of Marfa and find the next opportunity to invest my newfound wealth, I guess.

❖ ❖ ❖

The next few weeks were more about orienting to having money for the first time and thinking about opportunities that I never dreamed about before. Working as a congressional staffer in DC had essentially sucked out the life force, imagination and desire to accomplish much more than going to work every day and stopping off at the local pub to forget about what I'd had to do at work to keep a politician happy. It didn't start that way, of course, but the excitement of DC political life faded in months, not years.

In only a few weeks, Marfa had opened my eyes to what was possible in the open space of West Texas, unshackled from having to pretend to serve my country while massaging the ego of a career politician. I'd served in the Army and knew there were many ways to serve that didn't involve power trips. After only a week in Marfa, I also knew I could find new ways to serve right here, particularly now with some meaningful funds in the bank, businesses to run and workers to employ. I couldn't wait to learn what was next and to discover who I could be.

Thanks, Uncle Clive. You're my hero, even if I'd sort of forgotten all about you and my time in West Texas.

❖ ❖ ❖

In less than two months the warehouse was the Galería del Sol. Peruvian, Mexican and flamenco music streamed out the door and created a nice ambiance inside the gallery, that is when the trains weren't running, which of course was about thirty percent of the time. Even better, sometimes the vibrations from the trains didn't knock a single picture off the walls. Stacy was beaming. She kept saying something about "alignment" and "inner consciousness." I really didn't have a clue what she was talking about half the time. I mainly just enjoyed looking at her while she talked to me. Her energy rubbed off on me and even made me think about the ambiance that art, wine and "indigenous music" combined to produce. I didn't really feel that in the Hart Senate Office Building.

The gallery started off well. As near as I could tell, Stacy was doing a nice job of running it. That was good because I gradually had become more interested in the other things I'd inherited. Uncle Clive, as it turns out, was quite the businessman. He owned an 18,000-acre ranch ten miles out of Marfa, a defunct beer distributorship and several buildings in and around Marfa that now included the Galería del Sol. There was also a total of about six million dollars in several bank accounts, all of which came to me minus various but not onerous taxes.

I was still in a bit of shock. I had no clue that Uncle Clive thought so much of me. I did recall him telling me one sunset while bouncing around in his old rusty pickup truck on the ranch that I'm the only person in the world other than Pablo who ever really listened to him. I was the only real West Texan in the family, he used to say. That was curious since I was born and raised in Houston. I suppose it was more a state-of-mind thing, and I really did feel at home with Clive and West Texas.

My uncle was kind of a curmudgeon. I think he liked me so much because I'd laugh at his grouchiness. I guess I didn't know any better. I thought he was joking, and he'd kind of lighten up like he thought to himself to get off "his high horse." I remember one time we were at a corral on his place, and we were watching the local vet stick his hand inside a cow's backside to determine if she was pregnant, and he looked me in the eye and told me, "If the price a cattle drops one more penny, I'm gonna be scratching a po' man's ass a long time." I didn't' know the relationship between poking around a cow's behind and scratching another guy's ass, but it seemed really funny the way he drawled out the words. I busted out laughing not knowing he was serious, and he started laughing, too. For whatever reason, I had that effect on him.

Aside from Aunt Bess, the only other person I remember Uncle Clive being genuinely fond of was Pablo. Pablo was about my age and was Clive's housekeeper Teresa's son and my main playmate along with my cousins, Amy and Clark, while I visited. I remember how Clive seemed to get in a good mood around Pablo. I didn't always understand what they were talking about because they'd sometimes alternate between English and Spanish. Both languages were common on the ranch. People sometimes forget that folks have been speaking Spanish or Indian languages in these parts for more than 300 years. When they burst out laughing about something said in Spanish, I'd start laughing too, even though I didn't have a clue what they said. Clive and Pablo had a special chemistry for sure. That's why I was surprised when my uncle got mad about my cousin Amy marrying a Mexican American. I'd only seen Pablo for a few minutes when I first arrived in Marfa but was looking forward to getting caught up again soon.

3

I thought a long time about what I wanted to do with my inheritance. I'd initially thought I would come out to Marfa and dispose of everything. I figured I could probably walk away with about seven to eight million bucks, easy. Even being the poor investor I am, I figured I could live comfortably on about $250,000 a year in interest off modest investments and returns. Call it blessing or luck, I knew I was embarking upon a life I totally did not deserve, and I hoped to share some of this good fortune with the people I met and worked with. On the other hand, I might have more money now than a lot of people, but in America today, I'm not sure that six million in cash qualifies as that much money anymore.

Stacy kind of slowed down my plans, though. That is, Stacy and what came to be my little corner of Marfa and West Texas. My whole world was beginning to coalesce around a small town and all it had to offer. I was slowly learning why Clive and others like him lived here, and Stacy was becoming a bigger part of that discovery every day. This self-discovery thing seemed to be working out after all.

Though I hadn't a clue how Stacy felt about me, I had a pretty strong attraction to her. She was smart, yet free spirited, strangely spiritual yet often flighty. But she was pretty, a real West Texas lady and more real than any woman I'd met up to that time. She was originally from Austin but had moved to Marfa a few years before. She kind of bombed as an artist and then a writer but she never gave up. She finally figured out that her forte was recognizing art and getting the best out of a very quirky community of artists in the Trans-Pecos region. When she wasn't on one of her "prairie dog rescue missions" or "save the harelip whales" or "pro-hemp" campaigns, she was very effective in her business endeavors as an art agent and gallery manager.

She'd made Ms. Schultz, her old boss, a nice profit by running one of the few very successful galleries in Marfa—*La Libertad*. When I first met Stacy on the lawyer's recommendation, she was looking to move on. Ms. Schultz was quite stingy and extremely weird—even too weird for Stacy. When Ms. Schultz insisted that Stacy come over and make her spaghetti and trim her toenails, thankfully not at the same time, Stacy decided she'd had enough. She had a much better deal from me—half the profit and no toenail management duties.

I guess I should share how I met her. After the introductory call from Clive's lawyer, Stacy was standing just outside the Hotel Paisano the next evening, when I ran into her—barreled her over might be more accurate. Somehow, during the melee, I bruised her foot pretty badly. I insisted on taking her to get medical treatment, which is tricky in Marfa, especially on a Sunday evening. She asked if I could just get her home instead.

She lived in a tiny room above a stucco garage that looked to have been built in the Grover Cleveland administration—did they have cars then? Anyway, I helped her up her rickety staircase. The interior was about twelve by sixteen with a small bathroom added on the back. The interior was reddish orange with Mexican religious art scattered about. Three large windows made it seem less confined somehow. When we walked in, I smelled a strange incense, or was it pot? Unexpectedly, I ended up spending the night in her red chamber. We talked almost all night, while I pampered her with ice packs, iced tea, etc. Though I crushed her slender foot, I was at that time still kind of working towards dumping my Marfa assets and heading back to DC or Houston. Lord only knows why I thought I wanted to return to DC, and the big, busy lifestyle in today's Houston was only marginally more appealing.

I really had nothing to go back to in DC except a so-so paying job on the Hill working outrageous hours. I was probably working for the equivalent of about thirty-eight cents an hour staffing a senator on environmental, transportation and defense issues. She, the Senator, wasn't on any of those committees and didn't give a damn about any of those issues, so I was the only Senate legislative assistant on the Hill with that kind of hellacious portfolio. Most of my colleagues made more than what I was making to just staff one or two issue areas. It was a labor of love, as they say, since most janitors in the building made more than I did. The only highlight was that I had gotten her to do the right thing on a number of National Park bills, a pet issue of mine.

I also had an arrogant "girlfriend" that I am sure loathed me. She would only date me Mondays through Wednesdays. She said she didn't want to let her girlfriends down on the good clubbing nights. I was so downtrodden, exhausted and short of time that I put up with it just to get some female companionship. The two times I saw her out on the "clubbing nights," she wouldn't even wave. Both times, she called me about 3:00 am to apologize. At the time, I felt like a loser. My so-called girlfriend did have the best legs I have ever seen though, and I was happy for a while to be seen with her. She always said I was the "marrying kind," but she wasn't quite ready to settle down. She spoke with great confidence that we would make a great couple once she settled down a bit. I was never sure where she got the impression that I was interested in marriage, particularly to her, but I never could bring myself to point that out. I think I was actually a bit scared of her and what any future with a socialite might bring in DC.

Stacy helped me let go of those "great things" I had back in DC. She filled my head with big dreams of what I could do with Uncle Clive's assets. The galleries, an LGBTQ bed-and-breakfast, a new age ranch, help save a Peruvian brewery by starting to import some kind of beer she said was great that I had never heard of, and all that sort of "make-the-world-better" stuff she liked. She had so much energy and confidence that I started buying in.

Holding her pretty foot with the orange toenails and a dark blue bruise and the smell of her perfume may have influenced me as well. And no, I don't have a foot fetish, she just had pretty feet to go along with the rest of her pretty self. And besides, I at least knew women loved foot rubs.

Anyway, I left her apartment the next morning exhausted but invigorated about my new life in Marfa—plenty of sunshine, fresh air, no more DC Metro, no more traffic, no more asshole Senators, no more bitchy girlfriend. It was going to be new and exciting. Plus, I was finally discovering who I was.

◆ ◆ ◆

While Stacy ran the gallery, I focused on the beer importation opportunity. We had to shift gears on that one. The beer Stacy had in mind was from Paraguay-not Peru. It wasn't even what I or any other real Texan would consider beer. It was brewed with Yerba Mate, one of Stacy's favorite drinks that basically tastes like dirt. I really didn't think dirt-flavored beer would thrive here, but it didn't matter. The brewery had been destroyed by a clash between the government and a labor union. Clearly, the Paraguayan government agreed that dirt-flavored beer should be unlawful. It may have disappointed Stacy but would cheer Marfans and any other market I could find for our new creations.

No problem. We found a small brewery in Chihuahua, Mexico that was brewing an interesting beer that had yet to be imported in the United States. Chihuahua was an up-and-coming beer-making area, as Heineken Brewery's interest recently showed. Since it was kind of close, I was able to bring it in by rail through Presidio for about $3.50 a six pack, after duties. We could retail it for $7.50-$8.50 a six-pack in grocery stores where it could be competitive, and I could net $2.00 a six-pack if I could sell a boxcar load a month. At first, I did okay in the El Paso and Houston markets, but I couldn't give it away outside of those cities and Marfa. Stacy somehow convinced the art crowd in Marfa that it was socially proper to drink it since the people of Chihuahua are "so oppressed" by the Mexican government—at least that's what Stacy claimed.

In truth, the beer tasted more like a modern brew, sort of craft beer-like, but I think the baby-shit brown can and unusual label threw off some people. The brewery had been owned by a large company for a while by the name of "Bimbo." The large company had unloaded the brewery, but the owners liked the name and insisted on continuing to use it. Cerveza Bimbo was one thing but their crude efforts at translating the label resulted in the unfortunate moniker of "Bimbo Beer" in English. As soon as the label was redesigned to look more appealing in America and the name modified, my sales doubled in the surrounding area, so I was having a pretty good run with it.

Almost exactly during my first sigh of relief that maybe the beer thing was going to work, Stacy flaked out on me. When the Chihuahua brewery went on strike, there was unrest between the strikers and the Mexican government. For some reason, Stacy felt the need to demonstrate solidarity with the strikers by traveling to Chihuahua to protest. She took it quite personally and disappeared to Mexico for an undetermined time. It was the only time she truly bailed on me, but she picked a bad time to go south since my beer sales had also gone south just as she closed the gallery. I could go in and man the gallery floor a few days a week, but it was probably more of a chore than I was prepared for.

I could also have tried to run the Gallery full time, but I knew better given my temperament. Trying to hawk what passed for art in Marfa to well-heeled snobs from Dallas was not a good situation for me. My candidness would have killed sales and probably led to some kind of protest in front of the gallery or even lawsuits. I just kept it open when someone called specifically to make a viewing appointment.

Dealing with the stoppage in beer sales and shutting down the gallery wouldn't have been a financial problem except that I'd still only received a small portion of the cash from my inheritance and I'd taken out a short-term loan to fix up a small house I'd bought on Austin Street. Truth be known, I'd have been fine, but the thought of paying my team with no money coming in concerned me. I was still getting used to having some real money.

With Stacy's consultations, I'd started updating Uncle Clive's ranch house and I had no desire to live at what was becoming a "new age" ranch with a bunch of Stacy's bizarre acquaintances. I leased it to Feather, Light, Molina and Emerald for a year so they could engage in intergalactic research of some sort. They were willing to pay top dollar since they could see the Marfa Lights from the top of the hill behind the house. Light's dad was apparently loaded. Feather and Light ran off to Mexico with Stacy for a brief spell to also demonstrate "solidarity."

The main reason I hadn't received all the cash from the inheritance was because Uncle Clive's daughter, Amy, had sued to get her share of the inheritance. I have no idea where Amy found the resources to hire a reputable lawyer, particularly in such a small town. Clive's lawyer assured me in the beginning that the will would be upheld in any legal proceeding.

Unfortunately, the one thing the lawyer and Uncle Clive hadn't anticipated was the possibility of a family lawsuit. Amy probably hated me almost as much as my old girlfriend in DC. I had an extremely tense conversation with her upon my arrival in Marfa. She looked me up the day I arrived. I impetuously and unwisely offered to share a portion of the inheritance, to give her and her brother, Clark, each ten percent. Two days later, she cornered me as I came out of my hotel lobby.

"Twenty percent between the both of us? Twenty percent total? You cheap-ass bastard! You better triple that. You ain't got no right to all that money! You just a damn thief. That's right. You just a no-good thief. I hate you." Her eyes had a cat-like insane quality, but on the plus side, she was still the pretty little cousin that I used to play with when we were kids. I couldn't help but have a soft spot for her and her brother.

"I'm sorry you feel that…"

"Go to hell. Are you going to give me my thirty percent, and Clark his…or do I have to kick your ass?" She stormed away, giving me a temporary reprieve. I resolved to see what I could do for her and her brother when I met the lawyer the next day.

You can only imagine what Amy said when I very calmly explained to her a few days later that I could not, in fact, give any to her, according to the lawyer. I had planned to try to call her but had put it off, dreading the confrontation. Then I saw her walking into a store.

Once she saw me, she just froze in her tracks and glared.

"What?" she finally grunted.

"Bad news, Amy."

"What?" An even meaner glare and grunt.

"Not sure how to break this…"

Glare with doubled up fists on her hips. The daggers were already forming in her eyes as she swung her ponytail around and struck the most threatening pose imaginable. I eased back a step.

"By the terms of the will, if I do not take all of it, it must all go to Pablo."

"Pablo…Pablo, you mean that filthy little Mexican?!" Pablo was now Uncle Clive's ranch foreman, a term also called out in the will.

"Yes."

"What the hell did that damned worthless wetback do to deserve that?"

Didn't Amy marry a Mexican American?

"Maybe he was loyal to your dad? And, besides, Pablo was born here, Amy. He's from Marfa. Pretty sure you know that."

"He's just a dirty…little…conniving…Mexican!" She said very slowly in a cougar-like growl.

When I told Amy that he'd refused a substantial bonus I'd offered him as the foreman, it did little to cheer her up or redeem Pablo in her eyes. I decided against telling her that I was going to donate $50,000 to Pablo's church in his name since he wouldn't take any of Clive's money. I doubt if that would have provided her much comfort.

"You gonna regret this, 'specially when Clark hears! You hear me, cousin Steve," she spit out the word "cousin" like it was a piece of excrement. "You mark my words. Yo' gonna regret this."

"Clark's in prison."

"He's gonna get out before you know it. He may kill you just like he did that dealer fella up in Fort Stockton who tried to jam him!"

I wasn't sure what to reply to that—fortunately I don't get death threats all that often. I just eased back from her and walked away.

"Get back here you son of a bitch...I ain't through with you!"

Well, I certainly had a lot to look forward to. I waved good-bye with my best imitation of a smile that I'd give a rattlesnake as it crawled away...more fear than happy, in other words.

4

About six days after Stacy bolted to Mexico, I got an interesting postcard from her. She updated me about her protest activities. She hadn't been in touch with me since she left, so I was missing her around work and socially, too. I'd basically been kicking around the gallery, visited Big Bend National Park and pretty much just marking time until Stacy got back. I was also doing well in avoiding Amy.

Stacy wrote me that she was confident that the government was going to crater at any time and honor the demands or her downtrodden compatriots in Chihuahua. However, what really intrigued me was her closing.

She wrote, "I love you Stevo! Miss ya!"

I analyzed at length what this meant. Well, I suppose I could have overanalyzed it a bit, but it was important. I had to know: did she mean it? It seemed like finding a meaningful relationship with someone like Stacy was important to finding myself and my potential to behave like a grownup man. She may not be the one, but she was important right now.

Did Stacy really miss me? Why didn't she call me Steve, why "Stevo?" Miss me, hmmm. We'd only really hugged twice when we had a successful opening at the gallery and when she left for Mexico. Though she was becoming warmer—maybe even slightly affectionate at times—I really still had no clue how she felt about me. There was a certain innocence about her that always kept me off guard. I'd flirted with her a number of times. She always responded in such a way that could have been reciprocal flirting, but I wasn't really sure. If we were meant to be a couple, we seemed to be snake-bit. After so long in the government, I wanted to avoid any leader-subordinate or employer-employee harassment issues, so I played things low-key. But, every time I remotely hinted about wanting more than a business relationship, she seemed distracted or got a phone call or something. She seemed to be coming on to me on two separate occasions, both with less than pleasant outcomes.

One evening right after a busy day at the gallery, I picked her up so we could go over the books. In her apartment, we were sitting next to each other on her small sofa. At one point, she reached over to get something on her coffee table and her neck and face passed right in front of me. I smelled her perfume and became very aware of her. When she straightened up, she seemed to know what I was thinking. Her blue eyes locked onto mine. We just looked into each other's eyes for an awkward moment.

"Steve, I want to ask you something. Do you ever...?"

Just then her phone ranged. Her aunt in Dallas had died. The mutual awareness died as well—at least on her end.

The other time occurred a couple of days before she bolted for Mexico; she asked me to come by one evening. Now of course this was the day I unwisely chose to gorge myself on an unusually large mega-bean burrito down at Mike's for lunch. When it arrived at my table, I felt that I'd hit the jackpot since this burrito overlapped the plate by several inches. It was like a huge beached whale, covered in a delicious green and red chile sauce. I came to greatly regret that selection shortly after my arrival at Stacy's place in the evening. The slightly funky taste as I ate it should have tipped me off. I kept thinking I should have gone to Mando's but kept eating anyway...it wasn't that bad. Stupid, stupid me.

As I drove up, I saw Stacy sitting in an Adirondack chair on her flagstone "mini-patio" under a makeshift veranda crudely attached to the side of her apartment. She was a welcome sight in the speckled shade, barefoot and wearing an attractive, short dark olive dress.

"How 'bout some wine, Steve?" Nice smile.

"Sure. Where are you headed looking so nice?"

"Nowhere…I just thought you and I should visit—maybe a little dinner. You know, something simple. Here lately, we never just talk."

This was weird. She always dressed nicely, but she had never dressed up for me. She even wore a little make up this evening.

"Sure. I'd like that." I was on cloud nine…disoriented, but very happy. Of course, that's when the funky burrito began to work its magic. Gas started roiling in my stomach like never before. I was extremely uncomfortable. Of course, the true discomfort occurred as the gas started to seek an exit. I had a feeling the expanding airs would show their displeasure by producing a catastrophically unpleasant odor. The "beached whale" was hell bent for revenge for my having eaten him…all of him.

"Let's go in, Steve."

Stacy took my hand and led me up the stairs. I panicked. The gas was aggressively making its way towards the exit. I flung my hand away from her. She gave me a startled look.

"I…I need to…go to my car. Yeah, car. Be right back!" I ran back down the stairs.

"Okay…uh…sure." Stacy had a most puzzled look.

"I'll be right there!"

"Okay…"

Just then, the neighborhood should have probably been evacuated. It was the worst gas explosion I'd ever encountered. A toxic mega-bean burrito blast. It was awful. I probably should've had to pay some kind of fine to the EPA or something. Thinking the gas had expressed the brunt of its wicked fury, I oh-so carefully went up the stairs to Stacy's apartment. I had to regroup. The evening was shaping up to be promising other than my potentially offensive gastrointestinal challenges.

"Are you okay, Steve?" Stacy glanced up from her stove with a disconcerted look.

"Oh yeah, fine." With great caution I approached but made sure not to get too close.

"Have a seat at the table. Dinner's ready. I hope you like black beans and rice!"

I think I managed a faint "sure" and a slight smile that was likely more a grimace. I gingerly sat myself at the table.

"You're acting funny, Steve. Sure you're okay?"

"Oh yeah,...great." I strove to rally. I had to see what Stacy wanted to talk about.

As dinner went on, I felt a little better. I think I even mustered a serviceable smile or two. Needless to say, my appetite was minimal. We talked mainly about a couple of new artists Stacy was working with down near the border.

As I pecked at the dessert she served, vanilla ice cream with a dab of Mexican caramel, she said she wanted to discuss something important. She asked me to have a seat on her small sofa.

"I'll be right back Steve." She put the dishes in the sink.

Stacy returned shortly and sat right next to me. I was very conscious of her knee against mine.

"Steve, I don't know exactly how to start. We have such a great business relationship...and friendship. I don't want to put that at risk at all...but I was just wondering..."

Oh no. Of course, that was precisely the moment my body chose to accommodate that last, yet sure to be lethal blast. My stomach began a roiling from top to bottom. I bolted up, froze just standing there for a moment to contain the wicked beast and as sure as I knew I could make it to the door safely, headed out. As I made it to the door, I quickly looked back.

"Stacy...I really want to continue this talk but I'm feeling very ill all of a sudden...I gotta go. I'm sorry."

The blast occurred at 8:43 pm just as I raced outside. I would have been the only survivor had other humans been present. I kept trying to think of more pleasant odors like tires burning or diesel exhaust.

"Wait...Steve," was the last words I heard.

Later that evening after calm was restored to my digestive system and the freakish, funky mega-bean burrito had been dispatched, I called Stacy. No answer.

Thirty minutes later—still no answer.

An hour later, I thought I'd at least leave a message. Her answering machine answered, *"No estoy aqui, pero* lay it on me and make it worth my time."

I finally reached her the next day.

"Hello."

"Stacy…it's me. I am soooo sorry about last night. I was…"

"Steve…I'm cool with it. I dig it. This is Marfa man. 'nuf said. Look, I'll see you at the gallery Monday to meet Breeze?"

"Yeah, but…"

"See you Monday, Steve. I'm good. Don't worry. I'm cool with it. This is Marfa, man."

Click. "I dig it?" "This is Marfa?" She was the only person I knew who still said "dig it." "This is Marfa?" What the hell did that mean? What did it mean to be "cool with it?"

Now, I didn't think about it too much after she informed me she was leaving the next day to give the Mexican government fascists hell over the Chihuahuan unrest at the brewery, but her comments from the last phone chat lingered.

Despite any trepidation I had, our temporary parting was nice except for leaving me in charge of the gallery. As she said goodbye, she was all over me. She was hugging me and everything I thought a lover should do when a long absence was imminent. Full frontal hugs. Not any of that sideways bullshit like before. Real hugs. She even lightly kissed my lips when she climbed in the car with Light and Breeze. I was looking forward to her return. I would certainly not eat any burritos before that reunion!

5

Stacy returned eight days after she left. The night she returned, she called me at 2:00 am to announce her arrival. We made plans to get together later that day when she promised to reopen the gallery. There was a big weekend coming up in town with an art festival. Live ones, I mean customers, from all over Texas would be in Marfa with fat wallets. I needed some cash flow starting up soon! Also, fortunately, with the strike ended and beer production resuming, the next beer deliveries should start in about 10 days from what Stacy and the brewery managers told me. It had already been over two weeks since the last beer delivery and the gallery had only been open a couple of days a week during that same time, given Stacy's absence. I was getting very tired of pretending to run the gallery and ration out the beer deliveries.

In fact, some of my customers had written me off. Now I had to hustle to get the sales going again. It didn't help that my last orders before the strike didn't taste right. In fact, they were awful. I hoped that the boxcars hadn't sat out on a spur in the hot Mexican sun for weeks as the strike was ramping up. The Texas, Mexico and Pacific Railroad assured me that they hadn't let the shipments sit around, but they couldn't attest to the service of the other railroad that carried the beer in northern Mexico. The second shipment of three replacement boxcars tasted right. The brewery wouldn't take back the "edgy" beer. I tried to donate it to some organization without luck. Finally, the local liquid-feed plant accepted it. They claimed they were going to mix it in with their cattle feed. I was suspicious of that but hoped it might lift the spirits of some poor cows in the Trans-

Pecos region. At least I got a little good will from a local business in case I needed help with the ranch.

Stacy reopened the gallery when she said she would. She claimed she felt revived. Unfortunately, Breeze, her new budding artist, joined a commune in Mexico and didn't return. Stacy wasn't really very happy about Breeze's departure. She had great promise as an artist plus Light became a bit amorous towards Stacy in Breeze's absence. "It's cool, but it's just not my bag," Stacy informed me with an earnest, matter of fact look.

Stacy invited me over for dinner the next day. I carefully monitored my pre-date diet.

I arrived at her apartment right on time. Stacy was under the veranda looking just as sexy as before. This time she wore a simple brown dress. It was all I could do to keep from staring at her legs. She slipped her spare sandals on and gracefully stood up as I approached. I was elated. Her short dress swirled as she stood. I was thrilled to have an evening with her minus the hellish effects of a mega-bean burrito. That is, until she spoke.

"Hi Steve. I want you to meet someone."

I'd failed to notice her company until he stepped out from under the shade of the backyard tree. Bruce, with the stealth of a cat, emerged from the shadows.

"Hi, Steve." Big toothy grin, big white teeth.

Accompanied by a nausea matching the mega-bean burrito after-effects, my heart sank. I immediately knew what Stacy was doing. She was setting me up!

"Bruce, this is Steve. He's a very dear friend of mine," Stacy slyly informed Bruce. She had a satisfied smile that did nothing to render the same feelings on my part. It was all I could do to keep from backing away, out into the street, as I now came to grips with what "I am cool with it" meant.

"Steve...so nice to meet you! Stacy has told me so much about you." He flashed an all-knowing smile at Stacy. He was beaming. I was about to throw up, not because of Bruce, but because of the total misunderstanding and misdirection that was going on here.

"Nice to meet you," was all I could muster. I felt like bolting to the car just as before, but I knew I couldn't. I had to straighten out a person I was beginning to care for deeply.

"Bruce has a used book store, Steve. He loves books and also sells some art at his store, too. I met him at the gallery. He bought my last Breeze."

"That's great." I'm sure I sounded so sincere.

"I'll let you two visit while I finish up cooking. Steve…a cocktail or a glass of wine?" She smiled her sweetest smile as she eased up the stairs to her apartment.

Bruce pounced on his perceived prey. "So…Steve. Tell me about you."

"Not much to tell, came to Marfa a few months ago. Ended up staying a while. Really not much to tell at all."

"Oh, Steve. Stacy speaks so glowingly of you. I think you're simply being too modest. Don't you? I'm surprised you're not blushing from all the modesty! Oh, wait you are, aren't you?" On the surface, he seemed innocuous, okay, maybe a little aggressive. However, behind the eyes lurked something cold. He was looking at me like a piece of steak.

"Uh…no, not really. Well, I did leave out one thing—I'm crazy about Stacy."

"Oh…aren't we all? She's quite the sweetie."

"No Butch, I mean Bruce. You don't get it. I'm very attracted to her. I mean like physically…well, in more ways than that, of course."

"Oh…that is simply not what Stacy told me. You know Steve, you can be honest with me. *Yo comprendo*, if you know what I mean? You don't have to pretend. I quite simply understand these things." He still wore the same toothy smile with one "all-knowing" eyebrow lifted. It was also the third time Bruce had used "simply" in less than a minute. There was nothing simple about this situation, at all!

I took a deep breath and then it happened. I exploded and said a number of things I shouldn't have. I felt like hell as Bruce started to get emotional. I am not a phobe, but he "simply" pushed the wrong button. He ran upstairs as the jerk, me, calmly walked to my car.

On the drive home, I felt guilty. Even if Bruce was a predator, which he may not have been, I had no right to explode. I had several gay beer-drinking buddies in DC and had worked with people of all types and persuasions across the Hill. It wasn't a big deal to me, but he just got too pushy, too condescending or something. I asked myself would I have gotten that angry if he'd been a woman? Of course the answer was no. I might have even been flattered. I knew that was wrong and that realization made me feel ashamed, but I was also kind of angry about Stacy getting the wrong idea and sidetracking what I hoped was a budding relationship yet again.

I guess I should have gone upstairs and planted a big kiss on Stacy's red lips, right in front of Bruce, but I just had to get away from that situation fast. I needed the air. I drove around Marfa for a while. I noticed two new boxcars on the siding. I assumed it to be "Cerveza de Chihuahua" for Mr. Steve Miles, importer extraordinaire—hopefully a post-strike vintage. As I got closer, I noticed only one of the boxcars was probably insulated. The other was what I called Mexico's attempt at a 50-foot-long convection oven. More happy cows were likely in our future, enjoying the "enhanced" liquid-fortified feed they'd soon be feasting on. I headed up Highway 17 towards Fort Davis.

It was one of those incredible evenings in West Texas. It was fresh, with a good cool breeze. The road was empty, a gray strip over a dark yellow landscape. Only the tops of the hills to the east were glowing yellow orange from the reflected sunset. The patchy clouds painted the sky orange, red and purple with a brilliant blue background. The sky was all around me. It was huge. It was beautiful. And I was miserable.

I missed a few things about DC, but Marfa was beginning to feel like home. I actually wanted to be there. I was beginning to enjoy the art thing. Stacy was becoming very important to me. I didn't sleep well while she was in Mexico. At one point, I considered going down to check on her. I thought a Mexican rendezvous could be romantic. That was before she thought I was gay. Was she messing with my head?

Right at the Jeff Davis County line, I turned around. What I wanted was in Marfa, not Fort Davis. I had to see Stacy now. It was time to get things right between the two of us.

6

It was about 10:00 pm when I pulled in front of Stacy's. I climbed the dark stairs. No lights. I softly knocked. No answer. I locked a little louder, still no answer. As I hit the bottom step to depart, her yellow porch light came on.

"Steve?"

"Stacy." I raced back up the stairs. "Can we have a talk? I'm so sorry about tonight. I was confused and clearly off-base." Stacy looked sleepy-eyed, her hair was a little tussled as she stood in her doorway, her apartment black inside. She was beautiful in the soft yellow light of her stoop, even without make-up. She wore a big, red tee-shirt which just barely covered her hips. She just stood there trying to decide what else to say or what was supposed to happen next.

"Steve. Who are you? You keep confusing me…" It was then I flung her rusty screen door open and kissed her with every ounce of passion in me. There was a lot of pent-up emotion there, too! Her body felt unbelievable against mine—firm, soft, smelled great.

"Steve…what are you doing? What are you trying to prove?"

"I am totally into you. I just can't get you out of my mind." Time to take the chance and let her know how I felt, the hell with the consequences!

"What?" She was awake now, her eyes huge.

"I am not gay! And, I'm crazy about you!"

She just stood there looking into my eyes.

"Come in, damn it. You have me so confused." I'd never heard her use profanity before. She knew it was time to clear the air, no matter what time of night it was.

She sat across from me, legs crossed in the only armchair in the room. She'd turned a small lamp on, filling the room with a soft glow. It was a little eerie seeing the Mexican saints on the walls softly illuminated and staring at us. She looked at me a bit pissed.

"All right. Lay it out Steve! I mean everything."

"It's simple. I've been growing closer to you each day I've been out here. You've been on my mind constantly ever since I sat right here holding an ice bag on your foot. That's all there is. I want a relationship with you, to be with you every moment of each day. I can't get you out of my mind. I was worried sick when you went to Mexico. It isn't complicated. That's it!"

"Why the hell have you waited so long to tell me? You bastard! I've been trying to get you off my mind since then. You asshole. You've put me through hell!" Her vocabulary was expanding before my eyes. It did nothing to diminish my desire for her.

"What are you talking about Stacy?"

"I'm very damned shy, Steve. Do you have any idea how hard it was for me to come on to you!"

"What? Come on to me? Bullshit."

"You rebuffed me every time I flirted with you!" She clearly was stunned.

"What the hell are you talking about, Stacy!" I am sure I looked shocked as well.

"All this fricking time. I really like you, Steve. I just couldn't bring myself to tell you. It's that shyness thing around men I'm serious about. I've had it all my life."

"I don't get it. You certainly don't seem shy to me! I mean, I've watched you. You're great with people! Everyone I've ever seen you around likes you and likes hanging out with you."

"Yeah, with "people." But not with people I am attracted to. I clam up. I say stupid things…do stupid things, like going to Mexico. I mainly just avoid it. I've only dated a couple of guys in my whole life, and then only for a short time. I've mostly avoided relationships because I'm so shy and afraid of what to say or do. I don't know what's wrong with me. I know I'm attractive. I don't know what it is. I've always been like this. I guess I just have issues with relationships."

"I really don't get it, Stacy. I flirted with you so many times."

"Bullshit. Maybe two or three times. I flirted back as best I could."

"I must be the worst flirt in the world. I thought I was showing my attraction every day. I didn't want to harass you or anything, but I wanted you to know how interested I was in you!"

She looked so vulnerable—tears, messed up hair—in the soft glow.

"Stacy, can I hold you please?"

"Yes…I mean wait."

"What? What!"

"Are you positive—without a doubt—that you're not gay?"

"I'm definitely not gay, Stacy!" I said with the most sincere look I could muster.

"I don't want to go down this path unless you know."

I walked over to pick her up and sat her down next to me on the sofa. She was so light. I kissed her softly on the mouth and caressed her face gently and lovingly while trying to let her know I could see only her.

"Trust me, Stacy."

"I'm sorry, Steve. You know how much courage it took for me to come on to you a few weeks ago? You just rejected me. Every time I reached out to you, you ran like I was disgusting. You should have seen the look on your face. You looked like you were gonna be sick. I felt disgusting. I was mad as hell at you. Then it all made perfect sense. You were gay. I mean you're clean, you smell good, you are great to talk to, well-read, you keep yourself very attractive…and neat. You have this, like almost accidental style…that most guys don't have. You even listen to me…usually…or at least sometimes, which is more than other men I've known. You're mostly perfect if a little unsure about the art business stuff, and maybe a few other people-kinds of things.

"I thought I finally figured out," she continued, lowering her voice to a whisper, "why all those times we were here or at your house and you never made a move. You had to be gay. I thought I was making my feelings obvious. I know I'm not the most beautiful woman on the planet, but I'm not bad. And I've got a damn good personality. I can make a rock smile, usually laugh even."

"You're so beautiful. Such a totally cool lady. I'd have chased you all over DC! You have the best personality. You make me smile, laugh...you make me so happy, Stacy. You give me energy...an energy and hope that I've seldom had. You make me smile inside and out."

Her eyes were locked on mine, glistening. These words coming out of my mouth were mine, but I'd never said those kinds of things to any other woman before. My words, my thoughts and my affection...all for Stacy.

"I mean I was ready to dump all of Uncle Clive's stuff and run back to DC. I wanted to get the hell out of what I thought was just a sleepy, boring little town. I may be from Texas, but there's a lot of difference between Houston and here. You made me see Marfa and West Texas in a completely different light. I wouldn't be here if it weren't for you. I was going to go back to DC to a crappy girlfriend and pathetic job," I said, putting air quotes around "girlfriend" and "job."

"You gave me hope, vision, confidence. You opened my eyes to what art could be, although I have a lot to learn there. I never would have done any of this if not for you. You're giving me the soil and nutrients to blossom, even here in dry old West Texas," I said smiling as warmly as I could. I meant every word of it.

"You're allowing yourself to blossom, Steve. I just care about you and the relationship we've had together up to this point, even if I have been confused most of the time. You're doing the growing and blossoming though. I'm just your fan."

"Nonsense. You are helping me see beyond anything I've ever thought possible. A couple of hours ago, I witnessed one of our almost daily miracles—a beautiful sunset. I wouldn't have even noticed it before you. You have me noticing things I've never really seen before...I didn't even know they were a part of life. I love to just sit still and watch you—the way you admire a sunset, the laugh of a child, a flower, art."

I continued, "I was really kind of dead when I came out here, Stacy. I was more like a drone or a zombie. You awakened something in me. You're making a big difference in my life. I'm feeling creative for the first time since I can remember. I'm even thinking about doing some writing. Believe me, you didn't see what a pathetic loser I was before I stepped on your foot. Crushing your foot was probably the best thing I ever did. I'm sorry it hurt." I hoped the smile and weak attempt at a joke showed through.

"It was worth every writhing pain. Okay? On the gallery it's me, I guess, but you're a successful beer distributor and you are restoring a beautiful home."

I was dubious how successful I was in the beer distribution business, but at least I was making a few jobs for some poor folks in northern Mexico, the railroad and a couple of local dudes. The house renovations, well…I had had the fortune of finding finally some true artists to restore the house I'd purchased, as well as the ranch house.

"You're amazing Stacy. That is what I love about you. You might be a little too passionate about things sometimes, but most of the time, I love that about you, too. You're giving me way too much credit."

"Steve don't sell yourself short. When I met you, I was on the cusp of leaving Marfa. I mean, I bombed at writing and painting. I had a little success with Ms. Schultz, but I had to get away from that craziness. Did I tell you about the time she wanted me to sew clothes for her cats? She'd brought some cloth back from the Picasso museum in Barcelona…long story, never mind. Anyway, I was about to leave. I mean there is something I love about Marfa—what it is and what it could be—if we can just figure out how not to lose the traditional things. I love art, but I don't want Marfa to be just a bunch fakes, flakes and rich assholes like Santa Fe.

"Marfa's not Marfa if there isn't a rich Hispanic culture and keeping some of the ranching culture, too. I hope we don't run out all the folks with modest incomes that contribute the traditional cultures and that make Marfa what it is and has been for decades. The church here is amazing. It's alive with the culture of the original people who established it over a hundred year ago. Kindness and love really exist here. I mean many of the people here have grandparents who knew each other! It is so organic, so real.

"Steve, you're the only person in the world who has ever really listened to me. Most people wouldn't listen to my crap. Sometimes, I think I just care too much. Sometimes, I don't even want to hear my crap. Seriously, I was considering joining a religious order or something. I have a real spiritual void in my life, and Marfa has helped fill that, but your listening helps."

Stacy just looked at me for a minute. This seemed like something she'd needed to get out into the open for a long time. After the pause, I needed to confirm to her that I was still with her, both here and now, and in her future.

"I love how you care about stuff. So many people don't care. The rich folks who hang out here in Marfa just want their vacation trophy home or mansions back in the cities filled with trendy art and to hell with the world. But to hell with all that and those people. What about us?"

"I want to try to make an 'us.' I suck at relationships. You have to know that going in. There's something in me that I'm battling. I can't put it into words yet, though. I always figure out a way to screw them up. It's fact. But, if you're willing to gamble, I think I want there to be an 'us.' Let's please not lose the wonderful relationship just because our feelings have become stronger. Please don't let us lose 'us'...who we are now and our strong partnership. I don't know where we go from here. Sorry if I get flighty, but I feel we are on the verge doing something special with our lives, and right now I hope it's together."

"I agree. I just don't know where "it" is. I think we can do better than selling art to rich bastards and peddling beer."

"Steve, some of my art customers are great people!" She looked at the ceiling, took a deep breath, and let it out slowly before continuing.

"Let's take it slow and see how it goes. I don't think I could stand losing you no matter where we go or what kind of relationship we have. I may feel confused and sort of lost sometimes, but right now, I know that we must put us first."

"I like that, let's 'put us first.'"

I kissed her passionately. It was tough not to get too excited about the turn of events with Stacy, but suddenly she pulled back.

"I like this Steve. I really do like it a lot," she said with a deep sigh and looked away. After pondering her floor for a moment, she added, "Let's take it slow. Let's savor this. Let's take our relationship one step at a time. I admit that I'm still struggling with a few things, but…I know I care about you a great deal."

"All right Stacy. I'll take it on your terms. You…we…are worth the wait."

7

 Everything was great for the next month or so. The beer business was mostly flat those days but at least keeping itself out of the red. I was glad that Miguel left. He was one of my two employees. He kind of "managed" the warehouse. Chuppy, with Miguel's "help," unloaded the boxcars and loaded trucks for deliveries. He made a few local deliveries. Chuppy and Miguel were both good guys, but Miguel had the vexing habit of consuming a lot of free beer. At first, that didn't really bother me, particularly since he helped rid us of a good bit of the less savory beer that would otherwise go to the cattlemen. It was when he started supplying half of Marfa with free beer that I felt obligated to step in and reduce the losses once we started getting good beer from Chihuahua again. After several attempts at counseling and retraining as it were, Miguel left me to take a job delivering Budweiser over in Alpine. He said they would double his salary. I doubted that but I played along. In theory we were both getting what we wanted since Budweiser would be more generous with freebies than I could afford to be.

 As he was leaving on his last day, he stuck out his hand to shake and thanked me for the job because he was in a real bind when I hired him. Just as he was walking out the door, he looked back and reflected, "I would have stayed, but I really need to feel wanted, know what I mean? It's only right I get to take care of my friends, man, like you took care of me. What good is a guy if he can't do his friends a solid from time to time? But this new position you put me in, where I can't share the wealth, man, well, I just don't get that. I just don't understand you, amigo. Good luck, anyways," he lamented. I had to wonder if this meant there'd be lots of free Bud in Alpine soon—at least for a little while. It was kind of a confusing way to look at things, I thought, but it was all good, I guess.

Since the Chihuahua Cerveza part of my holdings were slowing down, I thought I'd spice things up a bit. I decided to try to cash in on the craft beer craze that was taking over the rest of the country, since it seemed to fit the original business model. After reading an essay from a writer named James Fallows about what makes small-town America great, I thought I'd try to pump up Marfa with one of the key ingredients of small-town goodness: a hometown brewery.

I bought used equipment since there were several small craft breweries going out of business around the state, and because I didn't want to take too much financial risk becoming a business victim myself. I set up the tanks and rest of the equipment in a modest former storeroom between the beer warehouse and a defunct restaurant I was converting to a brewpub. The new, if small, brewery was next to the much larger distribution warehouse that was home to the exclusive distributorship of the American versions of Chihuahua Cerveza Americanos, Ltd., my real pride and joy. How could I miss with good imports and good craft brew?

Beer-making wasn't quite as simple as the books and magazines suggested, though. I somehow managed to start cooking the beer wort from the tun over in the small boiling kettle, without fully locking down the seals when it went under pressure. Within about 30 minutes, there was a small explosion just before I was ready to start the separation and cooling process. Well, it was my first time, and I was the only one that had read the book, so that part of the story was never going to end well. The minor explosion didn't damage the restaurant part of the brewpub exactly, but it did set off the fire alarm and the sprinkler system in both the warehouse and the brewpub itself, which I think in hindsight might have been wired incorrectly; I think Miguel did that before he left. The fire sensor was burned to a crisp, so we couldn't tell about any bad wiring. The real damage was caused by the volunteer fire department trying to gain access to the closed off section where the tun, boiler and fermenter were located, not that I blame them for all that happened.

Anyway, it was all related to my initial mistake, so I decided to just take credit for it. But I decided no more free beer for a while for the volunteer firemen after they axed up my brewpub walls. They'd have to earn that privilege back.

If I ever try to make craft beer again, I'll hire a real brewer, not just someone who knows how to clean tanks and hoses. Despite the mistakes, it turned out well, and the anticipation of tasting my own beer was fun while it lasted. To recover from the debacle and to make it a real brewpub setting, I managed to get the Chihuahua brewery to send up some kegged beer so I could tap it and sell it in the pub as draft craft brews. No one seemed to miss the promise that my contributions to the taps would have added.

As I set up to sell our new beers from Chihuahua, I hired the cook from the hotel in Fort Davis to cook up the southwestern cuisine that a good Marfa-based pub would need. Stacy even spiced up his repertoire by adding some of her mom's Spanish recipes. The Fort Davis Chamber of Commerce got mad at me for taking their master chef away, but that's just business, as far I'm concerned. The hotel should have paid him better and the community of Marfa deserved the best of the best, anyway. Of course, the existing Tex-Mex joints in Marfa weren't exactly thrilled either, but I didn't care at all about causing discomfort to Mike's, the source of my funky burrito.

Other than contributing the recipes and explaining the finer points of the preparations, Stacy wasn't really that much into the endeavor so that helped explain why things went south, as it were, and why the best we could manage to do was set up a new art business for her to run. Yep, the semi-brew pub, as it were, ended up as one of Texas's first beer and art galleries. Stacy did like that, and I got to see her more.

It was my first and only attempt to add to the food artistry culture of Marfa, but it was fun while it lasted.

I imagine I made more from the write-off and insurance than I ever could from serving my own beer at the brewpub. I was just trying to be imaginative, as Stacy usually admonished me to be. I also enjoyed being a recognized contributor to the Marfa social scene. It was fun to give it a go, and we might have also helped a few people along the way: Marfans and visitors discovered the value of having another artsy congregating place, decent southwest and Spanish food and a place for Stacy to show off a little more of her creativity. It was almost a self-actualizing time for me, except for the brewery explosion, and I got to meet some fascinating characters that would be fun to think about describing in a book sometime.

◆ ◆ ◆

Stacy was primarily busy filling homes in Dallas, Austin and Houston with fine art. At least some of it was. What passed for art at times in Marfa never ceased to amaze me. It was great for her since she didn't have to travel as the buyers came to her. One buyer did offer Stacy a job to be her personal art collector, but she declined. The rich society lady art collector literally wanted to pay Stacy to travel the world in search of emerging artists. We seemed to have an abundance of those types of artists right here in Marfa and the surrounding area. We didn't need to travel far to find great works in our eyes.

When I thought about how to combine the art gallery and the brew pub, that's when things started to come together. It seemed like we were starting to hit it off as a Marfa society couple, and the Thanksgiving and Christmas holidays were about to hit. I could tell something was still holding Stacy back from fully committing to a relationship, though. It bothered me a little, but we were so busy, I tried not to think too much about it until we had some time together on a proper vacation away from Marfa, something we'd only talked about but not yet done.

I went over to Houston for Thanksgiving and caught up with the family there on what was happening in their neck of the woods. I shared details about the new Marfa world I was living in and even poked around for some possible new customers for the beer distributorship. I returned to Marfa after a week or so, anxious to get back to Stacy.

Stacy and I shared the rest of the holidays with some of her relatives she had in town and our acquaintances in Marfa, decorated the gallery and businesses in appropriate style and generally just hung out together as friends and business partners would. There was no uptick in the pace of the romance, but with the holidays it didn't seem to matter all that much. I was enjoying my first holiday away from DC and that part was glorious.

Amy had made one appearance but was laying off in honor of the season, I suppose. She had to be plotting something, so I knew that would be a short reprieve.

8

It was the next month, January, that the real funk hit: post-Christmas, gray skies, the weather would just not warm up past 50 degrees, as the locals promised me it would. Stacy and I were both were kind of listless. Our relationship had been good, but it wasn't growing. It was like we were kind of locked into how the relationship started. I mean the company, the conversation, the laughs were still there, but we weren't becoming more intimate.

There was sort of a combination psychological–physiological barrier we just couldn't overcome. I still felt tremendous warmth and affection towards her and, to my personal surprise, still viewed her as a potential life-mate. Unfortunately, there was a limit with how close she'd let us get. We were affectionate, but not intimate. I mean I didn't have to have sex right now...that wasn't all that meaningful to me unless the love and commitment were there. I certainly wanted to share a physical bond with Stacy, but she was so special to me that I could work on her timetable.

I wanted to talk to her about it, but I sensed there was something in her or something that had happened to her that made her cautious. Though she was confident and gregarious on many levels, she really was intensely shy in some ways. I felt there was some history I needed to know or that she didn't really see me the way I saw her. I felt there was a dimension to her she was hiding from me. I almost wondered if she didn't have another love interest. It bothered me a little that she didn't want to come home to Houston over Thanksgiving to meet my parents, and that she'd stopped talking about our vacation get-away to Cabo or Costa Rica.

By mid-month, I finally decided to pry a little. Our relationship was still good but there was that listlessness about us that had begun to surface fairly frequently. I invited her over for dinner. I cooked pesto and pasta—one of my specialties. I made the pesto with pecans; they were abundant in the area. I had two pecan trees in my backyard.

She arrived unusually happy.

"Why are you so happy?"

"I didn't tell you—Breeze is back!

"She's painting?"

"Better than ever. I really missed her."

"A gallery in San Antonio offered her a much better deal than we can, but she turned them down."

"How did the gallery in San Antonio know about her?"

"Turns out that I unknowingly sold that gallery three of her paintings. Word is they tripled their money. Breeze is a hot property, and she's ours!"

"Yeah…but we don't want to abuse her."

"I offered her more. She won't take it. She calculated exactly what she needs to live and only takes that much. So, I told her that you and I would donate ten percent of her sales to a local place that helps women recover from afflictions. I hope that's okay."

"Sure." I loved this woman. We finally hit something big, and she starts trying to figure out how to share the wealth. We'd never really make it big, but at least we'd sleep well. How could I criticize her? It was the right thing to do. I had donated money to Pablo's church, so she thought I'd be "cool with it."

Stacy was so positive that night that I was debating on bringing up the funk I sensed we'd both been feeling. I was carefully debating with myself as I heard Stacy go on and on about Breeze's new work, but then I heard a loud hammering on my door—pow, pow, pow—in very quick sequence. Before I could get to the door, the hammering went on again.

When I opened the door, it was none other than Clark on the

other side of the screen.

"Listen you asshole, yo're gonna fork that dough over now!"

He looked a thousand years old. I almost didn't recognize him. Though he was a year younger than I, his wrinkles had wrinkles. He looked to be about thirty years older than he really was—damn near bald. He wore a white WNBA tee shirt and a filthy, florescent green "Honk if Your Horny" ball cap. It had been years since I'd seen that oh-so-clever expression.

"Clark, what are you talking about? I explained it all to Amy."

"Amy may take yer shit, but I ain't. I'm more of kneecap buster than a listener."

"Oh really? That's interesting. I'm more of a parole officer-caller than a listener."

He just stood there with a really stupid look on his face staring at my forehead.

"Clark, I have company right now. If you can act more like a human being and less like a jail escapee, I'll talk to you later. You need to go away right now. My fingers are getting itchy to make a few calls on your behalf." I doubted he got the sarcasm.

"Now listen here," he said as he jerked his quivering head so he could peer through the screen door at Stacy. Hen-like, he cocked his head to the side as though he was having trouble focusing.

"I'm sorry ma'am 'bout the bad language. Dint see ya there."

Adjusting his focus back on me as best he could, he lowered his shaky voice a bit, "Now Steve, they ain't no need to get the law involved. Dis 'tween family!" He continued the annoying habit of looking at my forehead when he talked to me. I kept wondering if my hair was messed up or purple or something. I also wondered what kind of nasty, mind-altering chemicals were coursing through his bloodstream.

"Clark, I'll talk to you. But your daddy disowned you because you got mixed up in drugs. There's nothing I can do to change that. But I will visit with you…later…if you can behave yourself. I see you come charging over here again like some sort of maniac, and I'll get Sheriff Duncan all over yo' ass." I could hick it up too.

"All right. But this ain't over, cousin," Clark said, spitting out "cousin" in a nasty tone, just like his sister Amy. I guess the term didn't impress them as much as it used to.

"We ain't done by a long shot. Jus' cause daddy had some good summers with you and shit like that, don't give you any claim to what's rightfully mine…and Amy's!" Clark continued.

He craned his neck around the door one final time and manually adjusted his focus after removing his filthy cap.

"Sorry again ma'am 'bout my language."

A completely blank look came upon his face for about twenty seconds and then he adjusted his eyes to look at my chest and added, "Later Steve, you kin count on it."

Clark killed any chance of delving into the funk. We had a nice, pleasant evening, enjoying a relationship as Stacy prescribed it and not going one inch over limits.

❖ ❖ ❖

The next day I did something unusual. I went by the gallery in the morning to check in on Stacy. I figured it was better than watching Chuppy and the new guy, Jimmy Garcia, take their third half-hour long coffee break before lunch. I guess I could have protested but there was really no need. We didn't have that much going on since the explosion and besides this was Marfa. People just didn't get too excited about anything here except high school football, or the art gallery owners about new artists and how they could entice suckers from the big city to come spend $5,000 on a slab of graphite or a scratch on a piece of crinkled paper.

There was some real art being produced or sold in town, but some of it, by my parochial estimation, was a scam. In retrospect, watching Chuppy and Jimmy kid each other over the coffee breaks or talking football would have been much better than most of what I encountered at the galleries.

As soon as I walked into the gallery, Stacy darted a severe

glance at me.

"Paco, I'll be right back," Stacy blurted out and raced over to me and led me out of the gallery into the bright sunshine on the street.

"Steve, you have to make this, this woman, this thing, go way!"

"What?"

"This woman is driving me fricking nuts. I despise her. I have never in my life just naturally despised someone. I love everyone. Always making excuses for people, blah, blah, blah. I hate everything about her, and I want her away from me as soon as possible."

I peered in the doorway.

"Don't stare at her, Steve!" Stacy blurted out under her breath.

"Are you sure that's a she?"

She was the manliest woman I had ever seen. She had short-cropped blond hair, gold, wire-rimmed glasses and a wretched complexion. She wore dirty-looking man jeans, a red flannel shirt and wore bulky, brown "man" boots. She was disorienting.

"What do you want me to do?"

"Make her go away," Stacy said, stressing the "away" forcefully. "I don't care how you do it."

"She's a local?"

"Student—over in Alpine." Stacy quickly said while looking away and rubbing her forehead.

"She looks a little old for a student."

"She's getting a graduate degree or something. Look Steve, it doesn't matter. I want her gone"

"I'll get rid of her, but she may get angry."

"I don't care, Steve, please just do it! Do whatever you have to do. She's been here three days in a row." Stacy emphasized the "whatever" and I took that to mean this person had to go, one way or the other. I hated the imminent confrontation but was willing to do it for Stacy.

"All right. It may get a little ugly."

I struggled with what approach to use. I didn't want to touch on anything to do with her sexual orientation because I didn't really know what gender she might identify with, much less her orientation. Besides, gays were a pretty prominent and respectable part of the Marfa community. I envisioned a sea of rainbow flag picketers in front of the Galería Del Sol. Bruce notwithstanding, some of my closer acquaintances in Marfa were, partly because of the art scene I guess, gay, lesbian or trans.

I approached her as she studied one of Breeze's better works.

"Ma'am? May I have a word with you?" I cursed myself for saying "ma'am," but she didn't react.

"Sure."

"I own this gallery. I just wanted to ask you why you're spending so much time here without…well, without offering any particular interest in buying a piece of this fine artwork," I asked, without showing too much tongue in cheek, I hoped. Stacy had come back in and was in the back sheepishly peeking over, egging me on with her expressions.

"Well…?" I stared at her and she wouldn't say anything. That was it, "Well." She just kept studying the picture. "Is there something I can do for you? Are you simply loitering here?"

"I am just…absorbing the fabulous work you have here, if you don't mind!" She glared at me on the word "mind." She had a sultry, sexy voice. I concurred with Stacy, she was just completely disorienting. I felt sympathy for transvestites—for people who felt trapped in the body of the opposite gender. However, "Paco" made no effort to change her voice or minimize her large breasts. I think she was doing it to just to shoot the bird at the world or something. This stuff was touchy, so I made sure I asked myself if I would do this if she was any other customer. I decided I would ask her to leave, regardless.

"I really think you need to be going."

"Why?"

"You've been spending a lot of time here. This is not a museum, it's an art gallery dedicated to selling fine works of art. If you want to purchase something, we'd be happy to serve you. If not, probably best you move on."

Paco darted a menacing glare at Stacy.

"You can't do a thing about it. It's a free country"

"Why, yes...I can."

"Like what?"

"Call the sheriff."

"What can he do?"

"Arrest you for trespassing."

"This is a public place."

"Not when I ask you to leave, which I just did." If she would have been just slightly more pleasant, I wouldn't have taken such a direct approach.

"Are you discriminating against me?"

"What?"

"Are you discriminating against me because I'm omnisexual?"

"I don't even know what that is. I just want you gone because you're loitering. Look, it's been three days. It's really that simple."

"How do you know it's been three days?" She darted yet another glare at Stacy, who now was nowhere to be seen.

"I'll leave, but I assure you that you'll be hearing from the Marfa Omnisexual Defense Association!" With a very feminine air, she smiled and said on her way out, "Enjoy your last days of business and look for a Notice of Intent to Sue from MODA!"

Stacy was appreciative of the support, but I really didn't know what to make of Paco and MODA. I couldn't wait to see what happened from this encounter.

9

Life in Marfa was almost always interesting. Three days after Paco's ejection, Marfa's NPR station ran a story on Omniphobes citing the recent travesty at the Galería Del Sol. After we called the station to give them our side of the story and reminded them that we gave $1,000 dollars to the station that year, they ran no additional stories about the "travesty." I felt like a capitalist pig threatening our funding of them, but it was just so stupid. Apparently, an intern had slipped it by management when the manager of the station was out of town. The donation money probably didn't matter to them. They had plenty of donors from around the region and the state.

We never heard from MODA or any other organization, but Paco continued to honk and stick her man hand out the window of her rusty El Camino to shoot the finger at the gallery every time she was in town.

The day I ran off Paco was a memorable day in Marfa for other reasons, too. That was the first day I saw the "apparition of beauty" and on a less positive note, met Deputy Dudley, or as the locals called him, Deputy Dud or even, Deputy Daycare. The encounter with the deputy first.

His name was Deputy Dudley Morton. He was a big guy. He'd had played football at Marfa and was pretty popular in high school. He was about as dumb as a fence post, though. Everyone knew it except for me, well at least until I spent 20 seconds with him. That 20 seconds of "pleasure" came as I walked into the Chihuahua Cerveza warehouse.

"Sir? Hey, you thar?" he called out.

I turned to see the Deputy limping behind me out of breath.

"Yes sir?" He was kind of in uniform except he wore blue jeans.

"You own this place? You Steve Mills?" He was kind of tanned, maybe ruddy, with what I could only describe as a dumb look on his face. Must have battled hellacious acne as a kid.

"Uh, yes. The name's Miles." I put my sunglasses on to be able to stop squinting into the white Marfa sunshine.

"Yeah...well...I got some info on you. Need to talk." That's how he spoke: short choppy, nonsensical blasts.

"Okay." I just stared at him. I was astonished that Sheriff Duncan would hire this guy.

"Clark, told me 'bout the scam you pulling on him and Amy. And Miguel, you discriminated against him. Job discrimination, I think they call it."

"What?"

"Keeping an eye on you mister."

"I don't have a clue what you are talking about, deputy."

"You heard it loud and proud," he said as he limped away.

I knew the young deputy was supposed to be the son of the Presidio County Judge, but I couldn't see any resemblance of any kind. Marfans apparently tolerated the deputy because they loved the judge, who was going to retire soon anyway. I wouldn't be surprised if they looked at it like the city was giving the judge the perk of free daycare or something. No one seemed concerned he was packing heat and driving around in a city police car!

◆ ◆ ◆

The mystery next. I was driving down the street near the Catholic Church when I saw her. She was beautiful. Red hair flowing, pink shirt, short gray skirt, very shapely white legs propelling her bike. She had a beautiful smile, no make-up other than brilliant red lip stick. She was like a vision. I felt a little guilty being so aware of her. I had been so obsessed with Stacy that I hadn't thought of anyone else. Unfortunately, the woman I started calling the Red Angel kind of changed that. In fact, she became a mild infatuation for me. I never made any effort to speak to her, but I started to keep an eye out for her everywhere I went. I was sold on Stacy all the way, but I always thought of the Red Angel as I drove or walked around town. I would see her every few days or so. My pulse would always quicken. She smiled a beautiful smile at me with her brilliant red lips. She was a celebration of red and white and beauty and grace on a bicycle.

From the first time I saw her, there was just something about her, something almost other worldly. She penetrated my conscience with a mixture of unease and wonderment. I began to ponder what would possess a beautiful, twenty-something woman to ride her bike around Marfa. She appeared to be everywhere I went. Always a short gray skirt and red lip stick. How did she keep her legs so white in Marfa's blinding sunlight? She became a sort of obsession for me. I thought her behavior odd, but I selfishly enjoyed it. Over time, I started having a strange feeling about her.

One Saturday afternoon I was leaving the Hotel Paisano after having lunch with Stacy and her family, who had popped into town for the weekend. As I stepped out of the plaza of the hotel, the Red Angel rode by. She had a big basket on the back of her bike. She stopped across the street, stood straddling the bike, and stared at me for a brief second. She waved, smiled and rode away. My pulse was racing. This was the first time I had any contact with her other than brief visual exchanges. Suddenly, I felt an imposing figure staring at me from behind.

I turned around to see the "Marlboro Man" almost glaring at me. He was sitting on a bench cross-legged under a veranda. He leaned back on the bench, soaking it all in. He peered up at me. I could barely see his beady eyes under the brim of his hat. His neck and hands were very knobby and red, tortoise like. He was dressed just like the Marlboro advertisements. His filthy cowboy hat was hitched back. He had very strange eyes. He really looked a bit deranged.

"She gonna git ya."

"Pardon me, sir." I swallowed hard. He was creepy.

"She esss gonna git ya."

"What do you mean, sir?"

"Feller 'bout a month ago hooked up with her. Ain't been seen since." The goosebumps were kicking in good.

"What fellow?"

"Name was Highman, Marty, I think. Worked the YZ ranch, up near Balmorhea. Good fella. Too bad for him."

"Where is he now?"

The deranged, mystic Marlboro man spit tobacco juice out on the street, wiped his mouth with the back of his hand, then looked up towards the sky. "Up there, I reckon."

"You mean...up in that building?"

"Space, amigo," he laughed and snorted, and wiped his nose with his sleeve. "She works with dem dere alien aab-ducters."

"You mean she's an alien?"

"Use your head, man. What do you think?" I just stood there frozen by the strangeness of it all.

"All I gotta say, look out. She comin' 'atch *you*. She smiled at Marty just like that."

He laughed his deranged laugh again and spit another glob onto the street.

"She quite a package, that one. Gotta give her that! Man, dos' legs. Look out, sonny. Gonna be ugly. Don't say nobody warned ya. Course, then again, if she was afta me, not sure I could hep myself either. She some package there, fo' sure!"

He got up and started to limp down the street.

"Hey mister, who are you? How come you know so much 'bout her?"

He paused, looked back and started to say something. Just as he opened his mouth, he waved his hand in front of his face and chuckled. He limped around the corner without another word. He certainly put a new wrinkle in my "Red Angel" infatuation. Who the hell was she?

I didn't really want to share the fantastic story of the Marlboro Man with Stacy. She had already busted me for staring at the red-haired bicyclist one afternoon. Stacy got a little mad even though she said she didn't see anything but a blur going by. Stacy just saw my head turn like I was checking out another girl and nailed me. I was relieved she didn't actually see anyone in particular.

I decided to take the mystery up with Cecilia, the local historian, whom I'd befriended while looking at old documents to help restore my house. She'd given me the history of my house and the history of Austin Street in general. She said my house was designed by a prominent architect and showed me some pictures of the house and street from about 80 year ago. I had lunch with her one day.

"Cecilia, do you know anything about the red-haired girl that rides her bike around town?"

"No."

"You don't know who I'm talking about? Always riding her bike, red hair flowing…?" I thoroughly described her.

"Never seen her, Steve. Think she just moved here?"

"No. I mean she's been here a few weeks at least. I know you must have seen her. She's all over town on her bike with the basket on the back, like an old milk crate or something."

"I'll ask around. Never seen her myself."

I decided that a woman probably wouldn't be taken with her the way I had. Flowing red hair and shapely, bare legs probably didn't grab her attention. Then I got a brief chill when I started to wonder if only I could see her—just me and the "Marlboro" man.

◆ ◆ ◆

The next day, I got a call from Cecilia. She told me her friend was convinced that the Red Angel was Emmaline. I felt relieved that at least someone else had seen her, and that I wasn't totally insane.

"That's good to know. I thought I was going nuts."
"You don't know Emmaline, do you?"
"No."
"She haunts the Rincon Inn."
"What? You gotta be shitting me! Sorry for the language."
"No offense taken. Emmaline was killed in a horseback incident 100 years ago. She's haunted the house ever since. She's very benevolent. She's a pretty thirteen-year old with blond hair and wears a white dress. Numerous guests have reported seeing her in the bed-and-breakfast. You know the Rincon?"

"Of course, it's right down the street from my house."
"Yeah, well people also report her looking out the windows from time to time." Just another day in Marfa.

"Cecilia, that's great but this woman is twenty-something and has red hair. What could this ghost story have to do with the woman I asked you about?"

"Steve. I've asked a couple dozen people about the woman you've described. All of them hang out downtown a lot. Not one of them has ever seen this red-haired woman on the bike." Little goosebumps came back.

"I still don't follow the ghost thing."
"The only person who has seen her is Elizabeth Hart. She is our local ghost expert. She sees things that others don't. She's convinced that Emmaline has escaped the house."

"Why?"
"She says the woman on the bike favors Emmaline."
"But...what about the red hair?"
"You'd have to talk to Elizabeth about that. It appears you two have something in common. You two are the only ones who have seen her, except for maybe that crazy cowboy as you call him. By the way, it is true that Marty's family hasn't a clue where he went. They haven't heard from him in about a month." Bigger goosebumps now.

◆ ◆ ◆

I had one last encounter with the Red Angel in Marfa. I hadn't seen her in several days. One night I was walking from my house to the Hotel Paisano to meet Stacy and some of her art friends at the Jett Grille. It was named after Jett Rink, James Dean's character in *Giant* which was filmed around Marfa. According to the hotel, a lot of the cast stayed there while the Marfa filming was taking place.

It was one of those dark and eerily quiet nights where you think you may be the only person in town. It was about 8:45. I suddenly heard a bicycle coming up behind me.

It was the Red Angel. She slowly rode right beside me. Thoughts of abductions and ghosts paralyzed me. She eased her bike to a stop and leaned over on one foot. She wore the same short skirt. Her white legs almost glowed under the streetlight. She slowly turned her face towards me and smiled at me as beautiful as ever. She spoke in an almost English or Scottish accent, saying, "Farewell Steve. You're going to get hurt, but it's going to be okay. It's all going to be good; you'll see. Don't worry. Hang on to these words. Our paths may cross again." And with that, she was gone. I didn't even see her riding away, really…it was more of a feeling or memory.

My final thought of her was that red hair flowing as she passed under the yellow glow of a distant streetlight. The recollection of her on a lonely highway in the moonlight haunted me, but the temptation and obsession of the Red Angel was surely over. At the time, I figured she got my name from someone in town. I didn't have a clue what she was talking about, but I know I didn't like the words, "You're going to get hurt." My goosebumps were almost gone as I walked into the candle glow of the restaurant and the sight of Stacy.

10

The funk with Stacy was up and down but never totally went away. In my mind, we made very little progress in our relationship. I suppose we didn't really lose any ground either, but sometimes it seemed almost purely platonic between us. Somehow, strangely, the Red Angel episodes awakened in me a desire for more from our relationship. That was not really front and center on Stacy's mind one particular Friday morning while we were having breakfast together at the brewpub, though. I'd made us a traditional Irish breakfast with some imported Irish creamery butter and black pudding. I ate like a pig and Stacy kind of picked over the potatoes and eggs.

Stacy finally told me what was up. She said one of the big-city customers told her our gallery was kind of "boring and drab." She wanted to go see other galleries in Marfa to see how we now stacked up.

It'd been quite a while since either of us had visited another gallery except the opening at the small gallery Bruce built behind his bookstore. He had a very nice place that specialized in western literature and art books. To show there were no hard feelings, I'd bought a few vintage Zane Grey novels from him. We seemed to get along okay after the incident at Stacy's. I was happy for him to get his gallery up and running.

Bruce's opening was one awkward evening for me because of Stacy's former nemesis. Paco showed up and did her thing. She was attired in her formal gallery wear, I guess. She was in a camo-patterned dress and combat boots. She was hanging the arm of an attractive, well-dressed man who seemed, oddly enough, to be fine with it. She kept glaring at me throughout the evening.

Bruce, however, showed me he had a capacity for humorous sarcasm. I inwardly chuckled when he subtly ripped Paco a new one when she made a comment about a painting he was exhibiting. Surprisingly, Paco mumbled an apology and went outside. Wish I'd thought of that approach in our gallery. Bruce's opening was apparently a success, though, and the wine and hors d'oeuvres were good.

The next day, we began our tour of Marfa galleries. Stacy got a friend to cover the Galería del Sol for the day so we could tour several galleries. It was an education to say the least.

The first gallery we went to was called 4dimensions. It was an old house that had been painted white throughout with gleaming porch-grey wooden floors. The windows were cracked so a strange howling noise raced through the house. At first, I thought it was a clever sound track ambiance thing, but no, it was really the wind. In each white room small black squares and other shapes were hung on the walls. The black boxes as it turns out were not intercoms or doorbells but masterpieces by none other than Mary Yorkton. The prices ranged from $3,000 to $8,000. In the last room of the house, a severe looking fellow with closely cropped black and gray hair and dressed all in black sat at his computer with his back to us. He didn't budge. We left when he failed to acknowledge us. Outside, someone told us that it was really the owner, and that he was a very nice person and quite a successful gallery owner in Santa Fe. He was testing the waters in Marfa. Right after we walked out, I remarked to Stacy that maybe he too was also an exhibit: perhaps he was titled something like "Still Life in Boring White House."

In the next gallery, I really stepped in it. I fell right into their trap. Stacy was across the street saying hi to a friend on the street so she couldn't protect unfortunately. This gallery was in a historic storefront downtown. It was called Gallery 5. It was a white room about forty by twenty-five feet. The floor was black and white tiles. In the middle of the room sat two sinks—one white, one pink. The remainder of the room was bare. There was nothing else. A feminine voice rang out of the darken hallway to one side.

"May I 'elp you?" Strange, European accent—Romanian?

"When will the exhibit be up?" I turned to look at her and did a double take. She was about six feet tall, very slender, pale-skinned in a black sleeveless dress almost to the floor. Two very white, bare feet peeked out from the bottom. Her super shiny, straight hair was coal black. Her lipstick was very dark red. I did a double take because she was stunning but also because I felt I was watching her on black and white television or something—even her toenails were painted black.

"Deeze ees dee exheebeet. Zee de placar?"

The placard said, "Kansas City Materialism, 1958 by Chexo."

"I see. Fascinating." I looked her over one more time and thanked her. Stunning in a bizarre way. She was the exhibit in my eyes. She would have been even more stunning if I hadn't recognized her. I realized she was the blond that worked at the coffee shop down the street in the mornings. She faked a pretty good accent, I have to say. The intonations of her voice sounded like one of those overly-country sounding female recording artists in the coffee shop each morning. Quite the transformation. As I peeked in one last time, I wondered if the bottom of her very white feet were black; that would make the contrast complete. It was a pretty dirty floor to be walking around barefoot.

The last remarkable "gallery" we went to was a decaying old adobe warehouse named the Casa de Tifo. The sign out front said welcome in German, Italian and Spanish, but strangely enough, not English. German tourists were common in Marfa. The sign also announced "live art" by Claudia and Yaqua today at 1:30. We soon learned that once a month these two women stripped to their very skimpy underwear and played twister on a canvas where the dots are wet paint while accompanied by European technopop music. Their last "painting" sold for $3,000. A number of severe looking people from all over came to watch the painting being "created." Stacy and I only lasted a few minutes before we'd seen enough. We missed the bidding afterward. Our loss...or not.

We covered two conventional western-style art galleries as well. They were nice, but nothing unusual. Stacy and I agreed that the Galería Del Sol wasn't so bad after all. We discussed fiddling with the lights and "aromascape" as she called it. So, another day in Marfa went by without us growing an inch closer or further apart. Plus, I increased my personal skepticism about what counted as art, and our gallery was miles ahead in that measure, I thought.

11

After another mostly sleepless night, I decided I needed some counsel. Only thing was, pretty much everyone I knew was a friend I met through Stacy, most of whom I would never even consider asking advice. I had no interest in being told the answer is in yoga, some obscure eastern religious literature, watching smoke from burning acacia limbs or something else our ranch inhabitants would offer. Being that I was a marginal Episcopalian, I went to the lovely little stone Episcopalian church across from the courthouse. It's a beautiful sanctuary building with a lot of stained glass—it seemed like a smaller version of the one I attended as a child in Houston, so it was comfortable to contemplate visiting. I made an appointment with Reverend Judy Burkheisse for later that afternoon. I initially hesitated when I learned it was with a female pastor, but then I thought that maybe she would understand Stacy's perspective better.

All day I went over what I was going to say. I had that luxury because Chuppy was doing such a good job with my Chihuahua Cerveza enterprise that I didn't really need to come in more than a couple of days a week to do a little book work. We'd also started distributing some Spanish-oriented soft drinks from Miami on a trial basis, and we were getting good feedback so far. Our beer sales, coupled with the taps in the brewpub, were starting to pick up to a respectable level. We were still the sole US distributor for the Chihuahua brewery. We were also now shipping a couple of boxcars a month to Los Angeles to a distributor who had approached me with a special arrangement. It was nice. We didn't touch it. It came in by rail at Presidio and then it was turned over to the Union Pacific at Alpine for shipping to California—pretty easy money, 75 cents a six-pack came to us. I felt a little guilty about it when I thought what a pittance the brewery workers south of the border were likely paid. I resolved to send the workers a "holiday bonus" to express my appreciation.

At 2:00, I walked the few blocks over to the church. As I passed by the Courthouse, I noted Deputy Dud staring at me through his mirror sunglasses as he got out of his patrol car. Fortunately, he said nothing although he did express his disdain with a gaze over his sunglasses. I could only "disdain" back with my own glare. I wasn't about to acknowledge him any other way.

It was a typical beautiful early spring day in Marfa—sixty-four degrees, breezy with almost no humidity. It was very comfortable. A friend had called from DC the previous evening, highs expected in the upper thirties with a chance of flurries there. I took a deep breath and appreciated being where I was.

The church was beautiful in the bright sunlight. It and the office were shaded by large oak trees. In some ways, this part of West Texas was a haven in the high desert.

Reverend Burkheisse was a professional-looking woman in her forties. She had a mix of longish gray and blond hair that she flipped off her forehead periodically. Very pleasant, welcoming personality.

"How can I help, Mr. Miles?"

"Steve, please. Well, Reverend Burkheisse…"

"Judy, please."

"Okay. Judy, I need some advice. It's only semi-spiritual I guess."

"All right. Be happy to help any way I can."

"I have a girlfriend in town. She started off as an employee and then a business partner, really. I'm very fond of her. I guess I may love her. No. I do love her. Of that, I'm certain. Anyway, we have been together since early summer last year. We get along great. We laugh, we confide, we listen, we encourage. We're always there for each other. I'm sure I'd have left Marfa a long time ago if it weren't for her."

"Sounds like a great relationship."

"It is. Really is. Only, we seem to have reached a wall. It's like our relationship has peaked. The intimacy is no longer growing." I hesitated and peered out the window. "Look, this is embarrassing."

"Take your time. It's all right."

"We haven't been physically intimate. I mean, we're affectionate: hugging, kissing, holding hands with each other. It just seems there's a barrier."

Judy was a good listener. She knew how to pull it out of me.

"Is that very important to you?"

"Yes. Well, let me clarify. Eventually, absolutely. I'm okay for now, but I don't know if we'll ever get there. It's like our relationship is frozen. No forward or backward movement."

"How do you think she feels about this? Is she happy with the way things are?"

"I guess. She seems to be."

"Have you talked to her? Have you shared your concerns?"

"A little. I feel awkward talking to you about this, but I really want to do the right thing."

"A few things, then. One, you need to communicate. If you can't communicate about sex, your relationship is in trouble already. Two, you can't impose your preferences. You must have consensus on something this intimate and important. You'll achieve consensus only by talking. Tell me Steve, what are your real feelings about this from a spiritual standpoint?"

"I'm conflicted. I know pre-marital sex is wrong according to the Bible, although I don't refer to the Good Book much anymore these days. I know this is not the best approach I guess, but it's best to say that I'm just frustrated, and I can't wait to have that kind of relationship with Stacy."

"I can only point you to some references in the Good Book, as you call it, and you make your own conclusions."

"I know. You're right."

"I'd also like to prescribe some meditation for you."

"Meditation?'

"I do it occasionally. Some parishioners seem to benefit from it. But before I go into that, do you think there's anything about you that may be off-putting to Stacy?"

"What do you mean?"

"Well…do you think you're mature? Are you really an adult?"

"Do you think I'm being immature?'

"I'm really in no position to say, but that's essentially what I'm asking. It appears to me that you think Stacy is the problem. I just want you to assure yourself that you aren't the problem… or at least part of it. What you really think about your relationship is part of both the problem and the solution."

"Hmm. I don't know. I never considered that I was part of the problem, but really how would I know?"

"That very question may suggest you are in fact part of the problem."

"What do you mean?"

"How old are you?"

"Thirty-four."

"I know of many men who did not really mature until their forties or later, but you should know yourself better than you let on. Maybe Stacy has moral issues, maybe she has some things in her past, maybe she is waiting to see if she can help you grow up."

What she was saying kind of bothered me, but it was also making sense. I thought I should listen closely just in case she was on to something.

"In all honesty…and don't take this wrong, Steve…it kinda concerns me that you're talking to me about this when you should be talking to Stacy. I will say this though, I commend your effort to try even if you may be a little off the mark."

I just sat there letting the truth slowly filter in.

"Tell you what Steve. I have an idea. I want you to think about doing three things. One I want you to do some soul searching to try to identify anything attributable to you that could be giving her pause. You can call it meditation, if it sounds right to you. Secondly, I want you to come to our church tonight and sit in a pew very quietly and just think. Can you? If so, I will prepare the church for you, but I ask you to please be out by 10:00 when I get home from Alpine tonight. Finally, I want you to be direct with Stacy. You need to make sure you aren't the problem. Be here at 8:00, tonight?"

"Yeah...sure. See you at 8:00. Thank you, Judy...I think."

"I bet you'll be thanking me. I'm not going to tell you what to think about, but I do want to help you ponder this for yourself...I want you to resolve this issue on your own. Many people feel this church provides a great place to think. They say it takes on a spiritual, even mystical air at night. See how you're feeling about things after an hour or so of solitude and self-reflection here."

◆ ◆ ◆

As I walked up Washington Street that evening, I saw the little stone church differently. A couple of floodlights illuminated a U-shaped arch at the entrance. I arrived a little early. It was one of the first nights of an early spring where the night still feels just a bit cooler than usual, but almost as crisp as a fall evening. As I stood in front of the church, I just scanned the scene before me. Marfa at dusk. Wind whistling through the new spring leaves of the nearby trees. A few of the old oak leaves that had started falling were being kicked around in the breeze. Golden light was cascading down on the grounds of the courthouse. The orange courthouse took on an even more intense glow. It was a special moment.

"Steve?"

"Hi Judy."

"It's all yours. I'll be back by ten to lock up. If you are through before then please blow out the candle near the front of the church in the window so I'll know you're through in case I get back early."

"Thank you. Thanks for doing this."

"I know it sounds a little weird, but a little peace and quiet in a spiritual setting can go a long way towards focusing the mind. It's a rare commodity these days."

"You're right. Thanks."

As I walked through the screened-in entryway to open one of front doors, my eyes had to adjust to the darkness. Only a red candle was lit near the front and a white candle near the rear. The dusky light streamed into the beautiful stained-glass windows casting little red, green and blue highlights about the church. The large stained-glass window above the front door was also illuminated from the outside, casting more multi-colored highlights throughout the inside of the sanctuary. The front door stained-glass feature depicted a knight holding a white shield with a red cross and a white horse. The other thing I noticed was the sheer solitude and quiet. It felt like a deep peacefulness was engulfing me.

From the pew I chose near the center, I just sat still staring at the red flickers that came from the candle to the left of the alter. The candle cast diamond-shaped patterns against the wall. I kind of went into a trance, where I found myself breathing very slowly. At first, it was an effort to concentrate on that tranquil red glow. Over time, however, I found myself considering my plight. I focused on Judy's question: was there anything about me that could be holding Stacy back. What were my shortcomings in all this? Did I really have long-held biases or beliefs that kept me from understanding better what Stacy wanted? I knew there probably were some things in my past that shaped my thoughts and actions that just didn't pass muster with her. I couldn't put my finger on it, but those kinds of feelings tugged at me.

I realized I was immature in some ways. I wasn't giving enough. I knew I had a wonderful, beautiful, warm, funny, enjoyable woman in my life and all I could focus on was what I thought was our one weak spot—physical intimacy. Contrary to the crap I learned in the football locker room, I'd grown to think that love and affection were my main criteria for having sex. I needed to start putting that into practice. The sanctity of the marriage ceremony the church insisted on was only a secondary consideration up until now, and I still wasn't sure how I felt about that.

I went through many scenarios in my mind when I'd pushed the issue a bit with Stacy. I thought about how I was just focused on my needs. Maybe if I was more focused on her needs, we'd achieve greater intimacy and the sex would naturally happen. I know we would grow closer. She was such a giving woman.

I felt a little guilty thinking about sex in church. I entertained the idea that the church probably didn't even need to be involved. I then appreciated I needed to be thinking about our relationship, not sex. The sex would come, when it was right.

I also thought that perhaps Stacy was unable or unwilling to articulate moral values that guided her behavior. Maybe she'd been hurt by some other unthinking and uncaring man in the past. Maybe she viewed premarital-sex as a sin. I started feeling disappointment with myself for not trying harder to understand her. Perhaps I needed to work more to understand me as well. I'd only really been sexually active with a very small number of women, one of them being the one who most likely hated me in DC. I think she just came over and used me, and I was nothing more than a willing co-conspirator. I thought I enjoyed it at the time, but I always felt guilty, even unclean, afterward. I thought it was because I was letting her use me, but maybe there was more. How did I really feel about it?

The whole scene was bizarre. On the one hand, I felt premarital sex, while not perfectly acceptable in the eye of the church, was not all that huge a deal. Almost everybody I knew had sex before marriage. What was so wrong with it? It was between two consenting adults. On the other hand, I knew something wasn't right—the post-sex guilt I always felt. What was there to feel guilty about? I know what the Bible said about it, but was it still relevant today? If so, why would almost everyone have premarital sex? How did I even know that "everyone did it?"

Why was so much written about it and why was it so glorified in the media? Was I reflecting my conservative, some would say warped, childhood, or was I clinging to ancient wisdom?

These were all questions that I'd never given a second thought to before.

I then begin to think about what difference it made what everyone does? Shouldn't what I—and my partner—think about it be the only thing that matters? I didn't want to be a freak or a prude. Sex is fun. Why did it have to be so complicated!

Then I thought long and hard about what could be wrong with sex. I knew what the Bible said. But I also knew what it said about some other things that didn't seem to make me feel as guilty, such as lying, getting angry, using profanity and probably a myriad of other things I did. Aside from the teachings of the Bible, were there more things about sex to consider? Disease was a no brainer. But something maybe even larger was its potential to diminish your view of yourself and take away from how special it could be with the person you really love. I mean I knew people who were very sexually active that did seem to have low self-esteem. I wondered how it would affect their relationship with the person (or persons over time) they marry. Will sex seem less special? I recalled the Bible raising the notion of man and woman becoming one. Did premarital sex harm that potential?

Again, I'd only had sex with a few women, and with each of them I'd had a meaningful relationship—except for the last one—so it wasn't like I was a sex maniac. I actually turned down sex with a few women when it just didn't seem right. The reason I craved close physical intimacy with Stacy is that I cared for her so much more than the other women. I just thought it would be incredible to be with her. If I really believed that, then I should be prepared to wait and take it on our terms, not my terms. She was worth the wait, I thought…I believed. I needed to slow down and let our relationship progress at the pace that seemed right to her. Some of my friends in DC would have laughed at me. They would say, "You have a right to sex, you two are dating."

But in reality, I knew I didn't.

I was astonished and ultimately ashamed that I'd never had this conversation with myself before. It spoke to the immaturity that Judy had detected earlier. Were there other internal discussions I needed to have? I knew there were. I had the money to be pretty much whatever I wanted. I needed to figure that out. I needed to stop just going with the flow. And just as important, having a lot of money didn't mean I should be able to have sex, or even extravagant cars or other material things just because I felt like it. It then occurred to me that a sense of responsibility to others or to the rest of the world was important, too. Otherwise, I'd just kind of be like an alpha animal that just took what it wanted whenever it felt like it, without regard to others… that seemed unsustainable over any period of time that I'd experienced anyway.

Perhaps just recognizing these facts was an important step in maturing. My visit with Judy would pay dividends well into the future, based on the way I was feeling now.

As I started to ease out of my pew, I sat back down and briefly prayed—prayed for really the first time in many years. I felt a sense of gratitude as I blew the candle out up front. I knew that somehow this experience would play a role in my future relations with Stacy, as well as my relationship with me.

I thought about how life today is a constant quest for distraction. Cell phones, tablets, technology in general. What are we so scared of that we run from distraction to distraction? Why are we designing a world where these inner conversations are growing almost impossible? Will we soon be so distracted from our inner world, that we'll in fact become strangers even to ourselves? Will we have no personal values? No inner compass? Just as when people don't see each other for a while, can people become disconnected even with themselves? That time in the church will really stick with me, I was certain. I felt it was one time in my life, when an hour lasted an hour. It was a time when I didn't cheat myself out of a little bit of my time on the planet.

I blew out the candle and headed home.

❖ ❖ ❖

As I rounded the corner near my house, I saw a small orange light hovering over the sidewalk. I realized it was a person smoking while lurking in the shadows under a tree across the street from my house. I stopped and stood in the dark shadows of a tree myself. I watched a while to see if the figure noticed me. In a couple of minutes, I could better see the figure's poor posture and I knew it was my dear, pathetic cousin. I eased up towards him as quietly as I could. He was so focused on my house that I got right up to his tree undetected.

"Reckon Steve's home, Clark?'

Clark made a strange gargled sound, jumped and unsuccessfully reached for the tree to steady himself and fell to the ground.

"Dammit to hell, Steve. You scared da shit outta me!"

"Really. Whatcha doing out here?"

"I was going for an evening walk."

"You seemed to be standing by this tree and checking out my house."

"I was just takin' a smoke break. Free country you know."

"Free…hmm…you reckon your parole officer would be interested to know if a judge slapped a restraining order on you?"

"Whatch you talkin' 'bout?"

"I don't know. I guess I'm just not comfortable with having you stalk me. I'm kind of funny that way."

"I ain't stalkin' you!"

"Well, I'm not sure about that."

"Look Steve, I gotta go. Can we talk soon?"

"I'll meet you at the courthouse tomorrow afternoon around 2:00."

"Courthouse?"

"The big orange building with the lady on top over there. Lots and lots of law enforcement folks hang out around it. Think you can find it?"

Clark looked a little worried and swallowed. "Yeah. See ya tomorrow," he said sounding very deflated.

After my chat with Clark, if that's the way to describe it, it was a bit late to call Stacy. I resolved to try to do something special with her tomorrow and maybe show her that I'd grown up a bit. In a very non-pushy way, I was going to talk to her about the issues I'd reflected upon that evening. I'd go over to the gallery tomorrow morning to tell her what I thought I'd learned about the experience. I fell asleep reading a mostly decent novel written by a friend here in town.

12

"That animal is back," Stacy said the minute I walked in the gallery. "It went around the block twice honking and flipping the bird."

"Do you mean Paco?" I still had no clue what an omnisexual was. And, I wasn't fully comfortable with calling another human "it" although in Paco's case it may have fit. She was so aggressive.

"Yes!" Stacy said, as emphatically as I'd ever heard her say anything.

"She'll go away soon. Thank God she doesn't live here."

Stacy took a deep breath then and said, "Good morning, Steve." A forced but nice, pleasant smile.

"Good morning to you, Stacy. I want us to do something nice tonight. May I pick you up about 7:00?" I added a little formality to the invitation, which Stacy returned.

"Yes, you may. I look forward to it." She was smiling brightly now, and the worries about Paco and any other distractions were gone. I was glad. The time last night was cleansing.

As I walked into the bright sunlight, I felt lighter, happier. I think I was starting to understand new and important aspects of life. I was learning to take life on my own terms versus allowing others to define what was normal or acceptable. I wasn't worried about Paco and I wasn't worried about the evening. Maybe I was growing up a bit after reflecting on last night. I had a great woman in my life, even if I was a little taken aback by her intensity over Paco. Stacy loved everybody, I thought. I guess Paco was so revolting that she was able to get under even Stacy's skin.

♦ ♦ ♦

I picked Stacy up a little after 7:00. It was dusk as we approached the Hotel Paisano. A nice breeze was blowing through the courtyard. We sat at a table outside across from Jett's Grille. Stacy looked great. She wore a dark brown sleeveless dress and stiletto heels that accentuated her legs. She often wore her hair in a short ponytail, but tonight it fell around her shoulders, nicely framing her beautiful face. She wore glossy, bright red lipstick. Her only jewelry was a simple string of pearls, with a silver crucifix adorning the bottom arc of the necklace. She struck me as a sophisticated French model though she was the product of fine Texas, German and Spanish genes.

Over a glass of a nice pinot noir, we unwound by joking about our week. It was great, other than seeing that Deputy Dud passed slowly by a couple of times peering at me through his mirrored sunglasses even though there was no great need for sunglasses at that hour. I loved the way Stacy could laugh about almost anything. She could always make me happy. After we visited awhile, I slipped into the Grille to order a couple of Chicken Cilantros to go. I'd earlier dropped off a picnic basket for the kitchen to pack up dinner to go. I got an uncorked chilled bottle of a pinot grigio to go also and placed everything in the car before walking back into the restaurant.

"I have a little surprise for you," I said as I approached the table.

"What?"

"I can't tell you yet. Be patient. I want to take you somewhere special. Ready to go?"

"Sure." Her eyes lifted with anticipation. I was so proud to be with her. Before long we were driving up Highway 17 towards Fort Davis. I wanted to get some passion brewing, so I played "Roots" by the Gypsy Kings. I had noticed flamenco seemed to stir her soul and make her more romantic.

The last vestiges of the sunset cooperated beyond belief. The sky was a swirl of deep blue, purple, and orange with white and yellow highlights. It was as though we were driving under a huge artistic masterpiece. The flamenco music seemed to make the colors more vivid. At Weber Road, I turned off the highway and went up a dirt road that led up to a canyon onto a ridge that was only a few hundred feet high but offered a great view. Marfa shimmered in the distance. It was near dusk. The courthouse was easily visible. I finally got to "Stacy's peak" as I'd dubbed it. It offered a 360-degree view from a small mesa. As I was popping a couple of chairs open, I noticed a tear in Stacy's eyes. She stared around the mesa in amazement—the view, the closing minutes of the sunset, Marfa in the distance. All were bathed in a fading orange glow. She was overwhelmed.

I set the little portable table up. The music was on. Different, more subtle, but still flamenco. I opened the bottle of chilled wine and placed it on the table to breathe in the mountain air. Stacy seemed to be shocked. I knew she'd like it, but I didn't expect this depth of reaction. She just sat across from me with moist eyes smiling, listening to the music, and staring into my eyes. Her hair being down and gently tossed by the light winds was exquisite. She was speaking to me without words. I felt no need for words. We were totally communicating.

After a glass of wine, she stood on song 13 and walked around the table. She took my hand and led me up. She put one of my hands around her waist and said in a most sultry voice, *"bailamos querido."* I'd heard her speak Spanish before, but it never sounded that sensual. If I'd known she could sound like that, I would have banned the use of English in our presence even if my Spanish was so poor.

This was a new dimension, almost overwhelming. She was so graceful. Her body was heaven in my arms. I'd never seen her like this. With burning eyes, she spoke to me in Spanish. I didn't catch most of it, but I didn't care. I wanted more.

She was light, deep, sexy, fun, all at the same time. I loved this Stacy. She actually danced a little flamenco for me. She had studied flamenco in Spain one summer in college while visiting her mother's family. This was a whole new "saucy" side of Stacy that she'd up until now concealed from me. There's nothing more amorous than flamenco dancing, especially when Stacy danced.

By now, it was dark and no moon. The billions of stars seemed about 100 feet away. The air was cool and fresh. The slight breeze kept swirling her hair. I'd hoped to talk about our problems. It was impossible. We had no problems that night. There were no problems anywhere. After the flamenco, I popped in some very soft Dinah Washington.

I put a blanket out and we just stared at the stars. As "Just One More Chance" eased up into the stars, we kissed like mad, passionate lovers. We kissed with more passion than ever, but I didn't make any moves beyond that. I'd finally learned to accept Stacy on her terms. I chose to let her control the pace of our relationship for a while. It seemed to give her the confidence to let her guard down a bit. It was an amazing night. My memories were forged like iron, and I knew I'd always feel the warm breeze and envision the lights down in Marfa.

I don't recall what time we came off the mountain, but I think it was getting lighter in the east. We didn't encounter a soul as we eased down Highway 17 into Marfa. It was morning gray and still. I was in a daze as I kissed Stacy goodnight, or good morning, or whatever it was.

"*Buenas noches, querida,*" she whispered, as she left me at the door.

13

I may have gotten two hours sleep when I heard Clark pounding on my door. Through the muffle of the door I heard him outside cursing.

I finally made it to the door. I didn't think it right for my neighbors to have to endure his screaming. I cracked the door. The screen was latched.

"Open up you asshole!"

"No."

"Where thu'ell wiruh?"

"What?"

"Where the hell wiruh, you som bitch!"

"Cut the screaming and the cussing, Clark!"

"Where?"

It then dawned on me that I was so busy scoping out Stacy's Peak that I had forgotten to meet him.

"I'm sorry, Clark. I forgot. Later. Today. Same time and place."

"You mean in about fifteen minutes?" I looked at my clock. It was 1:45.

"Give me thirty minutes. I'll meet you there."

"You'd better not miss it dis time!"

"Yeah, yeah, Clark. See you in a half-hour."

I showered. I was really looking forward to this discussion.

When I hauled my squinty self out into the bright sunshine, I tried to stay in the shade. As I rounded Washington Street, I could see Clark sitting on the side of the courthouse across from the white church.

"No Clark, let's visit on the other side. I like the view better from there." He reluctantly got up and followed. On this side, we had a good view of the sheriff's department and a dark foreboding jail replete with bars on all the windows. I thought the view would set the right mood for our chat.

Clark plopped down on the lawn and looked straight ahead with a grimace. He had a torn black West Coast Choppers tee shirt, filthy jeans and the "Honk if…" cap. His facial expression gave him a run of the mill thug-look—only less intelligent. He didn't even project the usual "street smarts."

"Okay, Clark, what's on your mind?"

"You need to give me and Amy some of our daddy's money. You got no right to it and you know it." He wouldn't look at me.

"Clark, I explained it to Amy. I can't give you a dime. I wanted to. I really did. But I can't."

"Why da hell not?"

"According to your daddy's will, any money I don't receive goes to Pablo."

"Why? Pablo's a good man, but he ain't blood. I yam."

"I know it's tough Clark, but you really upset your dad."

"I know. But I'm clean now. I haven't done or sold drugs since I got out. I'm clean. I could really use that money!"

"What would you do with it?"

"You'd piss yourself laughing."

"Maybe not. Tell me."

"I don't know. You wouldn't believe it."

"Try me."

"I don't even know if I could do it. I don't even know if they'd let me."

"What do you want to do?" I was seeing a different side of Clark, or he was putting on a heck of a snow job.

"I want the money to go ta college."

"Really?" I was holding back the urge to laugh. I felt like I was keeping a straight face anyway.

"Yeah. I don't know if I can hack it, but I wanna try. I like history."

"Why do you act like a maniac? Why don't you show this side when you talk to me?"

"You don't understand, man. I got mixed up with a bad bunch of guys in high school here. I got my GED then became a worthless piece of shit. I don't know why I did it. I put on a tough act because that's how it is in prison. Weakness gets you killed, man!" He was actually able to make and even maintain eye contact. Maybe I caught him sober or something.

"I want to help you, Clark. I don't want you to be a "worthless piece of shit," as you describe yourself. You weren't such a bad guy when I use to come out to see y'all a long, long time ago."

"Whatcha gonna do?" Clark looked at me with the hopeful expression of an eight-year old. I was encouraged to see at least one of his slightly quivering eyes looking me mostly straight on. Maybe there was hope for him, however minuscule it might be.

"Tell you what. Let me think on this. I may have ideas, but I need to talk to the probate attorney to see what I can do. I know I can't give you money outright, but I may be able to figure out another way to help."

"No shit?" Clark looked incredulous. It was as though he was asking himself why anyone would want to help him.

"No promises but let me do some research. How can I contact you?"

"It ain't easy to contact me, Steve. I am driving a wrecker truck up in Stockton a few days a week. Buddy owns the truck. I fill in for him. It's a haul up there. I really hate it. I live in a pickup camper. Can I come by in a few days?"

"Come by one evening next week, maybe Thursday? That would give me a few days next week to do some research."

"You've made my day, man. Thanks!" Smile of a young boy. I saw a fleeting glimpse of the cousin I knew a long time ago.

"Sure, Clark. Just to be clear: no promises, but I'll try."

"See ya Thursday, Steve."

"Clark, just a little advice." I knew I shouldn't have done it, but I "accidentally" dropped a few twenties on the lawn and said, "Check around the bench, you know how some people drop things out of their pockets when they get up...maybe there's some money lying around to buy some new clothes. Please work on improving your grammar and stop the constant profanity. You'll never get into college with such a rough edge. And try to drop the 'just got out of jail for selling drugs' look you've been sporting since I came back."

"Thanks for giving me a chance. Steve, ... I know I'm kind of a fuck-up, I mean screw up. I'll try...I'll try real hard, I promise."

Clark picked up the money, tried to smile at me, and walked briskly away carrying himself just a little less like a thug. I made a mental note to visit with the probate attorney next week. I guess Clark had the fortune of finding me in a good mood after my magnificent time with Stacy last night.

◆ ◆ ◆

When I got back home, I had no idea what to do with what little was left of my day. Our business was still pretty light, so the distributorship closed weekends unless we had a special situation. Most weekends were wide open. Last week, I had to go to Presidio on a Saturday since we had four boxcars of beer being held at the border because a German shepherd had a cold or something. The dog kept alerting on one of our boxcars like it had drugs on board. The Texas, Mexico and Pacific Railroad had this worthless agent that just sat on her massive ass in an air-conditioned office watching television.

The agent hadn't once been able to answer a single question I'd asked her, nor had she even gone outside to see what riled up the dog. She was hired because she was the cousin of some aunt of some cousin of some aunt in Mexico who was related to the president of the railroad in Mexico City. Every time I had to go see her, which was as seldom as possible, she sat with the door closed in her small air-conditioned office watching the Mexican soaps. She acted as though it was a major hassle to turn the TV volume down just enough so I could shout over her *telenovelas*. The last time I was down in Presidio, I had to pick up a filthy American flag which was laying on the floor in the hallway lead-ing to her office. When I handed it to her, she just rolled her eyes and said something in Spanish I didn't catch. I would have cancelled my business with the railroad right then if the rest of their crew wasn't pretty conscientious.

I also feared that if I bailed out on them, the Union Pacific Railroad would stop servicing Marfa. As it was, only my warehouse and the cattle feed operation—the occasional recipients of my funky beer—received shipments in Marfa. The feed operation got in tank cars of molasses. The Union Pacific very reluctantly took my boxcars from their interchange in Alpine over to Marfa. I felt it my social responsibility to help keep railroad service in Marfa. The Union Pacific didn't mind taking my pass-through traffic to Los Angeles. They just didn't like servicing tiny, old quirky Marfa. Not sure why, but like the ranching and Hispanic culture, I didn't want that part of Marfa's heritage to die. There'd been a lot of shippers at one time including an oil dealer and a grain operation. My uncle had shipped loads of wool at one point. As a kid, I remembered seeing them unload boxcars of feed at what was now an art foundation. I like a wide array of art, but some of the work shown in the exhibit hall in what was once Marfa Wool and Mohair looks a bit like the aftermath of fatal car crashes.

◆ ◆ ◆

That afternoon, Stacy wasn't at the gallery. Pilar was staffing it. Pilar was a very attractive college student who I thought was someday going to be a successful attorney. She always tried to pick a fight with me, pushing back on almost everything I said, just for fun. I enjoyed jousting with her because she was very smart and exceedingly pretty. She was tall and slender like Stacy with skin the color of cappuccino. She had shoulder length, black hair.

"Hey, loser. She's not here," she said. "Say *vato*, how'd that woman you worked for in DC feel about immigration?"

"She wasn't great on immigration, I'm afraid."

"Shit, she probably listened to you."

"She seldom listened to me."

"Well, at least she was smart enough to resist that, but still, she was one of those tea party types, wasn't she?"

"Yeah, I guess." I normally gave her as good as she dished out, but I was shooting blanks this time. I worked for a Neanderthal in DC.

"You gringos." She defiantly smiled at me. Damn she was pretty.

"C'mon, Pilar, you know not all white folk feel that way."

"What?" She looked incredulous. Her big eyes were expressive, telling everyone that her emotions were simmering underneath. "What kind of weed are you smoking, dude? I think you got hold of some really bad stuff. It's making you hallucinate, man."

Just to needle her, I said, "You know Bush tried to fix this mess. He tried to get consensus on how to do immigration right, which would have in turn helped heal our rift with Mexico. He tried you know, before the party flipped out on this."

"You're so full of shit!"

"I know, but I'm not all wrong on this."

"If Stacy didn't like you, I'd have to whip your smart ass." That was her style of flirting. She was tough. She was looking into a mirror and was arranging her shiny jet-black hair into a ponytail. Pilar had a nice, long slender neck.

"I like that. You should wear it that way more," I said.

"Don't flatter yourself." She jetted a glare at me through the mirror. So much for me flirting back with Pilar.

"All right. I take it that Stacy isn't coming in."

"You take correctly, dear. But thank you for coming in here and pissing me off." Ponytail arranged, she gracefully spun around and smirked at me, although the flirting undertones were still there.

"Don't mention it."

"Believe me, it isn't worth mentioning. Don't worry."

"By the way Pilarita, have you sold a damn thing all day?"

"You might want to leave." The smile had not left her face. She really was a smug, very pretty, very self-confident little smart ass.

As I walked out, I stuck my head back in, "Oh yeah, can't wait 'til you guys pick the prez. Y'all have done such a good job down in Mexico! There's a lot to look forward to when that rolls around." I had to get one last dig in, even knowing she and her mom were born in Presidio County. Truthfully, if I were a few years younger and I didn't know Stacy, I would have been asking Pilar out about every two and a half minutes. Kind of like the Red Angel, she was always a player in the back of my mind. Having what I had with Stacy, I tried to push that temptation away.

14

When I finally caught up with Stacy, her Aunt Phronie from Dallas had popped in on her. She wanted me to run by in the evening to meet her. Some of her relatives had unusual names. She said it was a rural Texas thing. Her dad was from Shiner, Texas, a couple of hours west of Houston, but he had a few relatives who lived in and around Dallas. Her mother was from Madrid. A Texas German and a Spaniard, hence the complex, delicious and funky temperament of Stacy.

I decided to check in on the progress at my house. It was finally nearing completion. I had been living in a half restored house for quite a while. My third set of contractors were out on the porch sipping coffee from the Brown Recluse, a local coffee shop. We have classy, in other words, expensive remodelers in Marfa. The first crew lasted three days. They were incensed when I expressed reservations about their taking my 70" flat panel TV and theater sound system away in their truck to "safeguard" them while they were restoring the hardwood floors. They calmly explained that it was standard for contractors to use their customer's gear while in storage. When I opposed that policy, they ceremoniously, or unceremoniously in my view, walked off the job. Over the three days nothing had been accomplished other than draping a few drop cloths over some furniture and my goods being prepared for "storage."

The second crew was great for a few days. They got the floors fully restored and then just never showed up again. They never even came to get paid other than the initial deposit. They did the floors and patched all the adobe and then disappeared. I wanted to think it was divine compensation for the previous crew's total lack of production.

The third and final crew was great—mostly. My only complaint is that they sometimes got mixed up on the ownership of the house. Their policy seemed to be that the customer was seldom correct. The crew leader—Navajito—was very stubborn once he decided what color something should be or what finish should be used. He would eventually oblige, but he would always end his opposition by flashing me a microsecond of a vicious glare that made me just a bit nervous. His work was truly outstanding once I could convince him that I should really get to have my preference since I was going to be living there, as well as paying for it. I usually accepted his methodology because his craftsmanship reflected his passion, and he knew what he was doing. He took real ownership of his projects. No less important, he and his crew showed up and worked when they said they would.

Only once did this tendency of personal "ownership" of his work become a big issue. He painted my living room terracotta with white trim. I had requested a beige. I told him it was lovely but too bright for my taste. This went on for three straight days. Over time, I started liking his selection and became confused as to what I really wanted. Every time I mentioned my preference for beige, he'd give me his micro-glare and bark something at Rojelio, his assistant, that always contained a few curse words in Spanish. When I finally gave in and yielded to terracotta, he smugly told me that, "I think you will be most happy with *your* selection, amigo."

Navajito not only did a great job with the restoration, but he became a watchdog for the house during the day. I'd warned him about Clark. Once, right after Navajito and Rojelio had started, Clark came around and began to eye some of my furniture and appliances that had been temporarily stored on the front porch. Rojelio quietly informed me on my next visit that "Navi" had a quiet conversation with Clark, a conversation that drained all color from Clark's ruddy, disgusting, wrinkled face. After the brief discussion, Clark grabbed his stomach and quickly staggered away.

Clark was to me what Paco was to Stacy. I could almost get past Amy's foul language, greed, bad grammar and slightly crooked teeth, because she was kind of attractive, even if she was my cousin. I had an interesting history with her. We weren't kissing cousins, well maybe once, but we did flirt with each other when we were young. Clark however had no redeeming qualities—none. On top of that, I still hadn't fully bought into his "I want to go to college" business.

Later on, I learned the meaning of "Navi's" name. Rojelio told me that Navajito means knife in Spanish. Navi had quite a reputation as a young man in Marfa and Presidio. But he assured me that it had been years since he actually knifed someone and that I had "practically" nothing to worry about since Navi liked me. Rojelio said that Navi often said, "Steve *no es malo por un gringo*." I felt most comforted…sort of. On the other hand, I was proud that Navajito had dispatched Clark so effectively. I was impressed with Navi beyond just his craftsmanship.

◆ ◆ ◆

By the time I got over to Stacy's house, it was nearly 7:00. She had just returned from mass. Black slacks, light olive sweater, heels—looked great even in her modest church attire.

"How often do you go to weekday mass, Stacy?" I felt idiotic. Why hadn't I inquired before? Maybe the Reverend Judy was right concerning my self-absorbed focus and lack of maturity.

"Every week. I usually go on Sunday. I also go during the week occasionally, typically Thursdays."

"Really? Why haven't we…discussed it?"

"What's to discuss? I'm Catholic. My mom is Spanish, Steve, you know that. There wasn't an option." She had a rosary in her hand.

"I know. I just…"

"C'mon up. I need to change."

Her small apartment was clean as usual. Even if she was free-spirited, she was neat. Her place smelled of lavender this time.

"Nice incense? Lavender?"

"Perfume. Wanna drink while I change?"

"Wine"

"*Bueno. Vino rojo?*"

"*Está bien.*"

When she returned with a glass for both of us, she sat down on an ottoman and removed her shoes. She stared at her feet a minute and blurted out, "Let's do something really fun tonight. There's supposed to be a great band at the Liberty Theater at 8:30. Let's go!" Who could refuse that smile?

"Sure…" Just when I thought I knew her, she'd always surprise me. Why hadn't she mentioned her Catholicism to me before?

"Let me change."

She came back in five minutes wearing a flowing rainbow skirt that fell to just above her knees, red fuzzy sweater and flats. Fresh, red lipstick. Ponytail. All that in five minutes. I still had a lot to learn about this woman. Well, I have a lot to learn about women!

❖ ❖ ❖

The placard outside the theater was an all-black square. At the very lower right-hand corner in tiny neon yellow letters it said "*BLEU -- SAT MAR 24 @ 9 or + @ Liberty.*" Big sign for just a small amount of barely readable text!

"What are you looking at?"

I was studying the sign. "I was just looking to see if there was anything else, picture, anything. It really is just a black sign, isn't it? Why would someone make a large sign that's almost all black? You can hardly read the damn writing in the corner, it's so small!"

Stacy opened her eyes very wide and slowly said, "Have you ever heard of Minimalism? We are in Marfa, after all."

"Whatever, I guess. Maybe I'm not as minimal as Bleu and the Liberty Theater is, then?" I playfully sniped as we strolled in.

The band was warming up as we entered. Bleu was interesting to say the least. Stacy informed me that they were an emerging lounge, techno-pop band from Belgium. The music ranged from slow, ominous flamenco-flavored pieces to slow techno-pop beats that allowed the singer to show off her husky voice. I must admit she did have an intriguing, sultry voice when she sang in French; not bad to look at either once you got past the blue makeup and black lipstick. Stacy obviously enjoyed it. She kept trying to get me to dance with her. I finally succumbed after adequate quantities of alcohol became part of the equation. On one dance, she almost had me in a trance when she started her flamenco hand movements and started waving her skirt. I had to stop and just watch. I wasn't the only one. I think half the people there began watching her.

At one point she was staring at me with a sexy, defiant look. Her hands crossed above her head and her fingers were spread apart making beautiful, slender waves. My pulse was racing. I felt as though she was making love to me through her dance. At that very instant she "caught herself." She realized others were watching and she plummeted back to earth.

She pulled me off the dance floor and meekly whispered, "I guess my skirt is a bit short for flamenco, eh?"

"Believe me, it was magical."

"I guess I'm ready to head out."

I sure didn't have a problem with it. She was like a vision. There was an amazing, flaming passion she seemed to struggle to keep in check. At times, it was as if there were a battle going on inside of her though I wasn't sure what forces were involved in the conflict. Perhaps, the Spanish roots were warring against the German roots.

We returned straightaway to her apartment. She turned on the corner lamp and excused herself to change. I peered around the room. I realized that it had been a few weeks since I'd hung out much at her little casita. The red walls glowed beautifully. I saw *L'étranger* by Camus on her bed. On her nightstand was a copy of *The Stories of the Rose.* I wasn't familiar with that book. I studied the pictures on her walls. Once again, I felt I didn't really know her as well as I thought. My relationship with Stacy was a process where a thin layer was peeled back every once in a great while, revealing a whole new dimension that kept me just a bit off balance.

Aside from the images of saints, her pictures were of a beautiful western landscape, an Italian or French village landscape and a black and white photo of her as a child with her parents. I had only really examined the family picture before. She had lit a candle as we entered. I loved the feeling her tiny room evoked: warmth and mystery at the same time. I loved the scent of the candle over on a small shelf near the Virgin Mary image. The candlelight danced on the image bringing out vivid reds and oranges in the picture. It smelled a bit like a church—burning candles and incense—with just a trace of her perfume lingering. I hadn't smelled the strange pot smell again that I encountered the first time I sat right there holding her blue foot.

Stacy reappeared wearing a huge black night shirt that dropped to her ankles. An hour ago, she was waving her short skirt as though it were a long flamenco dress showing half of Marfa her incredible legs. Now she was standing before me meek, covered neck to ankle. Her clothing selection was the apparel equivalent of a bundle of barbed wire covered with no trespassing signs.

"Stacy, I just have to ask you…do you ever smoke pot?"

She looked shocked.

"I mean I thought I smelled it the first time I came over."

She looked relieved. "Oh, that was Dayleen. She was visiting that afternoon. She was stressed about a boyfriend. She knows I hate the stuff, even the smell, but I put up with it for her since she was so stressed out."

"Just wondering."

"Do you?"

"Not in years. I tried it a few times. Didn't do anything for me. It stinks. I'm cool with folks using it though. Our laws on it seem kind of crazy to me."

"I agree. Though I do like the thought of escaping sometimes." She looked at the floor as though she was thinking about the concept of escaping something.

I watched her for a moment then blurted out, "Yeah. I guess I use alcohol sometimes to do that. Not too much normally, though."

I noticed Stacy was still deep in thought.

"What's wrong. Stacy?"

She looked up very solemnly and stared at me.

"What? What's wrong?"

She slowly cracked a grin.

"Let's get drunk! Just you and me. Right here. Right now."

"What…are you serious?" I was gob smacked.

"Never been more serious."

"El Cheapo is closed…"

"I got plenty of wine."

"What's going on?"

"I really don't like getting drunk and I don't drink much anymore. I just know I have never really trusted anyone until I got ripped with them. You see a different side of people then. Let's see what happens."

She lit another candle, put on Miles Davis' *Kind of Blue*, and went to open a bottle of wine. She was right. She had the booze. She had about 12 bottles of wine stashed in the cupboard. She was alive once again. Joking, flirting, smiling…I was astonished with the transformation. I was hard to process these changes in her.

About three glasses later, I realized Stacy was serious. She was getting us drunk. She sat cross legged on the floor, her night shirt was pulled up almost to her waist, once again revealing lots of leg. The shy Stacy had disappeared. Whatever conflict that was taking place in her had ceased for the moment. The side I preferred was in control!

We shared childhood stories, laughed at our very bad jokes, kissed, rubbed backs. It was like a drunken childhood slumber party in a way. It was odd and exciting at the same time. It felt sexual and innocent juxtaposed without any conflict. I couldn't get the image of her staring at me on the dance floor out of my mind. It was one of the most erotic images I'd ever experienced.

"What in the hell are you reading Stacy?" I kind of blurted out, to break the tension. I guess I was trying not to take advantage of the situation as much as I desperately wanted to.

"What?" Her eyes were a bit glassy.

"The book on your bed."

"It's a book about the rosary."

"Not that one; I mean the other. But what's up with the rosary book, too?"

"It gives the history of the rosary. I love the rosary. It gives me as close to a state of serenity as I ever experienced on earth."

She operated on a different plane. Why couldn't I have the depth she had? I knew there had to be more than my outlook on life. Was I as shallow as Reverend Judy indicated?

"What about the other one? It's in French?"

"Mais, oui."

"You speak French?"

"Je parle un peu. Je le lis mieux."

"Nice."

"I speak a little. I read it pretty well. I double-majored. Modern Language and Geography at Southwestern." She flipped her hair back and smiled. She became very expressive as she spoke, way more body language as the wine kicked in.

I'd never even asked her about her education. What an idiot.

"How did you come to pursue those subjects?"

"Dunno. I guess I love the world, travel, foreign cultures. I really don't know. I guess I felt led to study those topics to prepare myself for something. Something like that anyway. What about you Steve? You went to Texas A&M?"

"Yeah. Believe it or not, I studied forestry."

"Forestry?"

"Yeah…I had dreams of being a forest ranger or something along those lines. And no shit, I was the only forestry major that also studied French and Spanish. The tree nerds all made fun of me, but in some strange way I wanted to be part of something bigger. I was the freak."

"*Est-ce que tu parles français?*"

"*Je parle un peu, aussi.* It's weird speaking French. I haven't spoken it much since college…except for one embarrassing occasion when I tried to chat up a French girl in a bar in Georgetown. She couldn't really speak English, so we improvised. It really was an embarrassing experience. She was nice, but I could tell she found me only mildly amusing. I also spent a week or so in Quebec on a temporary assignment, so I got to practice it a little then, too."

"Speak to me in French. I think it would be a turn on, Steve."

I got goosebumps when she said "turn on." But true to form, my French failed me. I finally remembered a Voltaire poem I struggled through in school and reprised the struggle once again. Stacy made a strange noise and came over to snuggle up next to me.

"You have potential. I knew you did. I've never doubted your potential. You reek of it…if only…"

"If only what, Stacy?"

"If only you'd let yourself go…or something. If only you'd let yourself be what you could be. Isn't that what you used to say in the Army?"

"That was 'be all you can be.' Just what do you mean, Stacy? What am I missing here?"

She paused for a minute and looked at the floor. "I don't know…I just feel like you're holding yourself back or something," she finally said. "You're more than what you've been since I met you. I just know it!"

"How so?"

"I don't know, Steve, but you're not getting off the hook," she said as she got up to refill our glasses.

She came back with glasses full to the brim and sat right across from me. "All right, Steve. You got something on your mind. I can tell. Out with it. Let's go with it. Tell me what's on your mind."

"I don't know how to say it. You're amazing. I love you. I love so much about you."

"But what? What is it you don't love?" Stacy asked, looking as serious as I've ever seen her. The alcohol was making her more pointed now. She appeared to be edging towards getting miffed or at least impatient with me.

"I love you, Stacy. It isn't qualified."

"You said that but help me out here. I love you, damn it. You know that. Now tell me what you want to say. I need to hear it."

"You seem to be battling, too...holding something back yourself. Something is struggling inside of you...to get out or to get in, or something!"

"Are you saying I'm frigid?"

"No."

"Then what is it?"

She was becoming angry, and impatient. But I sensed it wasn't with me even if I was the target right then.

"Stacy, I want you to be happy, truly happy. I sense you're holding back on something. Is there anything you're not telling me?"

"Fine. If you want sex let's do it right now. Floor or my bed?" Wow, the wine was fully kicked in. This was a real change in direction!

"I don't want sex. I want love. If love means sex, then yes, I want that, but it has to be more than just sex! I want to know where we're headed, where this relationship is going. You keep holding back, damn it!" The alcohol was kicking in on me, too.

"Steve, I love you. I love you more than anyone I've ever loved before. But you're not going to force me into having sex with you until I'm ready. So, if it is sex you've got to have, you need to look elsewhere."

I just stared at her in shock. Where did all this outpouring come from? How did we start heading down this path?

"Steve, I didn't mean it the way it sounded. I'm drunk so I'm just talking straight off the top of my head. I'm not saying it's unfair for you to want that. I'm just saying I'm not prepared to give it to you right now."

"You don't really get what I'm saying, do you? We must be talking past each other or something! It isn't just the sex. I mean that's important, when it's time. For me, I want you all the time. You're driving me crazy. But, I can wait. This is…this is…way deeper than sex. I just sense something. I don't know, damn it. I can't put my finger on it. There's a wall or something!"

"I'm sorry, Steve." She was looking into my eyes. Her eyes were moist. A tear suddenly appeared and ran down her face.

"I'm truly sorry, Steve. I'm sorry I ever got you into this. I really am. I'm crazy about you, and I'm so sorry." She leaned over to hold me and started sobbing. It was like tears came gently and then soon started coming from the center of her soul or something. She was shuddering.

"Look Steve, I love you. Things will be clearer soon. I'm struggling with something. I hope to be able to say what's been on my mind soon. Don't think it's another man or anything like that. You're right. I am struggling with something. I have to have peace soon. It's totally driving me nuts. But I want you to know something…I'm drunk so give me permission to be totally candid."

"Of course, Stacy. Please say what you feel."

"I love you so much. But I think you're really immature at times. I see so damn much potential in you. I see something in you trying to get out. Like you have an energy or talent that you have not…will not…tap."

She stared away for a minute, then continued, "You have depth, but you hide it. In fact, you're very immature at times. I'd never tell you this sober, so thank—or blame—the wine, I guess. I wish you'd fucking grow up a little! You have so damn much to offer. You are funny, handsome, smart, even though you hide it, but best of all, you have a very good heart. I mean giving money to Saint Mary's Church for Pablo and trying to help that nimrod cousin of yours. You have so much potential. Just tap it! Stop holding yourself back."

She looked me square in the eye and said something that

will always stay with me as long as I live: "I mean you aren't in high school or college or the Army anymore. Follow your heart. Don't put an act on for the guys, drop the clueless shit. I think you're an artist or something. There's something screaming on the inside to reveal itself. I see how you look at paintings, landscapes, sunsets, beautiful women…don't think I didn't know about you admiring other women! I've seen you check out Pilar. I don't blame you; she's stunning! Not a big deal. You're human. At least you have good taste.

"My point is that you are attracted to art and beauty. There is something artistic yearning inside of you if you'll only listen." She had stopped talking loudly, dropping into a whisper almost. Wow, she was penetrating something deep in me. "Follow your heart."

As she pulled her hair back into a ponytail as though she was really getting into this, she said "Steve, I tried being an artist, writer, whatever, but it wasn't for me. I wanted it, but I didn't have it. I do know I have a gift. I just don't know if I can bear the burden that goes with it. I only ask that you don't let immaturity or fear hold you back. Your gift is way different than mine, and it screams for release to the world. That was another reason I thought you were gay. You have an eye for creativity. I mean look at your house. It's gorgeous."

"That was Navi. Not me. He's the artist."

"Bullshit, Steve. You called most of the shots whether you want to own up to it or not. Did Navi take those black and whites? Who picked out that painting as you walk in? Who picked out the spot towards Ft. Davis where you took me for a sunset dinner? You've got something, Steve. Don't hold yourself back. When you spoke French to me, I wanted to make love to you and horsewhip at the same time you for being so stupid. I've seen it in you since the first time I met you. I just haven't had the courage to tell you. I thought it would make you mad or uncomfortable or something."

After a long pause, she quietly said, "Steve, why can't you see what I'm talking about?"

"Stacy, I thought we were talking about you, then you pull this on me. Are we both screwed up beyond recognition? Is that why we love each other?"

"To be honest, I think we love each other despite how screwed up we are. Look Steve, I am absolutely spent. No matter how much I desperately want to continue this conversation, I'm going to be asleep in about two minutes. Besides, we're hopeless. Please give me a long, delicious kiss then get the hell out of here! And, oh yeah, don't even think about driving, you asshole. You're drunk, too. I thought you blathered something about not drinking that much. Bullshit. Leave your car here."

She kissed me like it was the last time we would ever see each other, like I was going off to war or something. I was truly in shock as I headed for the door.

My mind raced as I walked home. Marfa at 3:00 in the morning is a ghost town. Even Highway 90 was quiet. The only disruption was a Union Pacific freight train. I'd thought it might drop off some loads of beer. We were overdue for a shipment, but it was a container train that barreled through town, clattering incessantly at the rail crossings.

In the wake of the train and the utter stillness that was restored to Marfa, I pondered whether Stacy was drunk and out of her mind, or did she see something in me that absolutely eluded me? What was holding her back? It was obvious that she was just as tortured as I was. I'd thought all this time that my torture was exclusively because of her. Was I torturing myself as well? And what gift was she talking about?"

About a block shy of my house, the deputy pulled up to me. What the hell was he doing out at 3:00 am?

"Hey, Miller!" He called out to me.

I absolutely did not want to talk to him as loaded as I was. I just nodded and smiled and kept walking.

"Why walking…late hour?" Damn, was he drunk or me?

"Just going home, deputy."

"Huh? You make it raht? Clark, Miguel?"

"Sure, all is well with them and the whole world, deputy." I was almost home. He kept cruising right alongside of me. A half of block to go.

"You better...be making it good, friend." He was watching me like a hawk. Did even he have a clue what he was saying?

Finally, in front of my yard, I simply said "good night, deputy."

"Wait Miller," I had given up him getting my name right. "You hiring. Criminals?"

"Huh?" I was home, let me go dufus, I silently pleaded.

"Navajo, whatever his name is. He's killed. Fella."

"No, sir. He's a good guy. He's a great craftsman. Very happy." I could hear the Rolling Stones' "Under My Thumb" softly on his radio. What a strange moment. Not worth remembering but I remember the absurdity of that song at 3:00 a.m. in Marfa and the dud.

"Uh? Don't like this. Clark tells me stuff."

I was losing my cool, Stones or not.

"Look deputy, I found Navi by talking to Sheriff Duncan... the sheriff recommended him for the job. Sheriff Duncan's my friend. He hunts on my ranch. Why don't you talk to the sheriff about this? This is getting old."

"Clark. Wrong?" The dud just sat there looking up at me with a completely blank look. "You know Daryl?"

"Yes. I know Sheriff Duncan well. He's a cousin of mine." I think that's true. He was related to Uncle Clive somehow.

"Miguel? What about him?" He blurted out. Damn, if I didn't know he was an idiot, I'd swear he was drunk. Maybe he was drunk, too. Who knows? It was late and I was done humoring this idiot.

"Look, Dudley, I gotta go to bed. Nice visiting." I spun and went on up my sidewalk. His dad, the judge, couldn't retire fast enough! I heard him say "Amy" just as I reached my door, but I just went inside. As I peered out the window, he eased off into the night. Looked like he was shaking his head as he drove off.

15

He looked down at the ground, took his cap off and humbly looked up at me. I guess that was his effort at contrition, earnestness or something.

"Believe me Steve, you ain't gonna regret it!" But somehow, I couldn't believe that.

"I sure hope so, Clark. I want everything to work out for you. I really do." Well, that was true. I did want things to turn out better for Clark. It was probably the only way I'd get him out of my hair. At the same time, I realized the chances were slim.

"I feel a whole new Clark coming on," he declared. "First a job at the beer place and now this. I'm set. Yes siree. I am all set. I'm gonna have money and one day a degree, a real college degree! Hell Steve, I might just have me a girl 'for long." His job was with the beer distributor over in Alpine. I had nothing to do with it. He probably trashed me in front of Miguel and cinched it.

"You bet, Clark. It's going to be hard work, but it'll pay off. Remember, one failed drug test and the party's over. Please keep that in mind while you're on the road to the new you." On the counsel of the probation attorney, I funded a scholarship at Sul Ross for which Clark was a cinch, at least I thought. It was probably the only free ride ever set up for someone with Clark's credentials, or total lack thereof. I thought it was bullet proof until Armando Ramirez applied. Armando met all the criteria —busted for drugs on at least three occasions, served over five years in jail, native of Presidio County, between 30 and 35 years of age and he was a former ranch hand. To Armando's misfortune, he hadn't served time in federal, state and local jails; I never thought the "local jail" caveat would be the clinching detail! That distinguishing attribute alone resulted in Clark being the only "fully" qualified candidate. I felt like an idiot pushing this "targeted scholarship to reduce chronic recidivism among at-risk cowboys," but it was the only way I could help my hopeless, idiotic cousin without breaking the requirements of the will. I inserted the drug testing requirement in coordination with the probation office. Sul Ross State University was for some reason disinclined to monitor this portion of the scholarship.

"One tip, Clark."

"Whatzat, Steve."

"Maybe you should lose the cap."

"What? Why?"

"I don't know but it might offend some people. Just a hunch."

"Steve, it's a …you know, it's like a joke or something. I'm not really telling folks to honk if they're horny, you goof."

"I realize that, but …well anyway, just a suggestion. Not everyone has your sense of humor, you know. Have a fine Marfa day, buddy," I said, hoping to disengage from this little chat as quickly as I could.

"You know Steve…you may be raht about the cap. Here, you want it?"

"That's okay, but no thanks," I sure as hell didn't want to even touch it. "Now don't forget, no drugs in any way, shape or form, and go see Mrs. Potter as soon as the new class announcements come out next month!"

"Sho'nuf, Steve. Thanks millions! Man, am I gonna get high tonight to celebrate! Oh, I mean drunk!"

"Sure, Clark, but I'd advise against letting booze get the better of you, too. Good luck."

"I get free beer now that I work for Miguel. Well, almost free. Five bucks a case! Miguel gets it free, but you know, he's gotta eat too. I like to help out where I can…just like you, huh, Steve?"

"You bet, Clark…we're just two peas in the pod," I replied, trying to smile in a supporting way.

I could tell he wanted to hug me, but mercifully, he just

smiled and wandered off. He stopped after walking awhile and gave me a humble smile and timid wave. Sounded like Miguel had upped his game a little on making money on the side. I dreaded him trying to come back to work in Marfa after he gets fired.

❖ ❖ ❖

Stacy and I gave each other some space for a few days following our drunken soiree. A few days later one unusually hot, almost humid morning, I ventured into the gallery. Unlike my birthplace of Houston, humidity was an infrequent visitor to Marfa. The gallery appeared empty until I heard Pilar's voice booming from the back.

"Hey asshole!" That was her effort at a warm, welcoming greeting. I loved it.

"Yeah…back atch'ya, *mujer*."

"If you are looking for your lady, *no está aquí*," she said in her best exaggerated gringo-fied Spanish. "I'm back here futzing with the swamp cooler, trying to get it to work."

"*Ah, sí. Claro. Estoy buscando para ti, querida*," I said in my best gringo accent. It drove her nuts.

"Please desist from ever speaking Spanish in front of me, at any time…it's truly disgusting."

"I couldn't help it, you sounded so sexy. I thought I could, too!"

She laughed. "You better watch yourself. Your woman may get jealous."

"I highly doubt that, especially of you."

"Don't be so sure. But you know what? You're right. She'd know that I'd never take on a mercy case like you, *vato*! What does she see in you?"

"Dunno."

She wore a short skirt that fit her perfectly. She looked so good I didn't need much of an imagination with her. I quickly whisked those thoughts out of my head.

"Where is Stacy, anyway?"

"She'll be back. She said she had an errand or two."

"Tell her I came by, please...*por fay-boor*."

"Only if you take an oath to never offend the Spanish language again by attempting to speak it. Three or four hundred million people might suddenly change their native language if they heard your version of it."

"Want me to have Rojelio swing by? He's good with cooling systems"

"Nah, it's starting to work. The drain line was clogged."

"*Muchas gracias carita. Te amo demasiado, querido*," I said in my sexiest Spanish voice. I heard a string of lovely Spanish curse words as I made my hasty departure. I actually understood two of them. My, she had a wicked tongue. I don't know if I found her or her affectionate abuse so attractive—perhaps both.

I still had much to work through with Stacy, but she'd be worth all of it. I was feeling pretty good in some ways. The beer business was pointing towards a pick-up in volume and the gallery was doing okay. I felt now like I had the money invested well. Even though we hadn't seen each other much lately, I had a feeling that Stacy and I were on the verge of a breakthrough. Even with the trace of morning humidity, it'd been another bright, beautiful sunny day in Marfa. My world was pretty darn good these days.

Naturally, it was now that Amy chose to reenter my world.

16

She was sitting on my front porch as dusk was settling in. I saw her as I rounded the corner. She wore skimpy red shorts, a red and white checkered shirt tied about her waist. Red lipstick, yellow-framed cat eye sunglasses piled on top of her pretty hair. Pure fifties. It took me a second to recognize her. She was actually quite striking. In Marfa, you never knew if someone was being retro on purpose or not. Of late, pink lipstick and eyeliner only on the top was becoming all the rage. Real trendsetting town, Marfa.

I'd always had a slight crush on Amy from my days on the ranch. She was the first girl to kiss me. She was only technically my cousin. She was adopted. I'd never met her until I was about fourteen, and after palling around together on the ranch a couple of days, we had one of those strange teenage moments. Just a couple of kisses in the barn, but it stayed with me for years after. Some might think it was sick, I know, but probably not all that rare within the human predicament.

"You givin' dough to that crackhead and those frickin' idol worshippers. Now it's my turn, big boy!"

Big boy? Too many old movies I guess.

"Now Amy…"

"No 'now Amy' shit. I want it now. I want $250,000 now. Clark got his, now I want mine!"

"Wait a sec. I didn't give Clark anything. I set a scholarship which he happened to qualify for. I was shocked, I assure you." Okay, shock was a bit of an overstatement, but I figured I might as well really piss her off. "I don't know what you're talking about as far as 'idol worshippers.' Who do you mean, anyway?"

"Talk 'bout a waste of money. That crackhead can't even read, dumbass! What are you pulling? Clark scoring you drugs? women?"

"No!" the thought of Clark setting me up with a woman was more than I could stomach. It was patently offensive that my "dear cousin" would even suggest it. Talk about trying to get my goat!

Amy glared at me as she slowly lowered her sunglasses over her eyes. She gave me a pretty smile and said in her best mountain lion moaning growl, "Steve…are we gonna do this the easy way or am I gonna hafta fuck you up?" She slowly stood up and approached me.

I wasn't sure how to reply. I knew too late that busting out laughing was the wrong response. She suddenly hit me in the stomach. She actually hit me! She doubled me over, the little bitch.

"Steve…you brought this on yourself. I can't make you give me the money, but I can sure make you wish you had'da!" she said as she casually strolled down the sidewalk swinging her hips. Weird thing was…as sick as it may have seemed and as sick as my stomach felt, I still felt a trace of a crush or something. How could I still care one way or the other for someone from my past like Amy? Maybe there was some underlying trend toward masochism at play there? I still kind of cared. I guessed first kiss stuff or something. I figured that the days to come would take care of that.

Amy never did mention anything else about "idol worshippers" so I could only guess what that was all about. Maybe it was Stacy's friends out at the ranch. Speaking of the ranch, it was time to check that out again, and see how Navi and team made out. I'd sent them out to do a little work after they finished my house in town.

◆ ◆ ◆

The next day, I found myself bouncing around ranch roads

driving out towards the ranch headquarters. The sun was blinding as I drove west out of town to make my way there.

I thought the ranch was looking pretty good after turning it over to Stacy's "friends" or colleagues or whatever they were. The "ladies" hadn't run cows on it, and we'd had some unusual spring rains. There were quite a few green patches in the fields.

I'd called Stacy after my encounter with Amy and arranged to meet her out there so we could review the work Navi and his team did sprucing up the ranch house. She'd told me about something else she wanted me to help her with. Stacy was already there when I drove up.

"We need to do this," Stacy said in a strained voice, approaching my car. I knew what was on her mind. "You need to show some interest in the house and your tenants."

"We? Can't you take care of the tenant part? I mean they are kind of your friends. You arranged for them to rent the house."

"I'm not going in their alone. What if Light is there?"

"You think you might succumb to her delightful charms?"

"I told you, I'm not into that." She was almost beginning to glare.

"Seriously, what could happen? I just don't feel comfortable around your friends. In fact, I just plain don't like them. I don't think they like me much either, especially Light."

"You know we have to do this. This is your land, your house. We have to inspect it occasionally. Especially with these people. It may be painted purple or something."

"All right. I know you're right. Actually, it's good to be out here again. Maybe we should move out here. It would be tranquil, you gotta admit."

"It's beautiful, but I'm not sure I could take this much tranquility, Steve. Marfa has enough of the tranquility thing going on to satisfy me." She looked around and continued, "This is a lot of peace...maybe even too much peace for a big wide-open space like this. I got lost a few minutes ago by the water tower. Took a left instead of a right." She turned towards me and peered over her sunglasses. She was wearing long shorts and a conservative top. Light really did make her nervous. She wanted me along in case Light became amorous towards her again.

I admired the cluster of trees that surrounded the house as we walked up to the front porch. I always forgot how big the ranch was when I stayed away for a while. I'd only been out here a few brief times since coming to Marfa. I could see no structures from the house itself except a few outbuildings to one side. The house was nestled in a little valley, so it was out of the wind, which was nice in the winter.

It was a pleasant micro-climate. There was a large pond, or what they called a tank out here, a few hundred feet way. I'd gone fishing in it as a kid. Memories were rushing back. I reluctantly looked over to see the barn where Amy had kissed me long ago. The barn building was mostly rusty but still there.

The three women were waiting for us on the porch. I noticed a strange contraption in the side yard, perhaps something to study the stars? Or maybe an alien signpost? It was painted a bright yellow with something that looked like a target or crosshair in the middle of it. What the hell was this thing?

Light was in a long black dress. She was a nice-looking woman but she'd aged badly. She was dark and wrinkled. Molina and Emerald wore their usual tie-dyed flowing skirts and sandals.

"Hi guys, where's Feather?" Stacy queried.

"She's on vacation in Mexico, you know with all the stress of our work and all."

I just looked at Emerald as she spoke. What the hell? Stress of their work? What work?

We chitchatted about the weather and the beautiful night sky out here for a few minutes on the porch as we drank some weird tea. I sat down in a porch chair and just looked out across the ranch. I sat my cup to the side after I noticed I was starting to feel strange, kind of a buzzing dizziness. I had noticed that Stacy hadn't even taken a sip. She just sat her cup down on a railing and walked in the house.

"What kind of tea is this?" I asked.

Molina gave me a long incoherent response. I understood the word, "hemp." Probably spiked with a ton of THC. I hadn't recalled her having such a strange accent before. She sounded Jamaican or something.

"Molina, where are you from?"

"Why?"

"Just curious, can't place the accent."

"I was born Dorothy before my awakening. Dorothy was from Pittsburgh," she said, in a matter of fact tone, like that's how it was for everyone. I had to wonder who I must have been before my awakening.

"Oh."

I heard Stacy calling me in a strained voice from inside. I got up and entered the house. The front room was just as I remembered it, even after Navi's work. I'd only asked Navi to make the house sound. Fix leaks, repair the roof, patch and restore plaster and so on. I didn't want to change the character of the place. Even the smell was familiar in spite of the repairs. It dawned on me then that I hadn't spent any real time inside it since I was a kid. Some of Uncle Clive's furniture remained. I heard that Amy had come out and ripped off everything that would fit in her car.

"Steve." Stacy's voice was getting more urgent.

I found her in Light's bedroom and Light was standing in the doorway blocking Stacy's exit.

"Oh, Steve." She darted me a strange, exasperated look.

"Light insisted on me on seeing her new heart-shaped rock collection."

Light glared at me, "It wouldn't interest you. Why don't you go drink some more tea? You need to lighten up, brother. That tea will make you a better person. And please mind your own business. Let Molina take you for a walk. I think she's kind of into you." Her smile was disconcerting.

"Stacy, don't we need to be getting back for that big appointment with the folks from San Antonio?

"Uh yeah. You're right." Stacy made a beeline out of Light's room as she ducked under Light's arm. We made a quick walk around and then headed for the front door. I only saw two small beds in the house, but I wasn't about to ask.

Just as we reached the car, I shouted back, "Oh yeah, what's the thing there?"

Molina and Emerald just darted each other a very guarded look. They didn't say a word.

"You know, that yellow thing, machine, or whatever. Did y'all build that?"

Finally Emerald broke the silence, "It is a…uh…weather station."

"Oh. Are you sure?"

Molina lost her temper and in her faux Jamaican accent erupted, "Of course it is, mon. What else could it be? No worries, mon!"

Her "no worries" sounded distinctly like mind your own fricking business!

I smiled and reply, "Of course it is, what was I thinking?"

As we were walking to our cars, the three of them just stared at us. Just as we got to our cars, I looked back one more time. It was rather disconcerting to see them start laughing and hugging each other. I remember wondering if they messed with our cars. I regretted not locking them.

I told Stacy as she got into her car that I wasn't sure it was a great idea leasing the ranch to them. Stacy added that she wasn't sure if I would ever be to get the "wicked" karma out of the house. Stacy kissed me on the cheek and thanked me for saving her as she got into her own car. She said she had a headache and needed to rest. She said she'd call if it eased up. I actually felt a little weird myself. I was hoping Deputy Dud didn't have one of his sobriety checkpoints set up on the way back. I felt kind of high after only a few sips of that "tea." I now understood about why they made their "cosmic supply runs" to Colorado that Stacy told me about a month or so ago.

❖ ❖ ❖

Other than the unsettling ranch inspection, Stacy and I didn't really see each other until the weekend. I guess we still needed a period to absorb the candidness brought on by our wine night. Saturday morning, we saw each other at the farmers market. My pulse raced when I saw her. She was still a dream for me. She was beautiful in the bright sun. She was toting a bag of vegetables, organic no doubt.

We briefly hugged and chatted a bit. She said she had relatives in town. She invited me to church with her and her aunt. I agreed. I wasn't going to decline a chance to be with her. I had a quiet Saturday evening. I thought so much about what Stacy had told me about my artistic side that I wrote a little prose. In fact, I started a novel about a fantasy of mine. It was set in France.

I'd always fantasized about going to France and falling in love. I wrote about 20 pages and it was just mostly what I thought France looked like or how I'd feel in Paris or in the southern part of the country. It was okay, I guess, but I was just guessing. I'd never been to France, even though I could've when I was on temporary duty in Germany in the Army. I always thought I'd go back and see Paris, and maybe practice a little of my "great" language skills.

It was then that I hatched a scheme to embark on a grand writing expedition one day… one day soon…or at least as soon as I could get Stacy and me on the right track. I would have made more progress, but I had a visitor that evening—an unwelcome visitor.

17

About 9:30, as I was starting to wrap up the second draft of my first 20 pages, an attractive woman about my age softly knocked on my door. She was dressed nicely in a knee length skirt, heels and a small sweater draped over a pleasant, low cut blouse. She smelled very nice. Since I was in kind of a romantic mood from thinking about my dreamy encounter with Françoise along the Seine and slightly buzzing from a Beaujolais I'd picked up earlier, it would have been a most welcome diversion had it been a woman other than my dear cousin, Amy. I mean Marfa at night is kind of romantic and the cooler night air was invigorating. And she was pretty. But oddly enough that hard punch to the stomach had a pronounced anti-erotic effect. Plus, she was still my foul-mouthed cousin, and she wanted money.

"Steve, I need to talk…we need to talk. I'm very sorry about the other day. I guess I was just so angry I couldn't think straight. Anyway, I'm sorry. Can you forgive me?"

"It's okay Amy. Don't worry about it. Have a good night," I said gently as I tried to close the door.

"Steve…could…I come in? I want to talk to you. I really kind of need to talk with you."

"Well…I'm pretty busy right now, Amy. I'm doing some writing."

"Please!" She gave me a pleasant, almost sad smile." Way against my better judgment, I opened the door.

"Thanks, Steve. I promise you won't regret it. No hitting!"

I looked out the door to see if she had any goons hanging outside. I suddenly thought of her husband.

"Where's…your husband, Amy?" as I continued to peer outside.

She proceeded to gracefully sit on the sofa. She could be far less repulsive when she tried. She patted the cushion next to her and asked me to sit down. I quickly sat in an easy chair across from the sofa.

"What's on your mind, Amy? And, where's your husband? I don't think I've ever met him."

She crossed her legs and seemed to deliberately hike her skirt just a bit. She looked at her legs a moment then glanced up at me with a very sexy stare. The stare somehow suggested the kiss from many, many years ago. Dammit, was she trying to seduce me?

"Well…Steve, I'm confused. I've thought a lot about you since you came to Marfa. I can't decide whether I should hate you or treat you like family. I mean we had all those good times as kids. I even remember kissing you once. I dreamed about that kiss for years. The next time you came back to the ranch a year or so later, you acted like you didn't like me. You were so shy or something. I thought maybe you'd found a girlfriend in Houston."

"Gosh Amy, that was a long time ago. I think I just avoided you because I kind of had a crush on you or something. It was sort of creepy. We're related kind of, you know. I don't know, it was a long time ago." I couldn't believe I was having a normal conversation with her, and this is what we decided to talk about.

"Where's your husband Amy?" I asked again. I hoped that question might distract her.

"He split couple of nights ago. He hit me…a couple of times. This time, I punched him in the stomach. Kind of like I hit you." She said it so matter of fact, so calmly. "'Cept I hit him in the stomach and then kicked him in the nuts after he tried to hit me again! I care for you, so I left the kick off for you. I didn't want to hurt you there!" She said it like she had some sort of protection plan in mind.

"You have a good punch I must say."

"I didn't sleep a wink that night, Steve. I felt awful." She gave me that strange look. She *was* seducing me!

"That's too bad. Well I appreciate you coming over to apologize. Don't worry about it." I started to get up and thought I could lead her to the door. She didn't budge.

"I didn't apologize." She darted a sharp glare up at me. She quickly softened.

"I mean, at least, not yet. Hear me out, Steve."

She crossed her legs again, hiking her thin, black skirt just a bit higher. She was good at this. "After I hit you, you just gave me a funny look. You didn't try to hit me back or nothing. You were a real gentleman, unlike that prick I married."

She was staring at me.

"Well…"

"Steve, I mean my ex tried to kill me when I hit him the first time. That's why I had to nail him in the nuts the next time, you see? You are really a gentleman, and I appreciated it."

"I don't know about that…."

"Wait, Steve…I got to thinking. I deserve that…I mean I deserve a gentleman. I shouldn't have to put up with some bastard threatening me or hitting me. I'm glad that bum split. It saved me the trouble of kicking him out."

Legs re-crossed, skirt hiked a bit higher.

"Well, you're right." I was feeling a bit of resentment at Stacy for being so difficult and so damned remote lately. It was leaving me a bit vulnerable. I'd had three glasses of wine as I wrote, just to stir the creativity, of course, but that absolutely did not improve my judgment for this kind of situation. I was struggling trying to get the old Steve inner voice to shut up.

"Damn straight. I mean if anyone had a reason to belt me it was you. I mean I've been a bitch to you. You held back. I've been livin' with the wrong kind of people. Steve, are you listening? You seem somewhere else."

"Uh…maybe your husband was having a bad day."

"Bullshit. He's having a bad life. He's brought it all on hisself."

She looked down. She appeared to be studying a small mole

on her bare thigh.

"Amy, would you like something to drink? Water?" I regretted saying it immediately.

"Do you have scotch?"

"Well…I think so. Let me check." I wandered off to the kitchen trying to think what I could do to get her to go. Not sure why I offered her a drink. Painful as it may be to admit, in my mental state at that time—booze, novel writing, stress with Stacy—I was only about eighty percent sure she couldn't seduce me. I didn't want to take a chance. After all, it had been a long time for me—I was getting pretty antsy. Stacy was right, I had problems. I hoped the problems were related to being a man, maybe, not a total idiot.

When I returned, she urged me to sit next to her. The lower edge of her thighs were still on display.

"That's okay Amy. This one's my favorite chair," sitting down in the easy chair across from the sofa. It was lame, but at least I was still out of her reach.

"Thanks for the scotch. This is good. Do you have anymore?"

She chugged the damn thing! That was 18-year old single malt. Good thing I'd watered it way down.

"I don't think…no. That's it."

"Come on Steve. I'll just go check real quick, okay?"

"Let me look again just to be sure." I had a whole bottle of course, as well as a bottle of 21-year-old stuff that I could only hope she wouldn't see on the shelf.

She was smarter when I returned. She stood up to take her drink from me. She grabbed my hand and pulled me over to the sofa.

"Don't you want something to drink? Don't make me drink alone." An innocent, pretty smile. She was very good at this.

"I'm good. I had wine while I was writing. Don't want to mix booze, you know!"

"C'mon Stevey. I'll make you a drink. I used to tend bar. I'm good."

"I better pass."

She darted up and went to the bar. I needed to be an asshole, but I just couldn't muster it for some reason. The resistance wasn't in me tonight. She seemed normal enough. Kind of like the Amy I knew on the ranch—the one I played army and Clue with. She returned with a scotch for me. It was way more generous than I would have poured. I hoped she hadn't watered it down because that was going back in the bottle when she left!

She sat back down almost on top of me. "Sorry Steve. I guess the whiskey is getting to me. I'm buzzing a little! That's some good old scotch, for sure. Cost a pretty penny, huh?"

"Amy...I think it's best you leave. You know, it's getting pretty late."

"Please, Steve. I can't go just yet. I balled like a baby last night. I kept thinking about how it was when we were growing up. We used to play and have a good time. I guess I realized the other night that you are my last kin except for that piece of shit Clark and my Aunt Loretta down in Presidio. I need family. I'm so sorry about the money. I don't care about the money. My ex put me up to it at first. Then I was just on auto pilot or something. Plus, I had been taking took some kind of blue pill he gave me a long time ago to calm down. It messed my head up. Look, I'm not a drugger. I don't normally take shit, uh, stuff.

"Last night, in bed, I realized that's not me. I ain't no money grubber. Youz family." She was beginning to slur her words. She put her hand on my shoulder.

"You look wiped out Amy. Want me to walk you home?"

"I'm wasted, Steve. Can I grab a little nap on your sofa?" She really did look stoned. Her eyelids were getting droopy.

"Not sure that's a good idea. Let me get you home. Where's your purse?"

"It's over there." As I went to pick it up, she got up and tripped and fell. I helped her to her feet. She moaned and crumpled back on to the sofa.

"You okay? Amy? Amy?" She was out.

I had the distinct feeling of being totally hosed as I slipped her shoes off and covered her with a sheet. Her soapy smell didn't distract me a bit from the dread I had of calling Stacy in the morning to tell her I couldn't come to church. "My crazy cousin who hates me slept over." What the hell was I going to do about Amy? What was I thinking?

Turned out it wasn't a problem, sort of. About 7:30 am, I woke up, suffering from a slight hangover that I imagined was even worse for Amy. But I walked into the living room and there was no Amy. It was a relief, I have to say. Even though it was raining softly outside—a semi-rare event here—maybe this was going to be yet another great Sunday in Marfa. I found her note on the kitchen counter, near the coffee maker.

Dear Steve:

Sorry about last night. You were great. Thanks for listening. I look forward to spending more time with you cuz. I'm working through some rough stuff.

- Aim

I used to call her "Aim." I was perplexed by the note and the evening. Was she for real? Was she becoming her old self? I doubted it, but I didn't want to rule it out since we used to be friends, after all.

18

Stacy and her aunt picked me up right on time. Stacy wore a sedate, modest black dress. Both she and the dress were somber this morning.

I stayed mostly quiet on the way to church, unsure what we should talk about. But I felt generally at home during mass. There wasn't much difference between the Episcopalian services of my youth and Catholic mass we attended. It actually brought back a few good memories of stability and predictability in life.

After mass, Stacy was a little more animated. We had a pleasant lunch at a café on Austin Street. It was in an old house where a couple lived. Half of the house had been converted so it could be used as a café. Like the gallery we'd visited a couple of weeks ago, the walls were solid white plaster, floors were porch gray throughout. It was austere other than some colorful, Spanish-inspired works on the wall. Faint jazz was playing in the background. It was only open a couple of days a week, but it was very good, sort of a Mexican American fusion cuisine.

I spied Pilar's sister behind the order counter.

"Hi, Liz."

"Hey Steve."

She was a few years younger than Pilar, almost as pretty.

"What's Pilar up to today? She working at the gallery?"

Stacy chimed in, "Dayleen is working today. Pilar wanted off to go to Alpine with her boyfriend."

"Oh, well. Tell Pilar that Steve asked about her. I know that'll make her day." I said with a smile. For some reason, it annoyed me that Pilar had a boyfriend.

"Think so?" Liz said with a challenging glance and proceeded to go bus a table. I guess she was taking after sis.

When Stacy's aunt went to the restroom out back, Stacy took my hand and said, "Steve, we need to talk."

My stomach felt a pang of nausea. I didn't like the look in her eyes. It bothered me she wore no makeup. The night we'd gotten drunk, she wore pretty red lipstick and black eyeliner. But today, nothing. Still very pretty, but I felt she was communicating something.

"Steve…it's going to be okay. Never forget that, right?"

"What do you…?" Right then her aunt returned saying the bathroom was occupied and she'd wait.

"Steve, I need to drop Aunt Nelda off at the house. The gang is about to leave town. We'll chat more in a little bit."

I didn't like the feel of this little chat so far. I was downright uncomfortable by the time we walked out of the cafe. I declined the ride home and decided to walk back home, it was just a few houses down to my place. Stacy said she'd come over around 3:00 to continue the discussion.

I had the sense it was all over, reviewing everything that'd happened in the last few months as I walked back home. It may have been a rollercoaster with Stacy, but I felt that mostly we were on a good path. The reflections continued as I walked.

I kept asking myself what the hell had I done? Surely, she didn't think anything had happened between Amy and me. My mind was racing. I was listening to some older staples…Train, Lifehouse, The Fray and just sat in the living room while I peered out the front window at the now sunny early spring Marfa day. My world was frozen. It was warm outside, but I was cold inside. It was slowly dawning on me that it was all coming to an end with Stacy. She was pulling away. I was losing her, and I had no idea why.

This was the bright sunlight that used to bring me happiness. This was the same sunlight that reflected off Stacy as she not-so-patiently convinced me to open the gallery those months ago when I first arrived here. I could see her looking beautiful in that sunlight—blowing her hair up off her forehead in mild frustration.

Was it over? I mean "It's going to be okay," she said. What the hell did that mean? I was completely lost in looking back over the last few incredible months—massaging her foot the night we met…Stacy on the mountain top with the orange sunset reflecting in her eyes…Stacy sheepishly spying on my discussion with Paco…the flamenco vision of gorgeous Stacy at the night club…her innocent smiles…her right dimple…her slender neck…our drunken reality session.

The most vivid memory that flooded my mind was that of us running to her apartment in the rain one evening. Her dress and hair were clinging to her. She was so sexy. I still remember how pungent the scent of the rain was. It rarely rains in Marfa, so the smell of it can be overwhelming. The rain awakens a desire in me to be with Stacy. Her soaked image is still burned in my mind.

I was almost panicking thinking at the potential loss of her in my life. It just couldn't be happening. It was right then that I realized that music was also coming from just outside my back door.

I got up to look out the window and there she was. Only about two or three inches of red fabric separated me from seeing my cousin totally naked. Could the day get any or more difficult to take? She was topless but laying on her stomach on my outdoor recliner. At least she had good taste musically. I think she was asleep.

"Amy…Amy?" I called her from my door.

No movement. I turned down the music.

"Amy!"

"Whatch…Was…Steve!" She started to bounce up then recalled her lack of a top—just a hair too late.

"Steve, do you mind looking over there a minute?" She put her top on. It consisted of another three to four square inches of material in totality.

"Amy, what are you doing here?"

"Steve...I had such a great time last night, I came by to tell you. And thank you. I brought muffins. They're in the kitchen. Where you been?"

"I was at church."

"Oh."

"How did you get in...did you just walk in or break in or what? And why the hell are you in a swimsuit?"

"The door was open. I didn't think you'd mind me making myself at home. Hope you don't mind. I don't have anywhere to sunbathe at the apartment. I miss the sun! Well, actually, there is a small pool, but some creep always comes out and stares at me since my ex's gone. He's harmless, but who needs that?" She was glistening with sweat from the direct sun and sunscreen.

"Well, I do mind. What if I had had company or something? You can't just go barging into someone's house. You need to get some clothes on."

"Mind if I take a shower Steve?"

"No. Out of the question."

"C'mon Steve. I'm burning up. Just a quick one."

"Amy...all this sudden change of heart is so...I don't know. One minute you hate me. The next you act like we're friends or something. What the hell?"

"I told you Steve. I've finally come to my senses. I finally got that loser out of my life and out of my mind. He was poison. Daddy was right. I just thought Daddy hated him because he was Mexican. He saw through the son of a bitch."

"We can talk about this later. Please, get a move on."

"I'm fried. Please let me shower really quickly, please."

Without waiting for my response, she got up and proceeded to pad her bare feet into the house. She had her top off before she walked in the bathroom. At least she had taken care of her figure.

She came out of the shower with a towel wrapped around her head wearing one of my tee shirts. I didn't hazard a guess what she had on underneath. She slipped on some cutoff shorts and a pair of flipflops and started to dry her hair.

"Amy. You've got to go. I'm about to have company."
"Is it that girl at the gallery…Stacy?"
"As a matter of fact it is."
"You guys an item?"
I just stared at her. Didn't really know what to say.
"Okay. I am outta here. Sorry for barging in, Steve. I was just lonely and wanted to talk more—like we did last night. It brought back old times. That was special. I'm sorry. I'll see you later."

She went out the door without looking back. She didn't look angry. She just left. I am glad my tee shirts are big. She was well covered. I still didn't know how she got in. I still didn't know what she was up to. Maybe she was lonely, like she claimed.

Stacy should be arriving soon. I took a quick look around the back-porch area and the bathroom to make sure she hadn't left any underwear or any other clues that she was here, but it was clean. Time to face the music with Stacy, I guess.

◆ ◆ ◆

Well…the Red Angel was indeed right. In simple terms, it hurt something awful. A few hours after Stacy arrived at my house to have our chat I found myself numb sitting on a bench near the Paisano Hotel. I'd been hit by a freight train. It was among the lowest days of my life. Stacy had finally revealed her secret. I now knew why we hadn't grown in our relationship as I was hoping. About a year ago, I'd smashed into the girl of my dreams a few feet from where I was sitting, and the best relationship of my life had started. It was fitting, I guess, that this is where it all ended, too.

Stacy had fundamentally changed me, for the better, I thought, but I didn't have the maturity to see it while it was happening. Now, I was only able to focus on the fact I'd lost her. And I thought I'd lost any hope of being in a happy relationship with a woman. I truly came to see her as the "one."

Orange and purple clouds formed on the horizon as I replayed the event in my mind over and over. She walked into the house just a few hours ago. She was about thirty minutes late and she'd been crying. She gave me a weak smile and said, "Follow me."

She led me down the street without a word. I stopped at one point as said, "What's going on here, Stacy? Why are we taking this walk?"

She gave me a small, sad smile and took my hand. It was then it finally hit me that the world I'd imagined just a day before had just been turned upside down. It was confirmed. We were finished, finished as a couple anyway.

"Steve, I need you to meet someone," was all she said.

In a few minutes, I was standing before the statue of the Virgin Mary at St. Mary's Catholic Church. The statue was raised so the Virgin looked down on the observer. It's probably impossible to not feel at least a little guilty looking up into her beautiful face. Her eyes seem to pierce your soul. I knew it was just a statue, but it was powerful.

As I cast my eyes from the Virgin to Stacy, I finally got it. I didn't know it at the time, but I was holding the hand of the future Sister Genevieve. She was radiant. She looked so relieved. She was beautiful in the light of the candles surrounding the statue. Though she was crying, she wore a warm smile that helped mitigate my grief, but only slightly.

She was indeed luminous. As much as it hurt, I had a hint of reconciliation inside of me knowing that she was doing the right thing. My understanding that she was doing the right thing did not, however, stop me from trying to talk her out of it. Even as I spoke, I knew I was making it all about me again, but I didn't care. I begged her to give it some time before she finally decided. She said that the decision was a given, there was no need to take more time. There would be some short period involved in completing the process. But she said it was done. Someone else had made the decision.

19

I self-centeredly but guiltily tried half-heartedly for more than a week to talk Stacy out of it, scarcely thinking to apply the lessons I was supposed to have learned in Reverend Judy's church that night not so long ago. I was in full selfishness mode, and the worst of it all is that I fully realized it.

I went to Stacy's apartment three times during that week. We would sit on her little patio near her steps—the same patio where she wore the short brown dress, the same patio she tried to hook me up with Bruce. I made every argument conceivable. Even her appearance had changed. She was still beautiful, but she had transformed already. To the extent it was possible, she took on a less sexual air. Thinking back, it haunted me how she had subtly changed during the few months we dated. I was anguished thinking that my immaturity may have pushed her towards this decision.

She assured me that it was in the works well before I met her. She felt that God had let me meet her to tempt her and give her insight into human relationships and love; she said she loved me and always would. I was her only sorrow about joining the order. She regretted she couldn't be with both God and me, but that wasn't the way the church and the order worked. When I explained that she could always be devoted and be with me, she wouldn't even entertain it. It was settled.

Some people tried to help me get over Stacy—unexpected people. Pilar was actually nice to me, at least nice by her standards. She came over a couple of times. She sat on the front porch and drank beer with me. She was gorgeous but so young, I thought. I was shocked at her compassion. Our chat one evening really stood out.

"Steve, you've got to let go."

"I have, Pilar. I'm good. I'm doing better, really." I thought I was telling the truth...that I was starting to get better. Stacy had left town for some kind of training or orientation or something. I thought I was starting to let go since she was in my mind only about half the time, which was a great improvement. My heart didn't feel quite as broken.

"Couldn't tell it by looking. You still look low. Your shoulders slump and you shuffle around when you walk. I mean you don't even take care of yourself anymore."

"Pilar, I've probably looked like shit to you from day one. Remember, I'm just a dumb gringo!" I was getting surly.

"Steve, you're a great guy. You really don't suck too bad at all," Pilar said with a hopeful, sly smile. "Really, Stacy was lucky to have you. It just wasn't meant to be. You have a great life to embrace and you have to get past this!"

"What's it to you? When did you start being this philosophical anyway?" I was getting drunk, surly and stupid. I regretted it as soon as I said it, but it did pretty much express what I thought about all my friends trying to cheer me up.

"You might be surprised, asshole. You're acting like you don't know a damned thing about life." With that she got up and walked away. She looked great walking away from me in her very short cutoffs. I wanted to call her back, but I just couldn't do it. I was still numb. Nothing really mattered—not even Pilar. I wanted to spend time with Pilar because I was strongly attracted to her, her feistiness, her youth and vigor. It just didn't seem right, though. I felt like a widower, like I was grieving the loss of a beloved member of my family. Even so, I felt something important slipping out of my hand as she walked away. I resolved to avoid her because she reminded me too much of how I felt when I was with Stacy.

◆ ◆ ◆

Amy of course was not out of the picture either. She actually had become more normal, even to the point of acting sympathetic. She did have the odd habit however, of showing up at unusual hours to visit.

It was about 11:30 that night when I heard a knock on the door. I knew it was Amy. She'd dropped by late a couple of times after Stacy left town. She would usually have a beer and we'd commiserate about life. She'd normally leave in an hour or so. She'd just stand up, give me a quick peck on the cheek and parade out a little happier than she came.

I figured that I had become a brother figure to her, since Clark had won an all-expenses paid vacation to a federal penitentiary in Pennsylvania. Three weeks after starting at Sul Ross, he was accused of trying to sell drugs to the daughter of the President of the university. He claimed it was another guy using his name, but the authorities wouldn't buy it.

Anyway, Amy and I became friends. Sometimes, our get-togethers were normal social events, and sometimes it seemed strange. On this particular evening, it got very strange. She was drunk before she got to the house. And she was dressed oddly, at least oddly for her visits. I mean she usually wore shorts or other very casual clothing. But that night she wore a short black dress with heels. She wanted to "go out with me."

"I don't think it's a good idea Aim. You're drunk. I've been sleeping. I'm out of it. Not sure I'd be too festive."

"C'mon Steve. I need it, and you need it. I've been down and lord knows you've been scraping the bottom lately. I need to cut loose and so do you!"

"Looks like you already cut loose."

"I need to dance…or something."

She ran inside and cranked up some music. She started kind of swishing about and knocked over a table.

"C'mon Steve, dance with me…*please.*"

My, how life in Marfa had evolved over the months: highs, lows, exalting, pathetic. I could never have predicted that inheriting wealth could also lead to so much complexity in life.

"I was sleeping, Amy."

"So?"

She started dancing right in front of me. Even drunk, she had good moves. The dress was quite flattering. I felt a pang of panic come across me as I started to realize she was again trying to shift our relationship into something more than cousins or friends.

"C'mon Steve. I'll dance by myself if I have to. C'mon."

"Amy, what in the world is going on here?"

"Watcha mean Steve? Get a damn drink!"

"Don't think so, Amy."

"Why not? You always drink with me. We've become good drinking buddies."

It was true. We had shared a lot of booze in the last few weeks. We'd even gotten drunk together a few times.

"I don't know Amy. It's different this time. It just seems like…"

"What Steve? Say it…what?"

"It seems you are coming on to me or something. It feels different."

She stopped dancing and plopped next to me. She put one arm on me. She leaned over and kissed me.

"You're right. We need this Steve. I don't have anyone but you."

She stared into my eyes. "Steve, I need passion. I know it looks bad, but I need physical companionship, not just friendship. I'm lonely. I need to escape. You need it too. If you want, we can just use each other. Don't lie, you need it." She was right about my needing it! She continued staring me right in the eye. She reeked of perfume and booze.

"I know, Amy. I'm lonely too. But this isn't right. We're family."

"I know Steve, but you know we're not blood kin. You know I'm adopted."

"I know, but I still see you as my cousin. It still doesn't feel right."

"Don't you find me attractive, Steve? I really find you attractive. I feel like I'm starting to see you in a new light."

"Of course, you're attractive...you're a great looking woman! I've always had some kind of attraction to you. I think it's just an outgrowth of my crush on you when we were kids. You were the first girl I kissed." I felt the need to say something supportive because she was starting to look sad and pathetic. I really didn't want to hurt her. I'd developed real feelings for her, just not in a romantic sense other than an occasional feeling of lust, which made me feel even guiltier. Over the last couple of weeks, there had even been a couple of moments where I found myself becoming even more strongly attracted to her.

Maybe that was why I generally tolerated, maybe enjoyed, her presence. Maybe she added a little spark to the otherwise totally pathetic life I had these last few weeks. Strange times sometimes lead to strange company and maybe even stranger thoughts. Then again, maybe I just wanted to help because I cared for her.

She reached over to give me a deep, passionate kiss. I immediately bolted up from the sofa.

"Where are you going, Steve?"

"To brew you some coffee. I know I need some!"

I thought she'd pass out, but we ended up talking all night. We really opened up to each other. When I dropped her off at her house at about 5:00 am, she thanked me for helping us avoid doing something stupid.

We'd somehow miraculously become real friends. I think she just wanted to try one more time to sort out what our relationship really was. In her own way, she was smart about the world of men and women. But she was as confused as I was in other ways. She was a person I wouldn't have normally associated with before I came to Marfa. But our history and crazy family roots bound us together after all. It was a family tie that I could only categorize as strange but organic and meaningful.

That night I decided it was time to leave Marfa for a time and see if I could do some real writing and find myself. It was time to see if writing in and about France could really work for me. I booked the flights and initial accommodations right after Amy and I parted ways. I would leave in little over a month.

The next day, I asked Amy if she would become my acting manager of the Gallery and ranch. She had an associate degree from Sul Ross in something related to business and was keeping books part-time for a restaurant in town. During my visits with her, I detected an innate common sense about her. I offered to pay her well. By the requirements of my uncle's will, I couldn't give her the money but I could sure let her earn it, and give her a piece of the profits, particularly if she did well. I gave her a very nice "recruitment bonus" to get her to start working. It was my way of giving her some of what she should have gotten in the first place. Uncle Clive should have never cut her off for "marrying a Mexican." Given Uncle Clive's fondness of Pablo, maybe it was more about her ex-husband's lifestyle than about his race. Regardless, I learned from Amy that a lack of support from Uncle Clive probably facilitated her making some unfortunate decisions. She was good at heart and wanted to make something of herself.

I slept better at night knowing I had helped her in some small way. I figured Uncle Clive would have supported me helping her move past her mistakes. Though she declined to house sit, she agreed to watch my place while I was gone.

20

In late June, following my self-imposed "Discover Who I Am" agenda, I was ready to set out for France. After many chats with her and watching her in action, I was convinced that Amy would have the gallery and ranch on a course I knew would turn a small, but durable profit. That was something Stacy and I rarely did, so I felt comfortable about leaving Marfa for a while. Amy was even showing a knack for managing the beer distributor and working with the brewery and distributorship crews. It turned out she was a natural leader and good manager.

Amy also kept an eye on the brewpub, but it was doing okay on its own, thanks to my hire from the Ft. Davis hotel restaurant. I was still persona-non-grata over in Ft. Davis. We'd added another variety from the same brewery in Chihuahua which boosted sales a bit. Combined, the businesses didn't do a lot more than break even, but we chose to keep them going since they all employed local folks.

I hoped Stacy was right about one thing, at least: maybe I was an artist at heart. I had written quite a bit between drinking beer with Amy on my front porch and starting to exercise and get back in shape. I even dabbled in painting, although that was a stretch to think of myself as an artist with paints—in fact, no one really recognized my subjects, until I dropped a hint or two about what they were looking at. I was feeling partially alive again. I had read that art can serve as therapy. I still missed Stacy deeply, but art, writing and, oddly enough, my friendship with Amy rejuvenated me. I was back for the most part and ready to "discover myself," my true self, as I described it to Amy. All-in-all, the loneliness and depression awakened a creativity in me that I didn't know I had.

Amy and I helped each other. We gave each other confidence. The fact that we found each other companionable as friends that were also family helped. We enjoyed each other's company. She filed for divorce from her no-good husband. I helped her have the courage to do it. We'd come to rely on each other a great deal. I don't know how exactly, but over the last few months, but she became a warm, attractive person that I really enjoyed being around. Maybe she just needed someone to believe in her. I guess we all need that. She still talked a little rough, but she blossomed during our mutual healing period. Even her speech had become more refined and better suited for the gallery.

All of this contributed to her growth as a good business manager. She did something Stacy, and probably I, wouldn't have had the heart to do but badly needed doing—she fired Dayleen. She said she caught Dayleen selling one of her paintings we had listed at $8,000 for a bag of pot. The fact that the gallery owned it didn't present any dilemma at all for Dayleen. She told Amy that we owed it to her for all the "bad karma" that Amy had been throwing her way. Stacy had caught her doing worse but would never do anything about it. I told myself this could only happen in Marfa, but it might have been common in any artsy-fartsy town, with all the characters that hung out in those kinds of places.

We still sold Dayleen's paintings, but she didn't work exclusively for us any longer. Amy hired Pilar back as soon as she could. Pilar originally quit her job at the gallery citing her contempt for all the power-hungry gringos like me, but over time, Amy had coaxed her back and found out that Pilar really didn't hate me, after all. She just didn't like working for me. She was an excellent employee, as long as I wasn't around spreading the "gringo gossip," she told Amy. I really wanted to see Pilar one more time before I left, but somehow, she had sort of morphed into a memory of Stacy. When I thought of her, I felt the same pain I felt for Stacy.

It was a little tough leaving Marfa to go to France because I had a vague, gnawing feeling I was leaving something important behind. Even though we had become special friends, I was sure it wasn't Amy. I didn't know what it was. At the time, I thought it might be the memories of Stacy and the slight glimmer of hope I continued to hold, but that diminished more each day that passed. I also thought it might be because I'd started to see myself in a new light in Marfa. I was transforming and hopefully growing up. I still didn't know who I was for sure, but I knew I wasn't the same dude from DC that I was when I first arrived in Marfa all those months ago. It was time to go to Paris and find out who this dude really was.

21

A few days later, I found myself on a gloomy overcast day poking around Paris in pursuit of what Gertrude Stein and later Ernest Hemingway had called the "Lost Generation." I guess I was searching to rekindle what produced a torrent of great literature in the 1920's. I figured all I had to do was channel one or more of my countrymen who had preceded me here a century before, right after "The Great War." I studied World War I and its aftermath in college and knew some of the creative forces the war unleashed in art and literature. Surely the magic would work again, even without a war...there was enough conflict going on within me that I could simulate those experiences, I figured. Here I hoped could find my inner Hemingway or F. Scott Fitzgerald.

After I'd settled into a comfortable though mid-priced hotel, I decided to take what I was sure would be a discovery walk, in search of worthwhile landmarks and what I knew would be important experiences to capture in writing. Many good writers had traveled these steps before and probably would again.

There it was. Café Delmas. This, or an earlier version of it, was the bar that was so filthy that even Hemingway avoided it. I knew his first apartment in Paris was close by.

After a short walk up rue du Cardinal-Lemoine, I spied a modest white building which housed Hadley and Ernest shortly after their arrival. I tried hard to envision what 74 rue du Cardinal-Lemoine was like in 1921. I was compelled to stand here and take in some important American heritage in France.

Hemingway was something of a literary hero in college. Over 15 years later, I saw him in a different light, knowing more about his problematic reality here and back in the states after his return, but his writing still inspired me. I wanted to pick up a vibe to help me chart a course for my first novel. I wasn't looking for ghosts or spirits, like in Marfa, but I knew there was an inspiration here in some form. To help me have something —as Hemingway would say—true and worthwhile to write. I wanted to write something deep and meaningful that could stand the test of time. I wanted to entertain but inspire and provoke as Hemingway did and still does. He shared a good part of himself in his writings, and I was prepared to do the same...to find and reveal those things that are common to us all and allow us to learn from each other through experience.

I had a friend in the Army that used to talk about participating in the "Great Conversation" that had informed and inspired people for centuries. American philosopher Robert Hutchins spoke about the same thing years before. Being a part of that "Great Conversation" is something I think I've wanted to do for a long time.

I craved inspiration, something that was apparently not with me so much in Marfa. The right inspiration would not only shake me out of the Stacy doldrums, but spark good writing. I needed the long-term cure. I pondered what dynamic existed around here in the 1920's that fostered such an explosion of creativity by so many people. When they escaped to France, I was sure the Lost Generation must have felt freer relative to what Prohibition-era America was experiencing.

I walked by 39 rue Descartes to see Hemingway's old writing studio. It was just an old building. There was an inaccurate plaque on it saying that he lived there in the 1920s.

It was there the downpour began. I ran over to the awning of a nearby restaurant and shared it with another refugee from the rain—a man of African descent with a pleasant smile. He spoke enough English that we could chit-chat about the weather, but I wasn't comfortable enough with my French to engage him in a more meaningful dialogue. Even though my ear for French was coming back, I was afraid to sound stupid, at least when I was sober.

When the rain slacked a bit, I walked up rue Clovis to the Pantheon and spotted an English bar. About the time I entered, the rain intensified to a downpour. I could smell the rain on the streets and sidewalks as it washed off some of the dirt and wear and tear of the day. I sipped a Bombardier as I watched the rain bounce into the large doorways that surrounded the front of the bar. The brewery that made the English bitter has been around since the 1870s and was probably a favorite of some of the American and English writers of the days after World War I.

I watched the Eglise St. Etienne du Mont and Pantheon take their shower in the driving rain thinking about how Hemingway and some of his cohorts must have walked by these beautiful structures almost daily. What it must have been like to be an "American in Paris" those days. I experienced firsthand what inspired Hemingway to write here!

Still no strong inspiration for me yet, however. I ventured on.

As quickly as it had come up, the rain slipped away, and a glorious sun took center stage, bathing Paris in a warm glow. When this happens, apparently Parisians make like ants out of a disturbed anthill and come scurrying out to the cafés and sidewalks to enjoy the warmth. As for the women, I greatly appreciated the replacement of pants and black stockings with short dresses showing off their shapely legs.

From what I'd read, each warm day in Paris was like a small celebration up until fall when the warmth eased gradually into gray coolness. From my first days here, I'd found that pleasant warmth in Paris evoked almost the same feeling of semi-wonder one would get on a snowy day in DC where it normally only snows only a few times a year. It creates a brief, fleeting camaraderie among the observers that experience it that lifts one's spirits into a shared discovery. That is, unless it gets too warm, which happens occasionally. That's a problem in a nation where few people have air conditioning—generally there has been no need, although that seems to be changing.

I'd been to see some of Hemingway's hang outs: Le Pre Aux

Clercs, the place that was Michaud's where Hemingway had to examine and reassure one of America's other finest writers that his sexual appendage was of adequate dimensions; the original site of Shakespeare and Company at 12 rue de l'Odeon, now a boutique, but at least there is a plaque now; and of course, Gertrude Stein's apartment at 27 Fluerus.

Nothing occurred on the inspiration front. I learned a bit more about Ernest and his cohorts, but no immediate passion to change the way I looked at life. I was hoping the magic of inspiration hadn't been all used up by the "Lost Generation."

❖ ❖ ❖

The next day, a mild early July day, I continued my quest for inspiration. I went to the site of the old Hotel Venitia, now a bookstore, where Ernest had his torrid affair with Pauline Pfeiffer. Surely that would get my juices flowing.

No. *Nada. Rien.* Nothing.

I then ventured over a few blocks to rue Delambre, the site of the old Dingo Bar where Hemingway and F. Scott Fitzgerald first met. I was disappointed to see it was now an Italian restaurant. Surely where these two guys first met would provide inspiration.

Not so much.

Even if it looked like a nice place, somehow it was hard to imagine the *Aubege de Venise* as a place where the Lost Generation made magic.

No. I was starting to realize any inspiration was going to have to come from within me. I felt like the framework for creativity was in place, but I hadn't done anything yet to build on a few wisps of an idea that'd been percolating since morning at breakfast. I looked for a bench or outdoor café table I could sit down and be still.

I pulled out my notebook and reread something Fitzgerald wrote to an aspiring writer in 1938, "You've got to sell your heart, your strongest reactions, not the little minor things that only touch you lightly, the little experiences that you might tell at dinner. This is especially true when you begin to write, when you have not yet developed the tricks of interesting people on paper, when you have none of the technique which it takes time to learn. When, in short, you have only your emotions to sell."

"You've got to sell your heart, your strongest reactions." I wondered if that was something I could really do? Did my strongest reactions die in Marfa on the dreary day Stacy told me her own inspired news, her abiding commitment to God? Or were my strongest reactions yet to be born? I wasn't so sure I was going to be able to pull this off. The stuff I wrote in Marfa now seemed naïve, even trite.

The next afternoon, I selected a table outside at a nice cafe on the *Carrefour de l'Odéon*. The sun on the large circle of tables felt good. It was July in Paris which could be very nice or a tad cool. I scanned the plaza looking for inspiration, for a strong reaction. The breeze felt good. The sun was relaxing. Paris was, as usual, deeply stimulating.

First, naturally, *les femmes* surrounding me came to mind. The women in France were typically slender. Good legs were common, though often a little thin for my taste. As juvenile as it may sound, I started dissecting what made not just good legs, but great legs. I was looking to fuse my passions, my inner self, with sensations and emotional outpourings that seemed to drive most men: admiration of and physical attraction to women. Hemingway and Fitzgerald leveraged it, why not me? With the warmth, the short dresses were common, so I had a lot of research material. Truly, there is nothing more inspiring than a woman.

After much thought and a *cinquante* of good *Côtes du Rhone*, I found myself waxing "logically," or so I told myself for science's sake, of course. "Science" sounded better than lewdness. I decided that great legs were partially the product of the ratio of ankle diameter to calf diameter. A 1-to-2 ratio seemed to work pretty well. Of course, there were caveats. If the ankles were too thick, the whole formula was rendered useless. But, how to be objective in my measurements? That was where the real science came in.

So, I looked about to verify the Steve Miles "Great Legs" proposition. To my delight, there was more complexity than I initially posited—this would justify more study. In fact, how that 1-to-2 ratio is achieved is of equal importance. A gradual increase in leg diameter is not nearly as compelling as "the mildly bulging calf." Not Russian weightlifter bulges, but bulges nonetheless. Enough where the calf evokes the impression of being exercised strenuously on a regular basis. I coined the term, "stark departure" to capture this critical attribute. It was a "phase transition" in physics, I was sure. Ideally, the diameter of the ankle gradually increased up until there was a "stark departure" at the base of the calf. It led to a "cascade of exquisiteness," I decided, trying to "shape" this hypothesis, as it were.

Then, and only then, could legs be considered great in all respects.

After much observation—again, I rationalized it all as research versus lecherous behavior—I finally concluded that this likely had little to do with writing. It was pleasant and lightly inspirational perhaps, but not patently suitable for writing great fiction. However, I could easily see Ernest and Scott having such a discussion.

Suddenly, I got new inspiration when I spied a twenty-something year old man walk up to his motorcycle parked on the edge of the sidewalk partially blocking a *passage piétons*, or crosswalk in English. When he spotted a ticket on his machine, he unceremoniously tossed it on the ground and sped off. I was so intrigued by his actions, I walked over to retrieve the citation.

I sat back down and studied the 35-euro ticket. His plate was a CD plate—*corps diplomatique*. The plate number was 23. My quick smartphone search told me 23 was Sri Lanka. The ticket included an additional *l'amende forfeiture majorée* of 75 euros if not paid in 45 days. Having his address, I wondered why he had disregarded it. Certainly, someone at the Sri Lankan embassy would deal with it and be done with the whole thing.

Ego and an indulging employer were the first things that came to my mind.

From the table of my sidewalk cafe, this event led me to ponder egos. Capturing the egos of the characters authors write about seemed important in the wake of the loss of the "Great Legs Theorem." After all, in science, things build upon each other...nothing really stands alone.

I reflected on how egos had impacted my life. I always worked hard to keep my ego in check. Almost every time I failed to do so, I regretted it. When I did let my ego go, I noticed that it had a voracious appetite that required regular feeding to avoid irritation. Feeding it often requires the cooperation or even the indulgence on the part of others. At its base, ego maintenance is essentially a selfish activity, yet an activity often over-nurtured.

I started coining sayings about egos.

"Unchecked egos--the mainstay of failing organizations everywhere."

"A bloated ego is the cornerstone of miserable people and failing organizations."

"Be selfish, inflict your ego on those around you. Demand they maintain your ego to its right and proper place!" Maybe not this one, since it was practiced so extensively and profoundly in government and academic professions.

"Ego expedites eradication." This one was simple and direct...it had promise.

I thought back to my time under Colonel Swippes, my boss during most of my four years in the Army after college. No subordinate could have a good idea in his presence. There was room only for his underlings' bad ideas and his great ideas, because any good ideas expressed by the team were his before the ideas could make it around the table. There was only room for credit for one good thinker, and he was the one. Most people stopped feeding him ideas. As a result, my unit had to endure his consistently poor ideas.

Then I started thinking about whether some ego is necessary to succeed. Maybe it would embody the paradoxical label of "moderate ego?"

Ego is now a loaded term. You want someone to have some pride, some confidence. It's tough to know how much is too much, how much is not enough. I've worked with people who had no confidence. That's a losing proposition as well. Perhaps a dead-on accurate sense of self-worth—or just slightly more than realistic—is what I need to develop.

Somehow this line of thought, if not inspirational, offered more promise than women's legs as a point of departure to instill encouragement in writing.

As I sipped a cold beer, I thought how I might have been channeling Ernest a bit too much. I was still feeling the *rouge* a bit. I stared up at the old apartments ringing *Carrefour de l'Odéon*, and tried to figure out how I could craft a "true" novel about the danger of excess egos. My thoughts were cut short when I noticed her looking down at me and displaying a warm and engaging smile.

"*Quelle est la question? Avez-vous terminé?*"

Catching only about a third of what she said, I just looked up and returned the smile.

She gracefully walked around and sat at my table. Only a French woman could make walking around a table so provocative. She lowered her sunglasses and just continued to smile at me. Dark brunette. Shorter, French version of a Sophia Loren. Mid-thirties. Fresh lipstick.

"*Les miennes sont les meilleures ?*"

"The best…*le meilleur?*"

"Are you English? Néerlandais?"

"American."

"We must speak English?"

"I'm trying. I read the stuff and get by here and there…I am trying…*J'essaye.*"

"This could to be exhausting."

"What do you mean?"

She just raised her shades and smiled and looked away. Unused to being approached in this manner, I just sat there waiting for her to probably walk away—not that I wanted her to. I'd been told, contrary to American stereotypes of the French, the women tended to be generally conservative about interacting with men.

After being very consciously aware of the cool breeze, the sunshine, her beauty, her accent, her perfume, the surrealness of this sublime episode, I finally blurted out, "What did you ask me when you first walked over?"

"She laughed and said, "*Ce n'est rien*."

"*Comment?*"

"Never mind."

"I mean it. What did you ask? I'd really like to know."

"I said it before…before you were…American."

I laughed and said, "What's that supposed to mean?"

She slowly crossed her long legs, leaned towards me with a mischievous smirk and a slight half nod of her head upward, "I know what you do…were doing."

I leaned towards her and almost whispered, "What exactly was I doing?"

You were looking…judging, I think, all the women's legs. It was some kind of…*concurrence, compétition*?

"*Je suis* …busted. *Desolé.*"

"*Quoi?*"

"You caught me. But, in my defense, I was simply doing research for a book I'm writing. I'm simply practicing the scientific method of observation and testing, as we say in the US."

"You are writing this book to tell other men about French women's legs? Is that a popular topic in America? This is what passes for science, then? Well, were mine the best?" She ran her hand up the length of her leg, leaned back and laughed, very carefree.

"*Bien sûr.*"

Looking skeptical, "*Est-ce que vous êtes*…sure you are American?"

"Oh yeah."

"*Oye ya?*"

"Yes, *c'est* sort of *comme ouais*," liberally mixing English in with my very rusty French.

"There is hope with you."

"That's good. Why did you come talk to me? I'm glad you did, by the way."

She took off her sunglasses, small smile, one brow lifted, "I look at *tous les hommes*. You are the only man without a book or constantly looking at your phone. You just living *et* looking. I like...I liked that. Not what I thought of Americans."

"How about dinner tonight?"

"No." Feigned stern expression. "We meet, there is 10 minutes...ago. I do not know you. *Hors de question*."

Stern look melting, she continued "A drink, now that is something I can do. Not now."

"Okay."

She gracefully stood up, put her sunglasses on, smoothed down her skirt and then stuck out her hand. "Monique."

I stood up as well. "Steve," I replied, with a subtle American smile, and what I hoped was an appropriately firm handshake. I didn't want to appear too excited, after all.

"*Enchantée.*"

"*Moi aussi.*"

"*le bar -- Au Petit Suisse, 21h00 heures ce soir. Vous le connaissez? Ça marche?*"

"That would work very well. *Au Petit Suisse*. 9:00pm. *À ce soir.*" My French was coming back a bit.

She walked, a la fashion model, across the street and headed up towards the Odeon never looking back. Somehow, I was quite confident that I would never see her again. Upon further inspection as she walked away, hers were, indeed, *les meilleures*. Although the ego theorem offered more potential than the leg hypothesis as far as writing was concerned, there was indeed some promise for my keen observations of physical attributes of French women. What a wonderful place to practice good science.

22

As I walked up the rue de l'Odéon I was already thinking what I was going to do with my night when she didn't show. *Au Petit Suisse* was sort of a strange selection on her part. Though attractive, it wasn't particularly cozy. It had a small *belle époque*-inspired interior with multiple levels. The illumination consisted of flourishing light fixtures and large grandiose mirrors that seemed like they'd been there for centuries.

I really didn't know where to sit. Wine seemed to be the preferred drink. I walked up to the sweeping bar and ordered a *pression*. I grabbed a small table outside as a couple departed. Great view of the *Jardin de Luxembourg* through a beautiful gold tipped iron fence surrounding the park. The beer went down easy in the cool twilight.

My suspicions were correct. No Monique. It was nine-thirty when my new "best friend" spoke to me. The park was closing across the street.

"So, you're into drinking alone, eh mate?" Man, I was a long way from Marfa.

Enter Chester C. Coolidge III and his band of "chaps."

Chester was about 30. Tall, handsome. Strange half-American, half-English inflection, sometimes called a "transatlantic" accent. Sweater, loafers with argyle socks, the full monty. Was he F. Scott Fitzgerald reincarnated, or rather did he think he was?

"No, just waiting for a friend," recovering from my disorientation of being in a time warp. It didn't get better when I checked out his friends through the open doors. They all apparently climbed out of the same century-past dimension. They must have arrived in a 1926 Bentley Speed Six.

"A lady friend, perchance?"

"Yeah."

"I'd say you've been stood up, mate. Come join us. We can always use another American in our gang. I am a bit outnumbered, you see?"

"How'd you know I was American?"

"Heard you order."

"All I said was *pression*."

"Apparently that was enough," he smiled. His neatly trimmed blonde moustache was a definite throwback to the 1920s. Chester escorted me back inside to join the chaps.

Chester proceeded to introduce me to his group. Mike, short, dark eyes, bit of a perpetual scowl, was a writer from Kansas City. Jensen and Laars were Swedish I think, both blond, tall, good looking. Beth and another girl, whose name I didn't understand during the introductions, were from England. Both nice to look at except the other girl had crooked teeth which she hid well. Stephen was Australian…sharp looking guy, friendly. Very firm handshake. A pretty French woman, Hortense, linked up with us shortly after I joined the conversation.

The way they spoke to each other, I began to wonder if I was on the set of a movie. Was I starring in a production of "The Sun Also Rises?" The preppy, teasing way they spoke to each other and the way they dressed, I might add, produced an interaction like something between Brett, Bill, Jake and Mike, right off the pages of the Hemingway novel. I wondered if they were consciously doing this? I was just waiting for one to say, "What say we pop over to the Select?" I looked around. No video cameras were evident. No microphone boom hovered above us.

After about a half-hour of spirited conversation about some of their recent travels, which I found to be interesting, someone asked, "Say Steve, would you be up for some sangria?"

Chester looked over to me and in a conspiratorial tone said, "Beth fancies her sangria. Keep an eye on her when she starts to hit this stuff. She can become a bit of a trollop." He leaned back into his chair, looking at me with a challenging smirk.

"So what do you say, Steve? In for a round or two?"

Without a clue where any of this was heading, I smiled and in the "Lost Generation" spirit of the group, I simply said, "Rather."

My new friends and I didn't have far to go. It was only 200 feet up rue de l'Odéon to the "Le 10 bar." With its peeling paint, it looked defunct. Through the windows I saw a warm, orange glow. I realized then that it was next door to a place I'd visited earlier, the original site of Shakespeare and Company. It was here that James Joyce's *Ulysses* was first published. One account described Hemingway walking out on the street in front of the old bookstore to throw down a vase of flowers upon reading a particularly bad review of his work. Now I felt like I was trapped in one of his novels. I didn't mind being there, I should say, and neither did my companions. I was certain I could find inspiration with this group, and no doubt there'd be fascinating egos on display. Seems I'd forgotten Monique already.

Le 10 bar was a bit stuffy, air-wise but not pretentiously. It was old, maybe even ancient. It was filled with similar *belle époque* trappings such as large, ornate posters, printed in reds, yellows and blacks. It was very rundown, but delightful. The clientele was all thirty- and forty-somethings. The sangria served from a barrel behind the bar was great, just the right mix of sweet and tart. The bartender put a small scoop of some kind of spice in it as he served it. I wasn't crazy about the way he used the same bare hand to grab ice and money, but no one else seemed to mind. Indeed, almost everyone in Le 10 was drinking sangria.

About midnight, she showed up.

Monique and three other women entered and sat near the window in the front. My group was towards the back in a corner around a couple of tables. Black mid-length dress, modest, but just short enough to abundantly display her "stark departures," pearls, hair pulled back 60's style with a band. Striking. Not entirely what I expected, but then I again I didn't expect to ever see her again. She looked elegant but a bit displaced in this situation.

After about 10 minutes, she spotted me. I would say it was almost a dirty look. The sangria had fully kicked in, so I didn't really trust my observations all that much. In fact, I just kind of ignored her. Our eyes met a couple of times. She was having a very animated discussion with her companions using a full range of expressive, pouty facial gestures common in Paris.

We exchanged looks a few more times, but there were a couple of vague disconcerting things rattling around in the fog of my buzz. One, Monique was glaring a bit at me. Two, I think Beth was getting a bit affectionate with me, perhaps others. I felt her hand under the table on my knee several times. In my state, I somehow found it hard to reconcile these two sensations. There was something in the recesses of my consciousness mildly—very mildly—irritating me, but not enough to do anything about it.

About 12:30 a.m., we fortunately decided to break up the party. A few of the "chaps" were leaving the city the next day. Chester insisted on having a way to contact me. I wasn't certain if such a contact would lead me into the future or into the past, but I decided to give these new friends a chance to help me find a path to inspiration.

As we neared the door, I snuck a peak at Monique. She once again glared at me, but raised a finger, thankfully not the middle one, as if to stop me. She got up, walked over to me and handed me a piece of paper, never saying a word, never smiling.

I said goodnight to my *nouvelle* Lost Generation, and we all headed towards the door. I looked at the paper as I enjoyed the cool, fresh, strikingly quiet air outside the bar. All I could hear was a distant siren and Beth's heels clicking as my friends walked away. On the paper was a phone number. Perhaps she could also teach me something about ego *à la francaise*. Ah, more research? This writing gig was starting to grow on me. "You've got to sell your heart, your strongest reactions...." I was starting to feel something, something I could sense in my heart and something I could possibly sell.

23

As it turned out, Monique was not the most adept at facilitating the "strong reactions" I hoped would naturally emerge from the great inspirations I was confident I would find in Paris. I called her twice and left messages. At least I think it was her phone. I think it was her machine gun voice on the answering machine, but of course it was in French and I may have been too hopeful in my comprehension abilities. Alas, no response.

Rather than harass her, I chose to move on. Maybe she gave her number just so she could have the final rejection. I couldn't even figure out women from my own culture, so it would be hopeless to try to decipher the ways of Monique…whatever her last name might be. However, she'd taken my mind off Stacy and the slowly diminishing pain of Marfa, for the most part. It shocked me when I realized I had gone a couple of days without thinking of either.

On Sunday morning, I ventured down to the Jardin de Luxembourg with my laptop to try to get in a chapter or two. It was going far more slowly lately. The story was essentially about a younger version of me, sorting out the meaning of his existence and where he should go with his life. While it was set in France, I was still in my early adulthood in the novel. It wasn't easy inferring what coming of "adult" age would mean in the France of 15 years ago when I wasn't all that sure what it meant as I approached middle age today.

But the view was pleasantly distracting. The Jardin de Luxembourg feels like the grounds that would surround a large chateau or royal residence, which is exactly the history of the park. It's truly a beautiful respite. Long rows of manicured trees and hedges and flowers are everywhere. Tall statues surround many of the walkways. Small palm trees around the large pool give it a tropical flair.

Before coming to Paris, my conception of the Jardin was based on the American expatriate John Singer Sargent's 1879 painting, "In the Luxembourg Gardens" at the Philadelphia Museum of Art. It's a magical painting of people walking around the fountain at dusk. Sargent's use of lighting was mystical.

I scanned the park as I started to transition into my John's world, John being my protagonist. There were no "lookers" to distract me around the large round pool about which chairs were scattered ringing the water's edge. I suppose it was too early in the day for that sort of crowd anyway.

I didn't really come to Paris to meet anybody. I came to write. Though I was quite taken with the embarrassment of riches before me, I wasn't looking for women to strike up relationships, or men to befriend. I was open to something—or someone—plopping in my lap (figuratively or otherwise), but I just wasn't energetically seeking it—or her—out.

It became warm in the sun, so I moved to seek the shady refuge of the Medici Fountain.

The Medici Fountain is an impressive cascade and pool in the Jardin. It was built in the 1600s by ill-fated Marie de Medici who was the widow of King Henry IV. Henry IV was assassinated the day after her coronation as queen. She was rumored to have been involved in the assassination, and her life was never easy afterward. She essentially died in exile in Cologne, after plotting against her son, King Louis the XIII, one too many times. The fountain was originally located elsewhere on the site. It was moved to its present location about 150 years ago. It's surrounded by huge Sycamore trees which supply a wealth of shade, a truly lovely setting. Depending on the season, the flowers surrounding the pool can also be lovely, providing a colorful cascade of their own.

I claimed one of the chairs aligned along the lengthy, narrow pool before the fountain. People were starting to gather around, sitting near the pool: lovers, readers, families and me, the writer whose writing was so eloquent it read like a dialogue with Deputy Dud. Okay, that was irony, a writing technique I remember studying in freshman lit.

Being a Sunday, I thought it proper to ponder John's spiritual side.

I didn't want John to be a zealot about anything. I wanted him to be normal, reasonable and thoughtful, but I was no longer certain what those terms meant in a spiritual context. I had my beliefs, but I didn't want him to be an extension of me, certainly not in that regard. I intended to explore an alternate version of me through John.

It helped to recap what I felt when I thought about spirituality. My beliefs include a God because as nonsensical as the world appears, and despite my readings in science, I couldn't believe all this beauty in life and other parts of nature were random: the probabilities of chance interactions of molecular structures that somehow formed an early version of life seemed in fact improbable to me. It certainly could happen, but why and how?

As a young man, back when I took time to think about "real" stuff, I often pondered why there is anything. Why isn't everything just a vacuum? Why is there anything such as a vacuum? I decided early in life there must be a mastermind, an omnipotent actor-creator, perhaps. The Big Bang and evolution helped further a potential and even reasonable explanation about life, but never settled anything for me. Why is there anything at all in the first place? I could understand why rational thinkers could doubt a creator.

I'm not sure man has done a very good job figuring who the mastermind is, or even why such a creator could exist in the first place. Much of the Christian bible seems okay, but some of the Old Testament in particular is hard to figure out. It kind of feels to me like we got at least some parts of it wrong. It feels like the further the Bible gets away from the gospels in the New Testament, the less right it feels, like the writers took a shot at inserting their own "learned" experiences and of course personal biases into their writings. As a result, I've found in my own spiritual life that to the extent I have a moral fiber to do so, I focus on the scripture during the time Jesus walked the planet. His life makes more sense to me and feels like it had more purpose than anyone else who's ever lived.

From my own experiences in the military and working for members of Congress, I know too much about mankind to think we could be perfect once Jesus exited the scene. It troubles me there are so many rules that are held as essential in many religious denominations that Jesus somehow forgot to mention. One thing has always jumped out at me: I think Jesus saw women as equals. I've seen nothing that suggests he saw them as second-class citizens that some passages of the Bible or other religions' equivalent texts seem to suggest. Given the era, it's impressive how much Jesus interacted with women and used women to make his points many, many times. In a way, that helps me think the gospels are real. No one else during that time would have given women the attention Jesus did. The gospels were revolutionary, even radical, on many levels.

Now I know that's arrogant. People will charge me with heresy and acting omniscient myself. It's what I feel and there just isn't that much I can do about it. I'm not saying the rest of the Christian bible is wrong, I'm just saying what I feel from an experiential and even mostly pragmatic perspective. I know it takes faith to believe. I have faith, it just waxes and wanes. I'm human…guilty as charged. And, I also realize that not everyone believes in the God I consider to be mine. Given the diversity of humans and even their respective cultures, it's unrealistic to believe the everyone on this earth would have the same beliefs.

However, what I've read about Jesus makes me believe he was a truly remarkable man, God among men, as many writers speculate. Jesus saw great value in the role children played in society then and now. He sought to protect and nurture kids in ways that I'm not sure we still do, at least in America, especially when you consider all the stressors we expose them to online or in reality. A society that that loves its children would care about future temperatures on the planet or protecting their kids from the kind of weird sex and violence stuff online! Jesus's was a message of hope, love and learning about the great potential life offers us all, regardless of station. I liked that part of his lessons to us a lot.

I don't fear about my life, now or in the future. I know I'm looking out of a microscopic pinhole at the 360-degree infinite universe of reality, but it's the only vantage point I have. It's like looking out of a keyhole of one door of one tiny closet into a dark, tiny bedroom of a huge mansion and thinking you know what the entire universe looks like.

Ah…welcome to the human condition. With what burden shall I saddle John, who will likely be only an alternate form of my younger self? Even being an atheist has burdens to bear, so I won't go there with John. Thinking this is all random and meaningless is a burden I think neither John nor I are willing to carry.

I was so deep in thought that I jumped when a huge sycamore leaf came floating down upon me. Then a half-second later my cell phone rang. Obviously, adults aren't allowed to think about the stuff I was pondering. The universe would have to intervene. We appear to be obligated to simply accept one package of beliefs or another and move on. But, then it would suck if it were really like that.

"Hello."

"Steve?"

"Monique?"

"*Ouais. Qu'est-ce faites vous*? "

"*Je suis…*" I don't know if we spoke French or English or a mix. Anyway, I just told her where I was.

Long pause.

"Monique?"

"Yes. I was wondering if you would like to join me somewhere for dinner tonight?"

"Sure."

"*La Cambuse*? 20h?'

"Near *Jardin du Luxembourg*? Up the street from *Au Petit*

Suisse? Of course. Eight o'clock."

"What?"

"I mean *vingt heures*."

"*A ce soir*."

"Ciao." Why I said "ciao," I have no idea. I had never used the word before. It was probably a residual from the night out with the *nouvelle* Lost Generation.

I didn't expect that call. I went on to have a pretty productive afternoon and got a couple of chapters done. Damn if I didn't give my character John all the spiritual baggage I haul around even today…he was getting a real head start on me.

24

La Cambuse on rue Casimir Delavigne was a nice, if typical, French restaurant. Nothing fancy, but a good representation of what makes Parisian restaurants so desirable. The interior glowed golden. Bright blue woodwork framed the front of the restaurant. Walls cream-colored, lots of shelves with little statutes of *les coqs*, five or six simple tables clean white table clothes —the classic French family restaurant.

I was trying to decide between the coq au vin and boeuf bourguignon as I noticed the large ornamental clock on the wall showed in was 8:20. Not again!

To my relief, I glanced outside and saw her crossing the street. Sedate outfit—all black, heels, longish skirt, sweater with a white blouse and pearls. Not sexy, but classy.

"Good evening, Steve." Nice smile.

I stood up to *faire la bise*.

"Hello. Monique, is it my imagination, or has your English improved?"

"As you once said, '*je suis*…busted.'"

"What do you mean?"

"I teach English and American literature at the Sorbonne. I was playing with you or maybe I didn't want to let you know… I don't know. I just instinctively avoid letting Americans or Brits know I speak English. Sometimes they get clingy or needy. Monique, can you help me with my visa? Can you read this contract? Monique, will you read this government form for me? It gets old. I hide it until I decide I want to be friends with somebody."

"Does that mean you'd like to be friends?"

"Maybe…or maybe it means I am too tired to fake it. We'll see."

"I'll assume it is the former."

"*Comme vous voulez.*" Wane smile. She was hard to read. No quick friendship was going to happen here. That was obvious.

We went on to have a pleasant meal. She was friendly, witty and occasionally subtly flirtatious, but…I wasn't sure there was a spark. She was very attractive. She had a different persona once she dropped the seductive faux English with a heavy French accent schtick. Her English was almost flat with a bit of an Irish accent.

After the meal, when the coffee came, she became pensive. Quieter, more hanging glances out the window.

"You okay? What are you thinking about, Monique?"

"I don't like being confused about people."

"Who? What do you mean?"

Monique made a long sigh and looked out the window into the night. She said, "I don't know what the next step for me is. I mean, I feel like a child sometimes."

"How so?'

"I teach bratty, elite kids. I have a circle of spoiled friends who all still live at home. I am thirty-two years old. I felt jealous the other night when I saw you with that…that girl.

"When?"

"At the sangria bar."

"Beth?"

"That English slut was all over you."

"She was? Why do you think she was a 'slut,' as you say?"

"Look, we don't even know each other. I know almost nothing about you. I don't know why I reacted that way. Sorry."

"Don't give it another thought. It's nothing."

"I don't even know if I like you. I'm confused. I'm in a complicated stage in my life. If you want a friend, I'm probably up for it. Any more than that, don't bet on it. I mean, I barely know you and we have only seen each other a couple of times, and I don't know your intent. I don't want to sound arrogant and assume anything, you know, but I also wish to be honest with you. I may think I'm crazy. I am normally far, far more reserved. You're American, I'm just putting some stuff out there as you say. You have caught me at a strange time. French people are normally very slow to open up. You are American, so I guess I'm just doing something I never do--be open."

"I'm good with that. Hey, I think you're very attractive. I won't lie, but I'm not looking for a relationship right now. I'm in a day-to-day mode in my life at this point. I'm simply here to write, and Paris has become one of my favorite places to be."

"Is that the only thing you are here for, to write?"

"Well, mostly. Look, I'm complicated too, right now. I'm still getting over a traumatic relationship back in the States. It was a couple of months ago, but I'm still pretty messed up."

"Divorce? Sorry, I don't mean to pry. Not my business."

"No, just a breakup. I thought she was the one. I was wrong, very wrong."

Monique just looked at me. Her eyes glistened in the candlelight. She was very pretty. Had I met someone more screwed up than I was? I knew she wanted the story.

"It just wasn't meant to be. She was great. It just wasn't to be. I'm getting over it."

Just a glistening stare. Man, she was a tough listener.

"Okay. She became a nun."

"What? No way. Stop kidding around."

"It's true…sadly true for me."

"Wow. I'm sorry. You're just as messed as I am…no offense." She laughed, then a bit of a relieved smile, "Well, we can be messed together, perhaps." Warmer smile.

I just smiled. I wasn't sure what to say. I didn't really know what she meant—maybe she didn't either. I didn't want to push it right then. I didn't know what I wanted, myself.

"I have a 9:00 class tomorrow, but I would like to get a drink somewhere tonight and then say good night. How does that sound?"

"Sounds great, my friend," I said with a wink and stood up to pull the chair out for her. She smiled and slyly winked back, as we left the restaurant.

We got a table on the Carrefour de l'Odéon. Over a glass of wine, we savored the last of the twilight. A little chatting. A little semi-comfortable quiet.

She sighed and then slowly looked over at me and smiled, raising her eyebrows, "I guess it's time. Well, thank you Steve for a most pleasant evening. I have decided that I would like to see you again, if that matches your desire."

"It does. I'd like to see you again, as well."

"I have a busy week next week and I have to go over to England a couple of days for work. Let's see what happens. You have my number."

After a warmer *faire la bise,* I watched her walk away from me on the sidewalk. This time she looked back, smiled and gave me a little wave goodbye. I was still pretty sure I would never see her again. She had such a hesitant, uncertain air. Maybe I did too.

After she left, I ordered another glass and just sat there. I had no class to prepare for. I really had nothing to prepare for, in fact. Nothing. I had no schedule and no preparations, and it felt a little strange. Nothing to prepare for on the horizon whatsoever. It was strange to realize that. Uncle Clive had somehow, thousands of miles away and many years ago, made this weird moment possible. Thanks to him, I faced almost nothing threatening. It felt both good and bad.

Sniffing the last bit of wine, I reflected on how much I'd changed since I left Marfa. As painful as it was to think of Marfa, I knew it had forced me to grow up, at least to a degree. The Steve who just had an adult conversation with Monique was no longer the bumbling guy who spoke with Stacy out in the bright sunshine in front of the warehouse that day she sold me on opening the gallery. At least I wasn't as bumbling now as then.

I still remember Stacy blowing the hair off her forehead. I remember how the sunshine felt. How I smelled the creosote from the nearby railroad track. That moment was burned into my consciousness. I'd changed, though. If only Stacy could have met this Steve. Although, I suppose I did have a lot of really tough competition with God in her life.

Thinking of Marfa really for the first time in days, I looked up at all the illuminated apartments that surrounded *Carrefour de l'Odéon*. I just closed my eyes a minute and enjoyed how the evening breezes felt, how the city smelled at night. I took a deep breath and finally realized that I was a long way from Marfa in many ways—physically and mentally. In fact, I felt a long way from Steve, at least the Steve of DC and even West Texas. I was slowly growing, even evolving as a man. As I absorbed all the moment had to offer, I became very conscious of how I was changing.

I was becoming more of a man, perhaps even in the same way Hemingway and his fellow expats had become. At the same time, I sort of missed the old bumbling Steve. He was such an amiable but clueless chap. In reality, he was a train wreck. He blew it in Marfa. Or did I? After all, I was in Paris, experiencing all this. The "pre-Marfa" Steve would have been much less comfortable doing this. I truly was, now, putting myself out there.

I struggled as I sipped the last drops of wine; why was I now thinking about Marfa? Was I feeling pulled to go back? There was nothing there for me. I committed to finishing my book. My first of what I hoped would be many. By the time I finished that first book, Marfa would just be a distant memory—for good or bad.

25

The next morning, I was fumbling around looking for my phone after the brutality of an early morning ringing noise. I was experiencing a system shock after only beginning to awaken from very pleasant dreams of drinking a delicious red table wine with a beautiful woman in a warm and comfortable French café.

"Hey Steve, up for some fun, mate?"

"Chester?"

"Oh yes, it is I, the great transplanted troubadour of Paris."

"What time is it, Chester?"

"Dunno. You tell me."

"8:15."

"Excellent. What about it?"

"What did you have in mind, Chester?"

"Tennis."

"To play tennis. You and me?"

"Yes. Tennis. You and me. Today."

"Don't have a racket and I haven't played since college," I responded with more grumpiness than I meant to. I was groggy but my ancient memories were intact, and I recalled that I seldom demonstrated anything beyond mediocrity at tennis back in the day. Well there was that one time when everything clicked to defeat a pretty Norwegian classmate who was on the university's team. We dated a couple of times, but somehow it never worked between us after that one career game.

"Doesn't matter. I have a spare racket and a membership to a club near here. Meet you there at 10:30? Lunch afterward?"

"Okay. Where?"

"I'll text you the address."

"Ok."

"See you there. Oh, by the way, the gang is meeting for drinks tonight. Almost everyone is back in town. The Select at 9:00. You'll need to get a nap in today after lunch. Could be a late night!"

Did he just say the Select? Maybe this guy really was from the 1920's.

"Yeah. Sure. Probably."

"Check that Steve, just read the latest text from the gang. We are going to the Aussie bar in Beaubourg. It's on Rue Saint-Denis. Not too far from the Fontaine des Innocents. You know it? Bunch of jazz bars around the corner?"

"I can find it. What's the name of the place?"

"Got Oz in it. Has a crocodile on it. Can't miss it. We might take in some jazz. Beth has been wanting to catch a jam session."

"Okay. See you at 10:30 at the tennis club. Oh, and Chester?"

"Yes."

"I haven't played tennis in a very long time and was hardly all that good even when I did play. I won't be much of a challenge for you, old chap." That last comment was just to make Chester feel better about being a total anglophile. I could never talk like that in real life.

"No worries, mate. We'll just work up a good thirst and hunger and plot the evening."

❖ ❖ ❖

Tennis was mercifully quick in the cool of the morning, the lunch was good and the afternoon nap that Chester recommended turned out to be well-deserved and useful.

Café Oz was a large place, lots of wooden paneling. The Steinlager was cold and tasty. It was a decidedly "un-French" tasting beer, with a southern hemisphere feel to it, if there is such a thing. It was a welcome change.

I felt just a bit at home. It was nice hearing so much English for a change. The women working behind the bar were all twenty-something beauties with at least English, if not Aussie, accents. At 7:45, it was pretty busy. Most of the people were outside so they could smoke. Small groups were scattered about. There was one girl by herself across the bar. She was average looking: blond, hair pulled back, and she wore sunglasses inside, even though the bar area was quite dark. Not ugly. Not pretty, in between. I fanaticized she'd have a gorgeous Australian accent. Then, I imagined she worked at the Australian Embassy or some other exotic gig. In Paris, anything was possible.

She kept looking over my way. I felt sorry for her. Just to be nice, I thought about going over to say hi to her but couldn't. I didn't want to be selfish. Seeing her alone somehow depressed me a bit. I wanted to reject that introspective crap by cheering her up, yet I couldn't. I guess I wasn't quite together enough yet to do something like pick up a girl at a bar. I just waited for the gang.

I stopped looking over her way and let her get on with her life. I was starting to feel a funk starting to settle in and I didn't like it.

"Stevie." I heard Chester's voice. He was with Jensen and Laars, the Swedes, and Stephen, the Aussie.

"Well mates, are we doing a guys' night out tonight?" I queried.

"Heavens no, Steve. What's up with a question like that? Feeling a little light in the heels, my friend?"

"Ah, no. Can't say I've ever felt light in the heels."

"You Americans, so homophobic!" retorted Chester.

"Say Chester, I thought you fancied yourself an American."

"Quite. Doesn't mean I have to act like one though, does it?"

"So how have the rest of you been?"

Stephan grinned, "What mate on earth would ever have you drink piss?"

"What?"

"Why are you drinking that Kiwi slop?"

"Okay. What would you have me drink?"

"Silly question, mate. I am a Queenslander, after all."

"Okay. What does that mean, exactly? Does it mean that you can't enjoy another country's brews?"

"Sorry, mate, it means Fourex or else."

"Very well, please forgive my ignorance."

"Not a problem. I will buy you a suitable beer, dear chap. Never fear."

I called out, "Thanks, Stephen" as he hurried over to the bar.

"Steve, I've got some bad news," Chester whispered with a solemn look as though I'd be crushed.

"Yeah?"

"I thought Beth fancied you. Not so." More solemn stare. This was a "consoling Chester." Didn't care for this Chester. Upon reflection, I really didn't care for any Chester.

"Okay. No worries, though I have been told she was affectionate with me at the 10 bar."

"Oh, yes. That is true, old chap, but she is always like that when she brushes up against a *pichet de* sangria. I warned you."

"Okay. I don't mind."

"But not all is lost. It seems both her friend and Hortense find you fascinating."

"What is her friend's name?"

"Sarah."

"Okay." This conversation was depressing me. I was starting to become convinced hanging out with these "chaps" was essentially keeping me from discovering and writing. This was not what I was here for.

"I know Sarah has that…that…errant tooth, but she really is quite fetching. I also find her charming. Wouldn't you agree?"

"Oh, yes. Quite fetching." I wondered how convincing I sounded.

"And dear Hortense, not bad either, eh? Of course, she doesn't speak a word of English. Would that be a problem?"

"That would depend on what she wants to do."

"Woah, a little on the salty side this evening, aren't you?"

"Sorry. I thought that was expected from the tone of your descriptions, 'old chap.'"

Stephen returned with a beer I had never heard of, but quite good, "Sorry mate, gonna be 'or else.' Not a Fourex, but rather on the tasty side I trust you'll find."

Chester grabbed my arm, "There are the girls."

After a full round of double cheek kissing with female representatives of practically every nation in the entire western world, we all sat down. It took so long that I swore some other women must have hopped into the party or multiple kiss greetings were going on, but there was only Beth, Sarah and Hortense. Sarah's "errant" tooth was not quite as prominent as I recalled. Hortense wasn't quite as pretty as I remembered. Beth was quite cool towards me. The sangria the other night had apparently affected us all.

Hortense piled in next to me. Chester was right. She spoke not a single word in English. She had to be the first younger person I had met in Paris who literally had zero English. We struggled; the loud music wasn't helping. I sensed she was somewhat interested in me until she realized my French was so spotty. We were both getting exhausted.

When the women all went to the bathroom, I took it as my chance to leave. The evening was doing nothing to repair my spirits, or even to compare to the night before with Monique. The blond girl from before had left. I was sinking further into a complete funk. I had earlier thought of grabbing her and going to get drunk—maybe crying into a beer together or something.

Not sure why I was feeling down. Describing Stacy to Monique had somehow brought a nagging, draining feeling back to me. I'd severely regretted referencing Stacy at all. That was the last thing I wanted to bring up in what might become a meaningful Paris relationship. I thought I felt immune on the other side of the Atlantic. I'd come to mistakenly and foolishly think of the Atlantic as my emotional firewall. Had Marfa become part of me? How could I possibly think of Marfa sitting in an Australian bar in Paris surrounded by attractive women from across the globe?

The music was getting even louder. I had to be very close to anyone to be able to hear. I was positioning myself to leave. That's when Sarah piled in next to me, just as I was sliding across the bench and starting to make a break for it. At least we could communicate this close to each other. She was really a lovely girl. That damned tooth! It was all I could see at first. Silky brunette, green eyes, red lipstick, smelled great, slender, charming British accent, yet all I could see is the "tooth." I felt so stupid, petty.

That must have been some strong beer Stephen brought me. Sarah morphed into a giant cockeyed tooth with slender arms and legs. In a short flash of soberness, I briefly pondered whether my obsession with the tooth was a reflection on her or me. Was I just looking for excuses to protect myself so the pity party of one could rage on? She, and as it were, the tooth, kept getting closer to my face as the music got louder. Stephen was keeping the beers coming so I wasn't feeling any pain.

I hadn't been this close to a female since my arrival in Paris, so she was beginning to break down my aversion to her "special" feature. I found myself really starting to warm up to her. Between her perfume, green eyes, and the beer, I actually started wondering what it would be like to kiss her.

I caught myself staring at the texture of her supple, red lips and it was like a freight train busting through my conscientiousness. I realized I had to get out of there or else make a physical connection that I probably wasn't ready for. I let the moment slide. Beth proclaimed that we should all go to the *Le Baiser Salé* and listen to some jazz. Everyone agreed and I realized it might be a good time to make an escape.

Fifteen minutes later, I was sitting in the dark of night at the Fountain des Innocents feeling sorry for myself. The fountain sits on an ancient cemetery. The bodies were moved in the 1780s. The fountain is beautiful, yet a great place to feel sorry for oneself. A person can't sit there very long without kicking their own ass for being pathetic in Paris—in Paris, gee how stupid!

At night, the fountain is beautifully illuminated. It's like a tall stone house adorned with women on the corners and a large archway in each of the four sides. Within the archway is a fountain that spills water down the rounded staircase-like features on each side. It's truly a delight to behold. Unfortunately, during the day, skateboarders screw up the ambiance. But at night, it's a fantastic Parisian landmark. I sat next to the fountain and just watched Paris go by at night. Beaubourg is vibrant at night —great bars and restaurants are in every direction.

After a while, I felt a bit of a sober coming on. I guess I really didn't want to lose track of my group. They were as close as I had to friends in Paris. Funny how the term "friend" is relative. From my days in the military, I knew close friendships could be forged quickly under the right circumstance—lots of them. I was still nursing the funk but I wanted to lose it. I wandered over to the *Le Baiser Salé.* Turns out, I didn't especially want to be left alone with the damn funk after all. It was worse company than even Chester!

26

The jam session in the *Le Baiser Salé* was in full swing when I walked in. The leader of the session was an unbelievable bongo drummer, but the entire band was quite good. Not my kind of jazz in particular. That runs more toward the Hank Mobley, Miles Davis, Dexter Gordon and some John Coltrane, but this music was still enjoyable and the performance intense. We were in Paris, after all, and good jazz was as important here as in the US. This particular group had a bit of a Cuban influence.

The venue was upstairs and tending towards small. It might have seated a little more than a 100 people or so. It was dark. I had to wait until the jam session was switching some participants to pile in with my group. Some of the musicians stayed with the new group, and the improvisational essence took off in another direction. Chester was leaned back against the wall, smiling and had his arms around Sarah and Hortense. Stephen and Beth sat across from them to the side. The Swedes weren't there. All were feeling no pain and getting friendlier by the minute.

"Steve!" the group announced almost in unison. I thought I was in an episode of Cheers.

Chester grabbed his beer, "Here's to our new, great friend Steve. Such an earnest chap." What a windbag. Oscar Wilde would have felt right at home with dear Chester.

The jam session started up again, which prohibited almost all conversation. No glares from Beth. In fact, she smiled a few times at me.

It was party central the rest of the night, with beer, wine and music blending in a torrent at times. We were all great friends as we pub-crawled back to our side of the Seine. All of us were all staying within a few blocks of the *Jardin de Luxembourg*. The funk was gone. The "anti-Stacy" firewall was secure, back in place. I was back in control, at least as far as emotions if not sobriety.

The party, if that's what we called it, continued through the night. Somehow, I ended up walking Sarah home. With my personal guard apparently on vacation we had a great time carrying on and poking fun at each other's native land. She lived not far from Gertrude Stein's old apartment on rue de Fleurus. She was a sweet girl. I felt a little ashamed about bolting for the door at the Café Oz. By the green-white light of the Paris streetlamps, I felt like we had good chemistry after all. I saw her in a different way after we lightly touched lips as we kissed good night. She wasn't desperate. She wasn't a tooth. She was a warm human being caught in the same predicament as I was. Since being in Paris, I've learned this to be known as the human condition, and I wasn't the only one in the world experiencing it.

As we said our final good night, our eyes locked for a moment, I felt an urge to really kiss her. I still tasted her lipstick on my lips. I felt very alive. I sensed she wanted it, but for whatever reason, I demurred. We both knew though that we'd connected in a sense; we knew it because that's when a human's primal side takes hold and releases some sort of ancient chemical. I knew making love to her would be very satisfying. The mystery and tension had commenced. I cared for her. I knew I may never see her again, but we shared that moment, that human moment, a sort of spiritual linking. The kind we humans don't quickly forget.

It wasn't lovemaking, but it was fulfilling in its own right. In fact, as I quietly walked home alone, I was shocked to find myself thinking that physical coupling is more a celebration of that far more important rare, authentic connection. I wondered how Hemingway would think about that. At that moment, I didn't give a shit what he would have thought. What does he know? He only had a Nobel Prize in Literature to go along with his Pulitzer.

It seems funny how the perceptions of a person can change when they turn the asshole side of themselves off. Big deal if she had come on to me just a tad. I had to stop keeping my guard up so high. As a "writer" or even as a fellow human being, I needed to connect with people, lots of people, if I wanted to better understand the human condition.

I felt as though the physical connection was less important than the emotional bonding I'd felt with people like Sarah and even Stacy. For the first time, it dawned on me that maybe I had done the right thing by Stacy after all. For the first time, a brief swell of pride came over me thinking of how I had conducted myself with Stacy. Maybe our destinies were decided before we ever met. Maybe in fact, I'd handled it as well as anyone could have. Maybe it was time to stop the regrets trip, and feel good about what I'd done, and really move on. I needed to get past all this and open myself up to people more, to seek real connections.

"You've got to sell your heart, your strongest reactions, not the little minor things that only touch you lightly..."

In the military, I was asked to toggle back and forth between seeing people as belligerents, maybe targets, and people to be helped. Constantly making that distinction led me to have a pretty conservative approach in dealing with fellow humans. As a writer, I knew I needed to break that mold. That was easier conceptualized than done, but I had to do it to thrive as an artist, and probably even as a human.

I'd let my emotional guard down with Stacy and gotten burned. I had to move on and take responsibility to get myself back to being open to what the world throws at me. Paris was a great place to do just that, especially if I could get my French to the next level. Right now, however, I was a "stranger in a foreign land" knowing too little of the culture and language. I felt like I was even experiencing what it was like to be a "wetback." I'd never see immigrants back home quite the same. I knew that in the future, it would be upsetting to hear the word "wetback."

It can be demoralizing feeling second class, being reasonably intelligent with something to offer, but having the vocabulary of a five-year-old as an adult.

27

To improve my language skills, I decided to try to get a job —any job that would force me to use my paltry French. I first hit a couple of restaurants. I saw a lot of people who didn't look French washing dishes and cooking food. That wasn't really what I wanted to do, but it would help my language skills, I thought. My long-term visa was a problem when I sought a so-called real job.

After a couple of days of searching, no one wanted to get close to me, except for one ratty restaurant that said I could deliver food for them. I had such a bad feeling about the business, that after I said yes, I couldn't bring myself to even show up for the first day. Fortunately, I didn't need the money, but how desperate it would have been for me if I did! Again, I was understanding more and more about what it meant to be an immigrant, legal or not, in the US.

So, I ended up volunteering at a church which ran a restaurant in its basement. They offered good, if not great, French fare at a very reasonable price. Diners had to have an annual membership to dine there. The sales raised funds for the charitable programs of the church. That's where I became the "heart throb" to 10 or so older, and I do mean older women. I never saw myself in that light before, but it had some advantages. Being mothered and a target for set-ups with daughters or nieces or friends was not among the better of those advantages, however.

As it turned out, almost all of them had a relative or two for me to meet. Being "an American," I was sort of a celebrity with these women. They kind of became my family in what might otherwise be a comedy if it was on American TV. The church didn't pay me, of course, but I got decent free food, including lots of leftovers, and plenty of opportunity to communicate with the ladies and patrons. Best of all, my French exploded! On the days I worked I came home utterly exhausted but had learned and practiced my French constantly.

I mastered the food vocabulary and a lot more, and I learned a great deal about the culture and history of the country. At first, the women were friendly but so prim and proper. But over time, some of them started to let their guard down. Most of the ladies were a little on the "*coquine*" side, and they taught me some humorous if naughty words and phrases. They roared with laughter when I would say their dirty words out loud—not exactly what I expected in a "religious" setting, but it was fun.

French sensibilities when it came to sex were rather different. They loved to share jokes that had a double entendre. Sometimes my obvious naiveté in French played right into their hands to make the jokes even funnier.

There was one joke I heard about a man making love to a non-responsive woman. He kept asking her, "*Est-ce que tu ne sens rien?*" This roughly translated to "Do you feel anything?"

Finally, she said, "*Pourqoui? Est-ce que tu a pété?*" This meant "Why? Did you fart?"

The verb for "to feel" and "to smell" is the same: "*sentir*." I didn't understand all the subtleties, perhaps, but I got the message on dual meanings, for sure!

Who would have guessed I'd learn to talk off-color in French from little old ladies? Not what I expected, but it would be useful in future writing, I figured. The best part was my French became passable after just a few weeks and the two-to-three days a week schedule left a lot of time for writing, exercising and socializing. I very much looked forward to "going to work."

I never took them up on meeting their daughters, granddaughters, or other family members. I figured if I met one, I'd have to do it over and over and I wasn't prepared for that. I kind of regretted my lack of courage during the time I was on the job, though. If the daughters or other family members were as much fun as the older ladies, I'm sure I would have learned even more.

I left there after six weeks. They had a happy hour for me upon my departure where I finally met a couple of their nieces and daughters. At that point, I realized I should've taken advantage of the opportunity to "practice" my French with the young French ladies that my friends suggested, after all. That's when I finally realized I missed a great opportunity for extended scientific research. I'd be braver next time, I resolved.

28

Since I'd left my volunteer work at the church, I'd been cloistered for a couple of weeks with the story creation. I maintained a good routine: in the morning, write an hour or so; croissant and coffee downstairs at the café; nice walk; a couple more hours of writing; quick sandwich or something from Picard in the microwave; an hour of studying or reading French; a jog or some kind of exercise; a couple of more hours of writing or French; nap; a long meal at one of my favorite four or five haunts around the block from my tiny, sixth-floor hotel apartment; usually a little too much wine, but only a *cinquante,* occasionally more; sunset walk and then a little more writing to close out the day. Sometimes, I would go down the street to get a beer and watch a soccer match if the evening writing got sluggish.

I was making excellent progress on the book until I got to a climactic part which I was certain was either going to make or break the story. That's when I hit the proverbial brick wall. I knew enough about the Lost Generations writers that they would recommend I get away from the writing block for a while when this happens. However, I also decided I wouldn't go on a drunken bender while taking a break. After a couple of weeks of this and finding the wall, I decided I deserved a break. I needed some real human contact. I called Monique and left a message. I then decided to call Chester. He hadn't called me since our outing to Beaubourg and the jazz club.

He answered on the fourth ring, "Hullo."

"Chester, my man. How are you?"

"Okay," a little cool.

"What's going on? I haven't heard a peep from you or the gang in a few weeks. Can I inflict some of my bad tennis on you?"

"Sure, maybe."

"What's going on, Chester? Why the coolness? Are you well?"

"I think you know precisely what's going on."

"Can't say I really do."

"How many times have you two gone out?"

"Who?"

"You, Sarah. Don't play games."

"What?"

"As you likely know, I think I might like Sarah quite a bit. I didn't fancy you suffocating her the way you did a few weeks ago."

Oh brother. "Chester…I haven't seen her since that night."

"Nice try."

"It's true. I walked her home and that was it." Silence.

"Look Chester, she's a delightful girl. But there's nothing between us. She's all yours, old chap."

"You're…you're serious?"

"Absolutely."

"I haven't seen her either. I've called her five times in the last couple of weeks. She's not responded in the least. She didn't say anything about leaving Paris or going on holiday, did she?"

"No, she said nothing about that. Maybe she's out of town for some other reason, mate. Look, I don't know. All I know is that I haven't seen her since we all went out several weeks ago. I've been busy volunteering at the church I told you about, and writing…writing quite a lot, actually."

He was quiet.

"Look Chester, let me know if you want to get together."

"Sure." He was silent for a minute.

"Hey Steve, let's play tennis tomorrow. Sorry about all this rot with Sarah. Are you sore at me?"

"Course not. Try to book a court tomorrow. I need exercise."

"Sure, Steve. I'll text you when."

❖ ❖ ❖

A somber, almost morose, Chester greeted me at the tennis courts. It was a beautiful Paris morning. Sun, crystal blue sky, slight, cool breeze. Smell of sunscreen wafting off the nice-looking women playing doubles on the court next to us.

Chester proceeded to grind me into the court. He showed no mercy. His spirits seemed to improve with every smash down my throat. I was worse than rusty. I could have been humiliated by his assault, if I didn't understand his motivations. I stopped looking at the women next to us and tried to pretend they weren't there. I noticed that Chester started to check out the women as he pulverized me. He was getting a mojo on. *C'était dégoûtant.* I began to truly despise him. I decided it was time for a little "psyops" as we called it in the Army. I could exploit my military training a bit, using Chester as an unwilling subject.

Just as he was about to serve to me, I struck back in what some might consider to be a childish way, but I rationalized it easily. "Look Chet, I hope there're no hard feelings about Sarah. I can't help it if she digs me. What can I say? The fact she's into me shouldn't mess up our friendship. Don't you agree, old bean?" I had no idea if he even liked being called Chet, but I decided to go all in on my own version of tennis court assault.

He then tried to put a little something extra on his serve and ended up hitting it five feet past the base line. He ground the second serve into the net.

"I don't blame you for being into her. She's hot, after all, just like you told me that first time you introduced us. That night I kissed her goodnight, she did look quite fetching in the light of the streetlamps. I must hand it you, mate, you do have good taste in women. I'm sure she's just out of town, or she would have called one of us, don't you think? We should harbor absolutely no worries, old chap." I was grinding Chester back in my own way.

Chester ended up double faulting most of the time he had the serve from there on out. It was either an ace or a spectacular miss. His returns of my serves weren't much better. I ended up winning the final set. I noticed Chester stopped checking out the women before they left the adjoining court. I don't think he wanted to be noticed by them anymore, in fact. I felt a little shitty for doing it, but he had it coming, and I'd always wanted to try out that Army training in real life anyway.

❖ ❖ ❖

My cell rang about 7:00 that evening. It was Chester.

"Surprised to hear from you," I said in a slightly humbled tone. I didn't want to rub things in too much after that last set.

"Sorry." He'd left me without saying a word after the game, the fricking turd!

"You going to talk to me now, eh? Is that the deal, Chester?"

"I said sorry!"

"Okay."

"10 bar, 8:00 pm sharp tonight. Be there."

"What?"

"Look, Beth asked me to call you. I did it."

"Who's going to be there?"

I don't know. Beth asked me to invite you tonight and I did." His transatlantic accent was starting to have a vaguely "Baltimore" lilt.

"Hey Chester, there is nothing going on with Sarah as far as I'm concerned. You know that don't you? I was screwing with you! I mean, I can't ever rule it out. She's special. But really, I haven't seen her." I wasn't going to let Chester off completely.

"Yeah, whatever."

"Chester!" Who was this guy? Was he Robert Cohn reincarnated? I was starting to have Jake Barnes-type feelings towards him. Damn! Was I trapped in the *Sun Also Rises*, after all?

"Look, Steve, it's okay. I suppose I don't care all that much. See you at eight?"

"Probably."

"Good, I guess." So much for my new best friend.

29

Le 10 bar was packed. Cheap sangria was the primary pull. The place sucked other than that. I shouldn't say that. The oldness of it was compelling. It was *belle époque* meets shabby chic, and I do mean shabby.

The toilet was disgusting beyond description. It had a strange inscription, "*Mort la republique illuminati.*" When I looked up on my phone what that could mean, it was some nonsense concerning Robespierre and a pretext to end the "cosmopolitanism and atheism preached by Cloots," an ardent republican, blah, blah, blah. I couldn't see how that would appeal to the patrons of this establishment, or any other for that matter.

As usual, the sangria was tasty and cheap. The clientele was eclectic. Freaks sitting next to models. Babes from the Sorbonne cheek to jowl with the very eccentric. "Eccentric" in this case means what we say in Texas are butt-ugly people. It was interesting, in any event. The music kind of sucked, too, but it did have a beat of sorts. The bizarrely colored juke box was from the 1970s, and apparently so was the available music.

"Steve!" Beth shouted across the bar, running towards me and grabbing me. Oddly enough Beth was very clingy. I expected the French minimalist *faire le baiser*, but she gave me a full-frontal body hug, and I do mean full. She smashed them against me. Okay by me. Sarah gave me a similar treatment. I was liking this. Chester was not happy. There was no doubt in my mind I could beat him on the tennis court if we played right now.

"It's so very wonderful to see you, Steve."

"Great to see you guys."

All the gang was there except for the Swedes. No real loss.

Beth was quite talkative. "So, Chester continue, how is your business venture coming along?"

"Okay."

"Do tell."

"Not much to share at this point, really. I have a few tentative partners, we'll see." His transatlantic accent was back.

I chimed in, "What kind of venture is it?"

Beth jumped in, "He wants to move, in their entirety almost, about half a dozen restaurants in Mexico to Paris—kitchens, décor and workers."

"Well, it's tricky, of course…the supplies, what not. It's a rather long supply line. I want everything to be from Mexico. I don't want the faux Mexican food supplies you get around here from Belgium, sometimes Spain. The Spanish stuff is usually better, but still not Mexican, after all. Legal issues are complicated with the workers, as you can imagine."

"Fascinating. I'm impressed," I really was.

"I don't know if French people will eat real Mexican food. But I want to give it a chance and I want it to be authentic."

"I like it. If you need an extra partner, let me know. I might be interested. Having some roots in West Texas, I've learned a thing or two about Mexican food from a few roads trips into Chihuahua."

"All right," he didn't seem convinced. As much as I liked the idea, I wasn't sold on Chester as a partner, so I dropped it. I decided I was only trying to make supportive conversation, perhaps to ease the tensions.

"So, Steve, how's the novel?" Beth inquired. Big smile. I felt Chester's white-hot glare.

"Good. Making good progress."

"Tell us what it's about? Beth and I were just discussing how much we would like to read it. Would you like me to give you some feedback?" Another nice smile. I was kind of enjoying it. I did my best not to make eye contact with Chester. His eyes were rolling out of his head anyway.

"That would be great after I make a bit more progress." Not sure I wanted anyone's opinion from this group, but to blurt that out wouldn't have been very civil. I did like occasionally hanging out with the group and wanted to be agreeable, however. I could see several of them being represented to various degrees as characters in the book. In fact, they were all characters, in every sense of the word!

"Swell. Let's go dancing. I feel like dancing!" Beth stood up and started motioning us towards the door. She was quite attractive in her short black dress and sandals.

We all stood. I'd really had enough glares from Chester for one evening, so I began to beg off. In front of the 10 bar, we stood talking a bit. I was trying to extricate myself from the group and get away from Chester and his foul mood. A British couple had joined us by this time—Laurence and Gwendolyn. They were an attractive pair from London who could have been fun if not for Mr. Downer, my dear friend Chet.

"C'mon Steve, you really must come. You see we rather need partners. Beth was urging me to join them. It was then that Chester just walked away without saying a word. He set out towards *Carrefour de l'Odéon*.

Beth yelled, "Chessie, where you are going?"

Chester just gave her a strange waving motion without looking back.

"That settles it Steve, you really must come."

I did.

30

We hopped on the metro and eventually changed trains to go to Charles de Gaulle *Étoile*. We walked west from the station, up Avenue Foch. After a wait in a long line we each paid 20 euros to enter a very large and extremely loud underground bar, the name of which I didn't notice as we entered. The bar had four or five big dance rooms. A variety of music played in each, although a heavy bass sound pervaded everywhere. The constantly changing colored lights were common to all the dance rooms. The army would have required double hearing protection for this kind of environment: earplugs and noise dampening headphones.

It was mostly "techno-pop" by my reckoning, though I was hardly an expert in the genre. It mostly sounded like the same music over and over, but it achieved the goal of getting young people to dance. The more dancing the thirstier and hungrier people got, so it was probably good for the bottom line all around. It was already half-past midnight and I had the sense the good times were just starting, as far as party-time anyway.

I was occupied wondering how I was going to get home since the metro stopped running shortly, and Beth, Sarah and Gwendolyn seemed intent on getting drunk and staying all night. Lawrence and I tried not to keep up with them. We felt someone should have some wits about them. The ladies wound up with a whole bottle of vodka and shot glasses for everyone. I was concerned about their rate of consumption when I looked over and in the glow of a strobe light, I could make out a guy chugging vodka from a bottle and a girl with her top off for a brief instance.

I've been around the world a good bit—Germany, Macedonia, Japan, South Korea—and I'm kind of hard to shock, but that surprised me. I might have thought a guy could die from chugging vodka like that. I wondered if my eyes deceived me, so I looked again. The throng was starting to grow on the dance floor, so it was harder now to see. I saw the bottle go up again. Not sure who was taking it in. Didn't notice any more topless girls though. I wondered if others were shocked or if it was just a common nightlife occurrence in Paris.

Beth and Sarah dragged me out on the dance floor a few times. We could hardly move it had become so crowded. I guess I wasn't drinking enough vodka to get the vibe of the place. I was definitely not having a great time, and it must have shown.

"C'mon Steve, loosen up." Beth kissed me on the cheek. Sarah started hanging on my neck. It was okay with me. They kept whispering completely indecipherable things in my ear. I knew they were both drunk. They were just having a good time, a really good time. Having two attractive women hanging on my neck was fine by me. For a moment I recall thinking "fuck Marfa" after they both kissed me! English women were starting to grow on me.

By 1:45 a.m. though, I was quite ready to go, likely because I wasn't shitfaced like the girls. Actually, Lawrence and I were both more than ready to go. With great difficulty, we got everyone out of the bar. We made it to the metro in time to catch the last train to Chatelet. The number 4 line was closed so from there we had to walk across the Seine. No problem since the ladies needed a walk and some night air.

Once again, I ended up with Sarah as we split on our walk home. She was still quite drunk.

"Sarah, not to be preachy, but you may want to watch your drinking a bit. That stuff can kill you if you go after it all the time like you did tonight." She was leaning all over me.

Her speech was slurred, "So sweetsh, so sweetsh."

"I know Paris is pretty safe, but how would you have gotten home if I hadn't come?"

"Cab, silly."

"Oh."

"You so sweetsh."

As we walked home, I realized that my *nouvelle* Lost Generation had some limits to its appeal. I was angry at Chester for throwing his tantrum. Were it not for his little snit fit, I would have been sleeping in my bed rather than helping a drunk Sarah get home in the wee hours of the morning. Chester really was morphing into a Robert Cohn. Beth and Sarah both seemed pretty lost. Beth demonstrated some "Brett" characteristics. The whole plot and character lineup from "The Sun Also Rises" was coming to life right in front of me. I needed a normal guy like "Bill" in the novel to hang out with, but they seemed to be in short supply. I guess they always are. I wondered how much "fiction" Hemingway actually wrote, or was it just recounting observations of real people?

As I walked Sarah home, even though I felt connected to her on one level, I decided to give Monique a ring this afternoon, and make one more try. Monique was complex but might be worth the challenge of trying to decipher her. At least, I could carry on some meaningful conversation with her.

Meanwhile, Sarah and I had to stop every few minutes because she thought she was going to get sick on the sidewalk. It wasn't a lot of fun.

When we reached her door, I reluctantly offered to get her upstairs and make sure she drank some water.

"So sweetsh" repeatedly. "Not needed, really."

I got her to her door and made sure she got in safely and locked her door. She promised me she would drink water and rehydrate. I felt bad for her. I knew what later in the day would have in store for her. Not good.

"Love you, Steve. So sweetsh. Sorry. Wish I could make out with you. Sick. Kinda. You are a love…" was the last words I heard her say on the other side of the door.

What an evening. That night marked a total turning point for my time in Paris on many levels. I never saw any of my *nouvelle*

Lost Generation again. I was done with them. I did find Sarah and Beth attractive. I loved their accent, but they somehow made me depressed and feel old. However, one interesting thing came out of Chester's tantrum. Incredibly, I saw the ghost, or whatever, again.

A few blocks after leaving Sarah at her apartment, there she was in the early morning hours. Yes, right here on the streets of Paris. I wasn't sure at first, but it had to be the Red Angel. It had to be her. It was dark and quiet. I felt like we were the only two people on the planet. Other than a very distant siren, there was no noise but the sound of the tires of her bicycle on the cobblestone street. I wondered how much I had had to drink.

She was riding up Rue de Vaugirard coming towards me. I kept telling myself it must be just a girl on a bike that looked like her. I remember smiling for just a second, and then it hit me with a colder-than-ice chill. It was her! Red hair flowed, short skirt or dress, white legs, I couldn't see her face. It was dark. She was across the street. The darkness or something obscured her face. Even though I couldn't see her face, she looked over at me and I knew for certain it was the Red Angel. Barely audibly, she called over to me, "You're getting there. Keep on. You're getting closer. You'll be there soon enough." It had to be her. Why couldn't I see her face? Was I crazy? Could this be real?

She peddled on and turned up Raspail. It was as though she passed in slow motion. I had goose bumps for another 10 minutes.

I sat down on the curb a few minutes to steady myself. There was no traffic. Paris was sound asleep. I got up slowly and walked home in shock, haunted by that image of her speaking to me then slowly turning her head and looking straight head.

I hadn't forgotten the Red Angel, although up until now I still questioned my sanity when I thought about her. Occasionally, writing a part of my novel that took place in Marfa, I recalled the image of her riding down that lonely highway out of town so long ago. Paris at 3:00 in the morning was a dark, quiet and lonely place. Thanks to the Red Angel, it was also a spooky place now. I felt very alone and a very long way from home. It was the first time, after several months of being here that I felt totally out of place in Paris. Had I imagined it all? In Marfa and now Paris?

31

"You're getting there. Keep on. You're getting closer. You'll be there soon enough."

I kept thinking about those words. What the hell did they mean? Did I hear her right? Was the haunting red-haired girl really here in Paris, or was it my imagination? What really spooked me was that I couldn't recall a voice, only the words. I vaguely recalled her voice in Marfa. I couldn't for the life of me recall any voice from last night as she called over to me. Had she not spoken? Did I not really see her? A chill ran down my spine just like last night.

After struggling with the words and imagery, I decided not to let a ghost, if that was what she was, get inside my head. I came to France to write a novel and that's what I was going to do. She was a Marfa thing, not part of my new life. Marfa was the source of my ridiculous wealth, but other than that, I'd left nothing I needed or wanted in Marfa. Stacy wasn't even there anymore as far as I knew, and Amy was my cousin and business partner.

Still, I had a nagging feeling. There was a pull. I finally attributed it to nostalgia and homesickness. I'd felt lonely after I saw the Red Angel. I continued to replay her slowly turning her head to look straight ahead as she passed me. I still couldn't picture a face. It was just darkness surrounded by flowing red hair in the Paris night. The goosebumps came back when I thought of that scene playing out.

I decided to head south for a few weeks and leave Paris and the *nouvelle* Lost Generation behind. I also wanted to get the Red Angel out of my head. It was a struggle to decide where to go. I thought about going to the Irati to fish the same waters

Jake Barnes did in the "Sun Also Rises." As appealing as fishing sounded, I was starting to have an aversion to the whole Hemingway thing. The *nouvelle* Lost Generation crowd contributed greatly to the disenchantment, something I knew Hemingway would have ultimately agreed with. In fact, I was confident Hemingway would have told my so-called friends to go to hell. That was really one screwed up bunch of people. None of them other than maybe Sarah seemed to be real. They just couldn't get to real since they apparently had no idea what it was. They were trapped in a bad novel and I refused to join them. Maybe they'd been an extension of the Red Angel somehow?

It was really like they were just performing a role, and I had no desire to be part of that. Hemingway was a great writer, but I was starting to think that he had a real dark side and probably led a life filled with peaks and valleys not to mention what he did to numerous folks along the way. Was he too playing a role his whole life? Did he lose the ability to get "to real" also? His writing about his boyhood in Michigan rang true to me, but did he lose who he was and become who he fantasized he would have liked to have been? Who knows? Much of his literature appealed to me, but there was clearly a struggle going on within his mind and the minds of the 1920s Lost Generation. It really didn't offer any inspiration for me in this day and age, and in this place.

I just wanted a steady, at least mostly positive life. I didn't need to run with bulls and catch monster marlins. The military had given me plenty of chances to prove my manhood.

I just wanted to create something worthwhile. That was the reason for heading south—to figure out what that "something worthwhile" might be. I finally realized that walking in Hemingway's footsteps wasn't going to get me there, even if I did want to write the "Great American Novel" like he had. I had to be about discovering myself, not Hemingway and his Lost Generation.

Going in the direction I was headed in Paris would only result in being someone I wasn't. Oscar Wilde reportedly said

"Be yourself. Everyone else is already taken." No truer words spoken, I thought, even if all I could be was me. I just had to figure out how to make the best of who I really was.

After considering Italy, Spain and Portugal, I settled on Languedoc-Roussillon in the South of France. The countryside was beautiful, the weather and food were good, and I spoke the language well enough to get by now. I know Hemingway rendered a very sensual account of the South of France with his *ménage a trois* in "The Garden of Eden" but that's not why I wanted to go there. I wanted to go there to continue the self-discovery mission I'd embarked upon in Marfa.

32

"*Mas de Peuch.*" The name of the place had a nice ring to it. It was also very popular on an obscure British website that rated small accommodations in Southern France. Sarah had raved about it soon after we first met in Paris. The small farm setting was perfect for an escape from "Lost Generations!"

I checked out of my little hotel in Paris, packed my belongings and took a TGV train to Nîmes. It was one of the best things I'd done for myself since I got to France. The next day, I found myself in what was about as close to paradise as I'd ever experienced. I was staying in a small house which was part of a farm and vineyard a little outside Sommières, not too far from Nîmes in the Languedoc area of the Occitanie region of Southern France. I had a manageable bike ride to get to Sommières and Cavisson and very nearby tiny villages of Saint-Côme-et-Maruéjols and Souvignargues. Sommières had a couple of great bakeries and even through it was small, it had a quaint pedestrian way full of great shops. It offered a lot for a small town.

What I enjoyed most was sitting on the small patio outside my little house feeling the sun and watching the grapes grow. The patio looked out onto a pasture. The pasture was ringed with hills on which vineyards continued to the horizon. Again, it took only a short time to establish a wonderful routine around my writing time. I normally made coffee and had a portion *d'une baguette* and a little local fruit or honey on the patio in the morning. I made a point of celebrating the Languedoc sun every morning. The peaceful setting reminded me a little of Marfa, but right now I was feeling more French than Texan. I loved the brilliant white midday sun too. It was a little too cool the first couple of days there, but I forced myself to take it in each morning. It was healing.

Normally, to begin my day, I'd start writing as soon as I got up, even if only for a half-hour, just to clear the cobwebs from sleeping. My first cup of French coffee accompanied my early morning writing effort. *Carte Noire* brand was my staple. If I didn't feel moved to write, I went for a long walk or bike ride collecting inspirations from the French countryside and observations of the people who lived there. My French had become more than adequate to conduct business and even some small talk. I studied a little French each afternoon when I needed a break from writing.

It was a wonderful setting in which to create a story; the pleasant days turned into great productive days. *Mas de Peuch*, in the ancient local dialect, was the name of the property. It had a small pool which the owner made available to me. On really warm days, which were rare at first, I enjoyed a crisp swim in the early afternoon. It was a great way to break up the day. The owners were Emil and Fernanda Gichard. They had three mostly polite children—polite other than their incessant, serious faced, staring. It reminded me of the severe looks I'd seen in pictures of kids of the Depression Era from the United States. I'm not sure what they found to be so serious in my being there, but I responded with smiles and jokes in the hope of breaking any tensions I might have been causing.

There were three quaint farmhouses on the Gichard's property. Mine had been divided into two units or *gîtes*. There was only one other guest as far as I could tell. My unit mate was a small English lady who looked about 80-years old and who was either exceptionally rude or shy. I didn't really care. I only saw her in the early morning on those rare occasions I awoke very early. I often wrote well into the early morning hours. My "good mornings" were responded to by a brief grimace. She would be a good character study for my novel in case I need a British biddy.

To overcome loneliness, I occasionally rode my bike into the nearby Saint-Côme-et-Maruéjols in the evening and had a beer at the *Bar L'Alambic*. It was a little like a bar, but they sold a few food items and locally baked breads. They also sold some deli sandwiches on the freshest baguettes. The ham, croissant and butter sandwich was so good. I'm sure all the ingredients were from local farms or butchers. But the small shop mostly sold cigarettes, lotto tickets and beer—primarily Kronenbourg and 1614, or *seize* for short.

Bar L'Alambic was a clean place that had a family feel to it. Creamy, yellow walls covered with a few old black-and-white photos of soccer matches from an earlier era. François, the bartender, and his wife, Anaëlle, were pleasant, and always patient with my French. Anaëlle, who was young and attractive, had the interesting habit of sitting topless in small semi-enclosed yard behind the bar to soak up rays in the afternoons. I was surprised to see her kids playing around her one day, completely unfazed. It is France after all, I constantly reminded myself.

On certain nights, the bar would be filled with guys watching a *Ligue Un* or rugby match. Marseille was the local favorite soccer team, so it was all about rugby and soccer for the menfolk here. For an American, I thought I was really into soccer, but by French standards, I was ignorantly indifferent. It was almost a cult more than a sport. I learned several additional curse words watching games on TV in the café to complete that part of my education in French.

I didn't like riding my bike home in the dark, so I usually headed back before dark, maybe around 9:00 or even 10:00 as the summer wore on. The traffic was generally light out on the narrow country roads among the vineyards and farms, but I got off the road on the very rare occasions when big trucks roared by.

Surprisingly, for a small village of 700 people, on certain nights the café was filled with more than two dozen 30-something women—pretty and great smelling other than the occasional ashtray smell. They were often argumentative and only rarely did men accompany them. I usually left early when I discovered it was "ladies" night, but one night I somehow hit it off with a table of women who accepted a token American male friend. I found out there was a company training center nearby, and many of the women weren't actually locals. Among other things, the training center also served to teach American businesspeople and expats French as a second language.

It was there I met Pauline, who was a local, sort of. She lived in nearby Sommières and did contract work at the training center. I welcomed female attention; actually, I welcomed almost any attention. I'd been in southern France for over a week now and talked, really talked, to no one except Emil and Father Mike, a local priest, whom I befriended at the *boulangerie,* the bakery, in town.

Emil, the owner of the *gîte*, and I spoke on most days, but it was the usual drivel about comparing French and American ways…lots of smiles, laughs, confused looks, a bit of struggling for words…but of little consequence. Father Mike and I spoke every few days at the bakery, but the conversations usually centered on politics, baseball and his perceived need for me to go to his mass and hear his homilies, which I promised I would do. He probably gave good homilies if only I could have understood him a bit better. Being from Buffalo, New York, he spoke great English but for some reason, I had difficulty understanding his French. I normally understood Americans pretty well when they spoke French—slow speech, simple vocabulary. I found that I could now converse in French decently because I had some expectation of what people would say. But as for lectures, TV dialogues, homilies, and so on, it was more difficult.

I also liked to go into nearby Calvisson on nice days. I liked sipping rosé and watching earnest old men play *pétanque* in the shade of a large tree in the central plaza. I noticed I couldn't understand some of what they were saying. I wasn't sure if it was the accent or if they were speaking the old local dialect. Southern France was amazing on so many levels. The sunlight really did remind me of Marfa. It resembled Marfa on several levels but there was a rich cultural overlay of over a thousand years of well-recorded history, culture and cuisine that, to use a

Beth term, "gobsmacked" me.

Pauline wasn't my only female acquaintance. I was trying to decide how to better get to know Pauline when Brites entered my world and rented the *gîte* next to me after the old English lady thankfully moved on. Brites beautifully pronounced her name as "bree-tees." She was too young for me, from Brazil, loved sunbathing in her skimpy bikini, or often less, and was a spectacular physical specimen. She was also very funny —though I usually couldn't tell if she was laughing with me, at herself or at me. Her skin was the color of a *café crème*, heavy on the milk. I couldn't believe she, a single, young female had rented a *gîte* for three weeks right next to mine in the middle of nowhere. I still wanted to get to know Pauline, but Brites was a pleasant distraction.

This "nowhere" in which I now lived was beautiful, but we had only vineyards and cows for neighbors. I'd come to write and get away from Paris and enjoy the seclusion of the French countryside. Thanks to the Internet and its endless travel site recommendations, however, I had my good fortune to meet Brites. The website of the *gîte* just happened to be in English and Portuguese since the wife of the *gîte* owner, Fernanda, was Portuguese. It was very lucky for me. While I was hoping Pauline would be a part of my social life here, I knew Brites would be a great addition to these weeks at the farm and would most certainly be featured somehow in my writing.

As for other women I had met in France, I reflected on the fact that Monique could very well have been compelling had she mastered telephonic diligence. She returned my call after my epiphany with Sarah, but when I called her back, she once again went into radio silence. So much for my having a Parisian tryst. Sommières was looking good in that regard, perhaps.

◆ ◆ ◆

Within just a week or so of meeting, Pauline and I had really hit it off. We were just friends so far, but there was a tension that suggested that it could go further. At first, she just enjoyed hanging out talking about America, using her excellent English and sharing funny stories. Over a short time, we realized that we really liked each other.

She first heard me speaking French in the *Bar L'Alambic* with my American accent, and she zeroed in on me. She'd lived in the US as a teenager for a few years and fortunately for me, really missed Americans. As was often the case when they're abroad, Americans never really knew if someone liked them or just the notion of knowing someone from the US. At least that was still mostly the case in France.

Pauline was slender and about five-and-a-half feet tall. She dressed very conservatively most of the time—lots of black. Her hair was cut to fall just at her shoulders and she often wore colorful and richly patterned scarfs. She had a relatively dark complexion. She generally had a serious look on her face and didn't smile as much as I would have liked, though she was a very warm, engaging person. Pauline just had one annoying habit: she almost always had to be right. I knew lots of Americans like that, so it wasn't all that unusual, but it was an art form with Pauline. She was a strong woman and I knew she would hold her own in any relationship.

Perhaps her need to be right in every instance wasn't so much a habit as a national trait—I found it endearing, nonetheless. I'm sure she must have thought I had the unfortunate habit of just being plain wrong most of the time. She would go to great, almost comedic lengths to prove she was right, just for the simple sake of argument, or so I thought. One time, she just insisted over and over that Texas was still an independent nation. I couldn't fully refute that assertion knowing much of Texas believed similarly.

At first, I usually gave in very quickly unless her statement or notion was flat-out preposterous—which it occasionally was, especially when she pontificated about American culture. She would shrug in such a way that suggested that her observation was irrefutable and that perhaps I was a fool for not seeing that she was clearly right. I'm not sure which one of us enjoyed it more on those rare occasions I vigorously disagreed. I even found myself starting to reinforce my position with sweeping hand gestures. I was going native quickly. With Pauline it seemed appropriate, however.

Occasionally, I would even speak to her in French when I really wanted to refute her. She would always give me a glowing smile when I chose to take her on in French. French is a great "refuting" language. "*C'est pas possible*" with a pronounced shrug, arching of the back and opening of the hands sounds so much more authoritative than "That's not possible." With the correct intonation, "*C'est pas possible*" and a look away can also mean, "You are an idiot and completely full of shit." Our exchanges usually produced light-hearted smiles and even laughter in the end. It was all quite entertaining and it was great to see her smile more often.

Even though we were still friends who so far only flirted, Pauline was a little territorial when it came to Brites. One day when she dropped by to visit me at the *gîte*, Pauline looked very concerned when she noticed Brites' long bare legs sticking out from the partial privacy wall on my patio.

"Qui est là?" Pauline glared at me. It was unusual for her to speak French to me unless she was teasing me. There was no humor in her tone this time.

"Oh. That's Brites. Let me introduce you."

"*Qui?!*" Apparently, French was her preferred language of anger as well. I kind of liked it. Jealousy?

"My neighbor. She's from Brazil."

The glare continued.

"*Bom dia, Brites*"

"*Bom dia, Stefano.*" As she stood up, I prayed she was wearing her bikini top. She normally did. Of course, today was not one her normal days. Without the slightest reservation she crossed over to my side to shake Pauline's hand.

"*É um plazer*," Brites couldn't speak a word of French...or much English for that matter. We just communicated with gestures and facial expressions mostly. She could read French and English pretty well but could understand a few words of spoken English.

"*Enchanté.*" Pauline said with an exaggerated beautiful French accent as she smiled at Brites then snuck a micro-glare at me.

Brites gave me an awkward smile and said, "*Até logo.*" She spun around and went back around the wall and into her *gîte*.

"What the hell was that?" Pauline demanded. At least she was speaking English again.

"*Comment...Ça te dérange?*" I tried to accommodate her by speaking French. Didn't help.

"Does this girl...this topless...*salope* bother me? Is that what you are trying to ask me?" She was always correcting my French —not her fault; it was just another national trait. I just loved how French people would often repeat what I was saying as to make a point my pronunciation was quite deficient. Many times I craved saying, "Please stop repeating what I'm saying!" But I didn't. It was their national treasure. I just learned to accept it.

"Well...yeah. You look pissed, angry."

"I have to go."

"I'm sorry. Brites is just my temporary neighbor. I don't even know her really. We can hardly speak...she doesn't know English and I clearly don't know Portuguese. She's leaving soon, I think."

"*Oui...mais...*you don't need language for...you know what I mean." She muttered, "Bye," as she swung her handbag on her shoulder and walked to her car. No wave. Nothing. My proud, beautiful French friend was not happy.

"Pauline...," I muttered, but not too loudly. I was surprised at the intensity of her reaction.

After Pauline left, Brites came popping out of her *gîte*. She came over to my patio and plopped down, still sans *une t-shirt*. She did look great, as disorienting as it was to a prudish but quickly recovering American.

"Did I mistakes, Stefano?"

"Well..."

"*Desculpe, Stefano.*"

"Don't worry about it. *Sem problema.* Did I say it right...no problem?"

"*Muito bom!*"

"You know Brites, maybe you shouldn't go around too much without a top."

"Stefano, I on *ferias*...holyday. I need free." She gave me a very innocent smile and stood up and twirled around with her arms outstretched and looked up at the sun. "I free!"

"Yeah, I see your point and I am a big fan of freedom, but just try to keep it on when Pauline comes around. Okay, Brites? And the word in English is "holiday" not "holy day." Kind of a difference."

"*Não tem graça...não* fun." She pouted and retreated to her *gîte* for the rest of the day. I couldn't really blame her. If I looked that good, I probably wouldn't want to hide it either.

33

The next morning, I felt a sense of loneliness. I was afraid I probably wouldn't be seeing Pauline for a while. I didn't have anyone to talk to...really talk to. Another funk descended that I exploited to accomplish some good, pure writing. Depression seemed to bring out the best in me artistically at least, as I was learning how to channel the lesser emotion of "funk" or what I thought funk was. Surely, I had that in common with the great masters.

On that day, and during the night, I crafted some really good, sad, yet funny passages that gave me hope for the first time since I fancied myself a writer. Maybe this wasn't a bogus indulgence, my coming to France. Maybe I wasn't a fraud. Maybe I had potential. I was so into the story, I found myself almost crying briefly. It may have been the entire bottle of wine, the smell of the French countryside, the dark night sky and stars or maybe the night sounds, but it was great stuff. The writing flowed strong, lucid, spare. Hemingway would have been proud. No, he'd would have been jealous, the asshole.

It may also have been Brites. That night I'd momentarily fallen in love with Brites. About midnight she came home from somewhere. She was beautiful. She wore slacks, sweater and tall heels. She smelled strongly of perfume, smoke and wine. She plopped next to me. She looked me right in the eye, went on and on in Portuguese then kissed me like I had never been kissed before—it was more an attack than a kiss. At about the time she was getting out of control, she excused herself and calmly walked over to the fence next to the *gîte* and puked. She turned, smiled meekly at me and slowly staggered inside. She left her door open. I heard her stumble, and then it sounded like she collapsed into her bed.

I got up, fell back out of love as quickly as I fell in love, then got her to rinse her mouth and drink some water. I wiped her face with a clean wash rag I found in her bathroom.

The next morning, she didn't remember a second of the experience. My recollection is foggy, but I do distinctly recall falling in love for about two minutes. It was a great two minutes. Just me, beautiful Brites and the French countryside at night—no one else on the planet. It wasn't quite like the connection with Sarah. It was kind of raw, human sexuality, but a connection, nonetheless. It wasn't deep, but it was powerful even if fleeting. I guess Brites awoke something in me. It was right after that two-minute interlude that my best writing occurred —about two hours of magic: just me, my laptop, crickets, the French countryside at night, and moonlight. I felt hyper alive.

Over the course of the next couple of days, I kept up the good writing pace. I exploited the funk to its fullest. The great American novel was finally emerging—the ill-equipped American man encountering the world and finding himself. At least I hoped that's what it was. Unfortunately, I was also finding out how "ill-equipped" I really must be, but that's part of self-discovery, I kept telling myself as I wrote.

The off and on funk, however, broke the next day. I was kind of moping around town when I saw Pauline on the street walking home holding a baguette, of course. She was dressed from work—black sweater, short black skirt, heels, quite becoming.

"Hi, Pauline!"

"*Bonjour*, Steve." After the obligatory three cheek kiss customary of the south, she asked me to come have some soup she'd made the night before. For whatever reason, she stressed that it was not a formal meal and certainly not a date. That seemed important to her, but she also looked like she was happy to see me. It didn't matter to me. I was just happy to be with her.

I accompanied Pauline to her small apartment. It was a

stone building, probably two or three hundred years old. It reeked of history as did about ninety percent of the buildings in Sommières. Her apartment looked out over one of the nicer pedestrian ways. It was also across the street from one of the better bakeries that I'd visited when in Sommières.

In her apartment, there were only two rooms and a bathroom carved out of the bedroom. The walls were white throughout. She had six or seven paintings reminiscent of Matisse. The scent of lavender filled the air, although it may've been her perfume. There were only three windows, but the place had a very light quality, breezy and very classy.

Within minutes of our entrance she had jazz music on—soft, perfect background music. We each had a glass of a very delicious red blend of some sort, local of course. She told me what it was, but I couldn't catch her high-velocity French. Unlike most Americans, she didn't change. She prepared and served the meal in her black outfit though she was barefoot on the tile floor. She said she loved to feel the cool tile underneath her feet in the summertime. Pauline served an amazing vegetable soup and bread followed by a cheese course, naturally. She brought out a platter with four wonderful cheeses. We then savored beautiful *framboise* tarts with strong black coffee. I loved how every meal was a beautiful if fussy celebration in France. Even the simplest meals were elegant. In France, I always found quality over quantity.

"I'm so happy to see you. We haven't seen each other since you were over a couple of days ago. How have you been doing? Been busy?"

Pauline lightly bit her lip a second or two then quickly looked away.

"*Mais oui*, work and all," she said somewhat sheepishly. After a deep exhale, she asked, "More coffee or wine on the patio?"

"Patio?"

"But of course. My bathroom has a small door that leads out onto a patio."

She did have a great little patio. We walked through the tiny opening off the bathroom that was as much a window as a door, but it worked. It was shady and welcoming. The setting sun peeked through between two neighboring buildings. Vines covered two walls. After my experience with Stacy, I felt a silly panic when I saw a large statue of the Virgin in one corner. As Pauline padded across the patio carrying two glasses of deep red wine, she informed me that the statue was there when she rented the place last year. It was too big and heavy to move, but she said its massiveness didn't bother her.

Pauline sat across from me sideways on a chase lounge with her legs crossed. She seemed anxious to create a pleasant ambiance for a discussion. This was her habitat, bare feet, hair tied up in a ponytail and totally relaxed with herself. Pauline just being who she was. Deal with it, I said to myself. It wasn't difficult at all. I liked it, a lot. She'd cranked her jazz just a bit so it wafted out on to the patio. Cicadas and a gentle breeze completed the scene.

Her expression gradually became more serious. She pulled her hair back from her forehead and briefly stared at the bluing sky. When her eyes came back down and rested on mine, she half smiled and said, "Steve…I am trying to figure out what we are. Are we friends or…what? I am mixed of emotions."

"You have *mixed* emotions? About us?"

"Yes." She just sat and stared at me. I was waiting for her to express her displeasure at me subtly correcting her English, but she moved on. She often gave me a "micro glare" and brief sigh, but not this time.

"Yes. I really like you. But I am having trouble with your "Americanness" or something. We've known each other for almost a month and yet you keep me out of balance."

"What do you mean? We're good friends. I really enjoy your company." That was true most of the time, but her fussiness or "Frenchness" also made me "out of balance" as well.

"What are we?"

"We're good friends. Let's just see where this goes. I mean I feel a little off balance at times, also. I haven't known many

French people so I'm unclear what you're really saying or thinking at times. I view it as a little confusing, but I also find it interesting, charming or challenging or something…but, something good, you know. It's stimulating."

"*Tres bien*, we will be good friends and see what happens. *D'accord*?"

"*D'accord*."

From that moment on I felt our friendship could evolve. It was hard because I didn't know how long I'd remain in the area. I didn't want to hurt her, or me. I was very much attracted to Pauline, and I wanted it to turn into romantic love or something else at least a bit steamier, but a relief of sorts set in for now. The pressure was off for the time being.

We were into each other in some special way, without rushing into to sating our libidos. We had a very relaxed visit the rest of the night. We both shared childhood stories—some funny, some sad. We grew as friends. Some of the pretentiousness or tension, maybe even competitiveness, that characterized our relationship had dissipated. We shared a very special evening on that dusky, candle-lit patio.

We were just two people sharing time together, looking into each other's eye by the flickering light. No French or American stuff. And, while love wasn't quite hovering yet, a trace of it was beginning to envelope us, at least on my end. It was simply good and hopeful. I loved her openness. Not something I expected from French people. Actually, I was surprised she invited me up, but I was glad she did. I didn't think about my impending departure, whenever that might be.

I finally had a friend. Brites was nice but the language barrier was substantial. Smiling and laughing is great, but at some point, I wanted some real communications, a real connection with another human with whom I could share. There was still a barrier with Pauline, more cultural than linguistic, but it was becoming more manageable and even humorous at times. She was getting where she could laugh at herself. The sexual tension between us was not growing, but that was okay for now. However, the relaxed air that had evolved between us compensated to some degree. We'd learned to laugh together. We flirted, but it was almost as though neither one of us wanted to screw up the good friendship that was emerging. If things did go further, it would be on a good foundation.

Southern France was working for me. Lots of sunshine, good writing, good wine, quality female companionship, soccer matches down the road to get in a little guy time, and the food was awesome. It seemed like the time of my life.

34

Over the next two days, I got the book to a good temporary stopping place and prepared for my first get-away from Southern France since I arrived. Pauline and I drove to a small town in northern Spain along the Costa Brava. She asked me to come spend a few days with her and her sister's family. I extended my stay at the *gîte*. What the hell? It wasn't like there was a lot waiting for me in Paris. I'd made good progress on the novel. Why not take in Spain? I really craved some "Texas" style heat.

Her sister, Yolanda, had a small summer get-away in the coastal village of *Llançà*. It was a great spot. They had a modest house a couple of blocks off the smallish beach. *Llançà* is a living post card. White structures with red tiled roofs, ultra-bluish-green Mediterranean, little but beautiful beaches framed by picturesque rock outcroppings and often filled with young, Catalan-speaking topless beauties, and lots of greenery right up to the beaches. Magnificent. How does life get better?

The first couple of days, we hung out with Pauline's family. Yolanda was great. She was probably more outgoing than Pauline and just as beautiful, in her total "Frenchness." Her husband and two children were pleasant to be around, and were all happy to speak English, perhaps to practice, or simply to make me more comfortable. The kids were young and occasionally fussy, so Pauline and I stayed mostly to ourselves except at breakfast, which we all shared as family. We ate mostly traditional Spanish breakfasts of tostadas and churros, with French coffee, of course.

One night, Pauline and I decided to go out on the town. We went to a great restaurant near the center of town. We enjoyed

Catalan cuisine, which is amazing, and a lot of good wine. "So, what do you think?" she asked me as we just sat there relaxing and finishing off our second *pichet* of rosé as the sun made its very last light for the day. We were outside on a terrace of the restaurant. The Mediterranean shimmered in the distance.

"Of what?"

"I don't know. All of this—Spain, us, my family—you pick."

"I want some more of the garlic, butter and anchovies stuff," as I nodded to the waitress, "*Un autre, s'il vous plaît.*" Given the whole political separatist dynamic in Catalan, it was usually better to speak French than Spanish in Catalan and way easier for me.

Pauline smiled and sighed, as though I missed her point.

"I hope you share this plate, or otherwise you won't let me kiss you tonight, it's so deliciously garlicky" I smiled. "Seriously Pauline, I like it. The food and wine were great. The restaurant and setting were magnificent. It's been a wonderful chance for us to be together. A chance to get to know your sister. All good to me." I immediately knew I should have listed the "us" thing first. I struggled a bit on how to respond. I wasn't sure what Pauline expected for an answer, and I also knew I was still hedging in terms of pointing towards any commitments. Something was clearly holding me back from saying what I felt about being together with Pauline.

"I like you being here with you, Steve."

"Good. I like being here." I grimaced inside, knowing I was being less forthcoming than Pauline. She liked being with me, I could only say I liked being here. I knew this was a different relationship with her than with Stacy. Pauline seemed to be interested in a commitment, but I was the reluctant one this time.

She looked me right in the eye and pointedly asked, "When are you going back to Paris or wherever you are going?"

"Well I have the *gîte* leased for a few more weeks. After that, I don't know. I really have no plans."

"Okay. Fair enough." A trace of edge.

"I really don't. I have a strange, almost wandering life these days. I still need to decide what all this means, I guess." I couldn't stand that I was unable to include Pauline in the description of my life here in France. Her willingness to commit was hard to balance against my hesitancy. I hated this. I felt a trace of the old Steve making a comeback. Still, I didn't want to hurt her.

We sat there for a few minutes just absorbing the moment and each other. It was getting dark. I was in Spain with a beautiful French woman. The temperature was slightly warm but becoming more pleasant as the evening wore on. She was striking in the candlelight. She wore a flowing red dress and matching flats. Her lipstick matched as well, coloring her beautiful face, framed by her lovely dark hair.

She smiled at me a few times. Neither of us felt a need to communicate with words. We were just being together. She grabbed my hand and held it awhile.

After a few moments, she said, "Let's go for a night swim."

"I'd love too, but I didn't bring my trunks."

"You don't need them!" She just stared at me.

When she saw my shock, she blurted out, "Just kidding! They're in the car. I threw them in. I got them out of your luggage."

"Kind of sneaky, huh?"

She just gave me a devilish grin. She then leaned in close to me and whispered in French with a wink, "But…if we can find the right place, they could be optional."

She looked at me closely in the darkening evening and eased back in her chair. "You're cute when you blush. Your French is getting better, *cher*."

A few minutes later, we were pulling into the parking lot ringing the beach. It was getting dark. Bathing attire on this beach was indeed optional. It was mostly deserted and there were a lot of rocky nooks and crannies along the water.

I got out of the car and let her change. Then I took my turn. Moments later, she took my hand and led me out to the water. The nearly full moon was just starting to come over the horizon, shining a long beam on the water. There was a soft, gentle tide, rippling the moonbeam that delivered a relaxing ambiance. We walked out into the water to our knees and held hands as we strolled in the moonlight. It couldn't have been planned better. *Llançà* glimmered to our right in the distance.

She gave me a flirtatious smirk and said, "Let's find some privacy."

We went around to the side where there were several huge rocks jutting out into the sea. I followed her up and around a few of these until we came to a small private beach surrounded by huge rocks topped with pine trees. It was beautiful and we were alone. She was truly stunning in the light of the moon. It was one of the most romantic moments I've ever experienced. Marfa was far from my mind.

The now stronger moonlight on the Mediterranean was overpowering. The view of softly illuminated *Llançà* by night was magnificent. If sex had been part of our relationship, it would have been the absolutely perfect setting. Her slight chill about my upcoming departure lingered between us, so that sort of intimacy wasn't going to happen tonight. Fortunately, her chilliness wasn't enough to keep the moment from being one of those memories that will never fade.

◆ ◆ ◆

The next two days were amazing. We had a great time with her family during the day, and the two of us had a great time by night, exploring the little village of *Llançà* and getting to know each other even better. The chill had diminished, and we seemed to be back on track with building a wonderful intimacy. I was convinced now that if we ever did make a permanent commitment, this friendship would be at the core of what would happen in our lives together.

The next day, after we returned to France, I found myself back on the terrace outside my *gîte* relaxing in the sun. Pauline and I had enjoyed an amazing few days in Spain. Now what was I supposed to do? I was supposed to return to Paris in two weeks. I was going to truly miss Pauline and the sun of Languedoc, the two things with which I had made a true connection in France, as well as the wine, the bread, and increasingly, the language and culture. I knew I had to decide about the future of us, if she was willing to talk about it, and I could overcome my hesitancy. I wanted to talk to Father Mike about my situation but felt uncomfortable with his roles as a priest and as a friend. I was reluctant to talk about sex and intimacy to him. I decided to give it a shot, since I was sure he was trained to talk about it in objective terms. And, I knew I really needed objectivity in all this.

35

Father Mike looked like a tall Yogi Berra. The sincerity of his smile, which was never simply a polite affectation, could probably put the whole world at ease. He had been my spiritual and American refuge during my weeks in Southern France. Even when I expressed great reservation about the Bible or dogma, he never judged and managed to gently counter my contentions without the slightest rejection of me. The subtle absurdity of a dude in horn-rimmed glasses from Buffalo, New York dispensing wisdom to a wandering Texan in Southern France, was not lost on me. We'd shared more than a half-liter or two at the bar in town, and perhaps more than a bottle of wine at a single sitting. He had become a good friend.

I took a chance and dropped by his place with a bottle of wine. Luckily, he was home. He was on his patio having an animated discussion with an older woman that appeared to be concluding. I waved to him just outside his side gate and laughingly flashed the wine as though it was a forbidden pleasure or something. He waved back and flashed the French sign for just a minute and then laughed as he put his fist over his nose and rotated it a couple of times and then pointed at me. He was asking me if I was drunk in French gestures. It was important to know the gestures as well as the words. Things we might say or signal in the US could have totally different meanings in France and throughout Europe.

His guest looked a little startled as she turned around to see me. She got up to start to leave. Father Mike smoothed things over with her and they departed laughing.

Within minutes, Father Mike and I were at a nearby park

enjoying the sunshine on a bench. Our conversation took place amid the sounds of metal balls colliding as a group of men nearby played *pétanque*. Periodic outbursts would occur as the men celebrated and poked fun at each other.

"I brought plastic cups so you could be discreet in the company of a crude Yank!"

"Steve, this is France. Relax. What's on your mind? I can tell it's something a wee bit serious and that's been on you mind for a while."

"Okay Father, I mean Mike. This isn't like a religious discussion, okay? I just need you to help me process something."

"Okay, so you want Mike the friend, not the priest?" he smiled.

"Exactly."

"Okay, I'll try. It's kind of a package deal you know."

"Got it. Just do your best."

Father Mike laughed.

"It's about this woman…"

"Yes, go on. How'd I know it'd involve a woman?"

"Yeah, well, I think I might really be into her, but there's this tension."

"Tension, eh?" Damn, Father Mike knew how to draw me out.

"Well, I have to leave soon. I really need to wrap up my book, check on my affairs in the States, and I didn't really come to France to be here forever, and certainly not looking for love, if you know what I mean. Between Paris and here, it's been close to half a year."

"Go on."

"I want to be, well, sorry Father…intimate with Pauline. I need that closure to see if we can connect on that level. She's really taken my mind off something that has been pretty painful for me for a while."

"You're saying she's a useful distraction, in a sense, that is?"

"No, Mike, not like that. I know I need to go, but I want to connect with her, perhaps on a permanent level. I'm really growing close to her. But I also want to be fair to her, too. Given what happened to me before I came to France, I want to protect both of us, but admittedly, especially me."

"Let me get this straight. You want to have sex with her to see if there is a connection and you want to leave soon. Is that what I'm hearing?"

"Well, not exactly.... Darn, Mike, when you put it that way, it doesn't sound all that good to me, either. At least not the self-defensiveness I seem to be taking here."

"What is it then?"

"Well, I want to see if we connect on that level, you know? I meant her being French sometimes throws me off. And I know I throw her off."

"So, help me understand. Would you stay for her if you really had sexual chemistry?'

"Well, no, well, maybe. I honestly don't know."

"Uh huh."

"I know, Father, I sound like a dick, I mean jerk. The more I talk about it the worse it sounds."

"Call me Mike, especially for this conversation." He smiled.

I just looked at him. I wanted a response.

"Look, Steve. You need to decide how much you care about Pauline. If you're really convinced you're leaving, you shouldn't do things that make her more attached to you, as sex most assuredly would. You get that, right?"

"Yeah, I get it." I looked over at the men tossing the metal balls around. Why couldn't my life be simple like that?

"I know you want Mike versus Father Mike advice. Honestly, it's the same. I'm not able to easily change my advice on an issue like that. This isn't a soccer game, or baseball, you know. And, first and foremost, I should be telling you that sex outside of marriage is wrong. Just getting that on the record. Ain't easy being a priest, you know?" He grinned playfully.

We just sat there in the quiet, sipping our wine. After a few wordless, relaxed moments, Father Mike excused himself to visit a person in the hospital. As he was leaving, we stood. He put both his hands on my shoulders, looked me in the eye and said with a grin, "Steve, I'm eighty percent sure you are going to do the right thing."

"Only eighty percent?"

"I've seen Pauline, you bastard. Let me know if you need a confession sometime."

He smiled again and slowly strolled away into the white glow of the Languedoc sun.

◆ ◆ ◆

That evening, I met Pauline in town for a dinner at a nice little vine-covered restaurant near her house. The walls were faded, and the plaster chipped in places, but it had "olives" in the title on an attractively designed light yellow and dark green sign hanging over the entrance. Something to do with olives, anyway. I'd been drawn to it since my arrival but hadn't visited there yet.

Pauline was happy to see me. Nice kiss upon my arrival. Well into the *plat principal*, she turned a bit pensive.

"What's wrong, Pauline? I'm so very happy to share the evening with you…the whole week, in fact. Spain was so amazing. It was unbelievable—so very, very romantic."

"I know." Uh oh. I could tell where this was going.

She gave me a strange look. She was beautiful. She had her "Spanish tan" and she wore a tangerine short, sleeveless dress that put her radiance on full display. Her nails were the same color. So striking.

"What is it, Pauline?"

"I was just thinking…well…ah, nothing."

"What? Don't leave me hanging. What's up?"

"Well…honestly…I was just thinking that I wish you were French. It would make things so much more…doable."

"Doable?"

"Yes. Doable." Her command of English blew me away sometimes.

"How?"

"I mean...sometimes I'm glad you are not French. Sometimes French men are impossible—they are often basically assholes. But I usually don't understand where you're coming from...at all. I mean, there are times I think I do, but then you confuse me. Plus, I don't know how long you're going to be here. I mean, Spain was great, but what did it mean for us? Is that it? You leave and I never see you again?"

"I...I don't know. I didn't expect to meet someone like you. What do you mean you don't understand me? I think we communicate very well. I communicate better with you than almost any American woman I've known!"

"No, you silly dough-shit. I understand you. I just don't get you. You are just so un-French. I mean, sometimes that's good"—often that's good. I don't know, I just don't sense you're in touch with who you really are."

"What do you mean?" I wisely let dough-shit go.

"You're sometimes without clues to what is going on around you or maybe even in you. Maybe that's just how Americans are. Maybe you do know, but you hide it. I'm not sure how to explain it."

"I wish you could explain it. I'd like to know."

"There, right there. I love that. That's a thing I love about you. You're quite thoughtful in many ways. You are more thoughtful than most Frenchmen. I mean you seem to really care what I think about things. And, you haven't pushed for us to be intimate, apart from the intimacies we share in the moment, like the beach in Spain. That's a good thing. I mean French men fake caring about the woman in order to take them to bed, but we know...believe me, we know."

"That's good, eh?"

"Yes. Yes, it is." She gave me a sweet, but exasperated smile. She blew her bangs up with a sigh.

"Hold on, Pauline. Please try one more time. I need to understand what you're saying."

She smiled as she eased back into her seat and glanced out the window as she assembled her sentence. She smiled and looked at me. "Okay. Don't be hurt. I feel like you are in some ways…immature. *Comme un enfant.*"

"How?" Trying my best to not sound defensive. This sounded painfully familiar. If only she had seen me before. I knew I'd grown up so much since Marfa.

"You just don't seem to understand what really matters to you. Don't feel bad. Maybe it's an American way. I mean Americans have iPads, cell phones, high speed internet for your video streaming and such. You all are so electronically connected to the world. Yet I don't sense you are connected to yourself."

She looked me in the eye and continued, "Does this make sense? It seems like Americans don't think much. They pick sides and are told what to think in order to be member of the side they pick. The US really has only have two political parties, for God's sake! We have dozens. I mean, surely, the issues don't line up cleanly on two distinct sides for all those people! What if you are pro-environment and for limited government? What if you are against abortion and for taking care of the poor? What the hell! You people are crazy! Likewise, I sense that you don't reason through what you think about things. Like you don't have personal preferences, or something. You just pick a team and stop thinking!"

I was haunted by past conversations with Stacy and the reverend in Marfa that covered similar ground. It seemed unfair, in some sense. There were some issues, like the environment, on which I was very strong.

"I think I do have strong inner feelings, Pauline. I may not seek to inflict them on those around me, but I do have those feelings. But I also agree that many Americans don't. They just follow their tribal leaders. And, after all, you all have the same technology we have."

"Yes, I know. It's bad for us all, in too many ways. We seem to be losing the quality of living in the moment and relishing the world that's around us rather than some televised or video enhanced picture or explanation of a world someone else thinks is important. To be French is to be independent, to think for ourselves. I once thought we perfected the democracy America created."

"Okay, Pauline. This is the deal. I'm a work in progress, just like America is a work in progress." It was hard not to be a little defensive, but I knew it was a difficult argument to defend, after all.

"Some of what you say is true but…I am trying," I continued. "I kind of hid from this during my time in the military. I was busy doing the manly soldier thing. I didn't have to think about who I was. The Army gave me an identity. That's the way they like it. Your army is the same way. Individual identities make team building harder. And it worked for me. You can be both manly and immature at the same time if your team succeeds. Maybe the Army expects so much out of a person, it tolerates the immature ways of soldiers. It could have been worse; I could have been enlisted. I was an officer. It was a little better, but the team was still all-important.

"Maybe that's partly…maybe mainly…why I'm here…why I'm in France. I'm looking for something that helps me identify who I am. Maybe I'm trying to access an inner voice or listen to nature better. I left something very important behind in Marfa. Well, really, I guess she, or maybe it, left me. It's more than that; I feel I left something more than a girl I thought was my destiny. I'd pretty much convinced myself that we were supposed to be together forever, you know? I was starting to imagine that I belonged in a small town in West Texas. Now, I don't know what I think. I'm maybe losing a narrative that has been driving me whether I liked it or not. That's a loss that now I think is a good thing. Maybe you've been part of my evolving narrative. I don't know, but I feel that you are. I also feel the need to go back to Marfa to get closure and make sure there aren't other things I need to lose, or gain."

Pauline looked at me with sympathy, silently urging me to go on and get this off my chest, I suppose. I seldom fully opened up like this and it was cleansing.

I kept going. "I know I'm going to have to go back and retrieve whatever I left of me…if it's still there. Or at least I have to try. I'm a bit angry I don't know what I'm supposed to do or who I'm supposed to be. But I do know this. That girl, Stacy, thought I had a talent, a talent that I was hiding from myself. She thought I was somehow keeping myself from becoming who I'm supposed to become. I thought I could come here to France and write a book—a special book—that could help me find myself. Maybe it can help others, I don't know. All I know is that I'm committed to trying. I need to grow before I go back. I've already made a lot of progress. You should have seen me before! Since I've met you, I've started thinking maybe I'll recognize what I'm supposed to retrieve if I grow up a little more." I didn't want to tell her about the Red Angel. She'd surely think me worse than immature.

Pauline smiled warmly and reached out to hold my hand. If I hadn't been fooling myself with Stacy for so many months, I might've confused that look for love.

"I'm impressed," she said. "I've never had a Frenchman open up like that. They play games, you know? You don't."

"Thank you for trying to understand me, Pauline. I don't think I could ever play games because I just don't know the rules. I certainly couldn't play games with you. It would be a waste of precious time."

She just glanced over at me with eyebrows raised, with an air of subtle, very subtle approval. Her mind was working. I think she was starting to see me in a different light, a better light.

"Yes, Pauline. It's not every day I have someone go to such great lengths…to illustrate just how screwed up I am. I love it and hate it at the same time!"

Giving me a sexy look, "*Je suis très spécial, n'est pas?*"

"I am inclined to agree, *Mademoiselle* Ferrand." She and I were an making an emotional connection, maybe even approaching a stronger than emotional intimacy. With Pauline, the fact that the intimacy was apparently now emerging on multiple levels gave our relationship a delightful edge.

36

I dreaded the next couple of days. Brites was leaving soon and for reasons that both relieved me and worried me. I'd become attached to her, kind of like an admiring cousin or uncle, perhaps, but not as a potential paramour. She was an important part of my French country life. Brites somehow helped me see what was here in the South of France and then how to write about it. She was due to leave France on Saturday morning, but it was only Thursday. She caught me outside adjusting the brakes on my bike.

"Steve. Let us drunk."

"What?"

"I want celebrate."

"What do you want to celebrate, Brites?"

"I am at France. I have two days. Please."

Beautiful and sexy but oh so young. Against my better judgment, I found myself saying yes. I always try to accommodate the pretty young lasses, apparently.

I wasn't fond of being seen in Sommières with Brites in case Pauline was out, so I suggested we go somewhere in Calvisson. She suggested a nice restaurant bar in Villevieille. Villevieille was next to Sommières but still far enough from Pauline's hangouts, I was hoping. Brites and I had tasted olive oils at an oil cooperative a few days before near the restaurant, so I was familiar with the area.

The restaurant was on the first floor of a large structure overlooking the valley on the upper level of Villevieille. The building was sort of like a square castle. The restaurant and bar were dark and wistful. It would have been a good venue for seduction, had that been either one of our intentions.

When we arrived on our bikes, Brites quickly slipped her tennis shoes off and put on black heels. Even if we arrived on bikes, she always looked very classy. It felt strange riding a bike to certain destinations in France like a nice restaurant, but we didn't have a lot of options. Fortunately, the summer afforded us enough daylight to get home afterward.

"You like da neck-lass?" She held up the string she was wearing.

"Very nice. It's you, young Brites!"

"Bought at Montpellier makes week."

"You mean a week ago?"

"Yeah. I say that, yes?"

"Yes, that's exactly what you said. Your English has become so good, Brites."

She just smiled and looked very comfortable. I'm glad she was.

They put us in a quiet corner with a window looking out onto the village. She looked great, even radiant.

"I miss you."

"You mean you are going to miss me?"

"*Sim.*"

"I'll miss having you as a neighbor. We've had fun. Many good chats and I've learned a lot about Brazil, as well." It was true that she'd awakened something in me. I guess it was because she was so alive, so free. Maybe this is why Hemingway and Fitzgerald loved it here so much…they were simply so alive in France.

Her eyes were moistening.

"I've heard I've got an English couple moving in after you leave. Probably will be a stuffy old bunch."

She snuffled and smiled weakly. She excused herself. Upon her return, she had let her hair down and freshened her lipstick. She seemed to be working up to something.

The meal was very good. We shared a bottle of excellent wine. Brites appeared to be nervous, fidgety.

"Brites…is there something you want to say?'

She blurted it out. "I tink I have *sentimentos por...*," she started, unsure of how to say it. "Dunno exactly how you tell in English, but there are boy problems home."

"What?"

"I like you *muito* o boy like you."

"Huh?"

"Silly." I had no idea what she way trying to say.

"We don't know each other that well. I mean you are a wonderful young woman. I've really enjoyed getting to know you. And you are a beautiful lady, Brites. Any man in Brazil would be lucky to have you."

"*Sem problema*...No problem. No need say..."

"We've had great time together."

"I know I say silly. I sorry. *Desculpe*."

"Don't apologize. I am greatly flattered. I am older. I had no idea."

"We have fun, much."

Language was making this even more interesting than it had to be, but still fun. It had to be tough for her to attempt to communicate weighty stuff in English. I wasn't sure what she was trying to say, and this was no time to be jumping to conclusions.

"Brites, I am also sad about you leaving France."

I was perplexed about what she meant, but felt I had to say something if it was as painful as it looked. She excused herself again.

When Brites returned she had cheered up a bit and suggested we ride home. We had a solemn ride back to the *gîtes*. When we returned, she hugged me and started for her door.

"Wait, Brites."

"What?"

"Let's share a bottle of wine on the patio. It's a beautiful evening." For whatever reason, I wasn't ready for this evening to end.

She thought it a moment and finally nodded.

Brites followed me into my door and watched me open the extra bottle I'd purchased down at the store near the restaurant. Out on the patio, I poured each of us a glass and placed the bottle on the table between us. I watched her carefully take her tennis shoes off and neatly place them next to her chair. She was avoiding eye contact. The sky had a hint of pink to the west that made her hair shine in a way I hadn't noticed before.

"Gonna be a nice sunset. Do you get nice sunsets in Brazil?"

She smiled without saying a word. I don't know if she understood.

We sat there sharing an overwhelming silence for several minutes. Exasperated, I asked Brites to standup. In her bare feet she seemed so small. I stood and walked over to her, looked her in the eye and smiled. I lightly kissed her right cheek and then gave her a long embrace. At first, she was like hugging a board but she gradually relaxed. I gave her another light kiss on her left cheek and sat her down. I sat on the ground next to her and looked up at her. I gave her an incredible pep talk, ninety-nine percent of which I meant, and probably ninety percent of which she had only a vague understanding. She started to laugh and apologize. The laughing threw me off, but we were still communicating in non-verbal ways that overcame the words.

We talked—language barrier and all—until the wee hours of the morning. We almost finished two bottles of wine, accompanied by some bread, cheese and olives. I recall hoping that this would be an important conversation for her for a long time. I know I learned a few things and sorted out a little bit in my own life. But the biggest thing I learned was that I had misunderstood almost all the conversation at dinner. All the time, she was trying to tell me about her problems with her fiancé. I'd jumped to the wrong conclusions and the more I thought about it, the stupider I felt. We shared a good laugh after we had our translation breakthrough. I guess I'd gotten a little cocky, maybe deluded, after some of my more recent French encounters.

At some point, she couldn't stay awake any longer. I tried to get her to budge but she was out. I found myself taking her next door and putting her in her bed.

I walked back to my *gîte,* a bit embarrassed after understanding that she just liked me as a friend. She was sad because she was really, really going to miss me as a companion. She'd never known an American before. She described Brazilian men in such a way so I could see why she liked me. She found Brazilian men sexy but very difficult to be around—very chauvinistic. I was slightly crestfallen because I'd misread her in so many ways, but also relieved. I didn't want more complications. She was a wonderful young lady and I was happy she had a good life ahead of her back home.

When she departed, she hugged me very hard and said she was really going to miss me. Brites was a very brief, but deliciously enriching chapter in my life. Interesting how a person can enter your life a few weeks and "stick with you," perhaps forever. I admired her sense of freedom and playfulness. She harbored few inhibitions, nor should she have.

Sitting on the patio in the morning shade, everything quiet in her absence, I began to reflect on my time in Southern France with Brites and Pauline. Since the time I'd first come to Marfa, I found I could have intimately friendly relationships with women, without a physical, sexual aspect. I think I finally realized that love and lust were separate sensations and I'd probably been confusing them for some time.

I discovered that I could be attracted to women for who they were and how they thought and separate that from desire and the drive to consummate the attraction through sex. It was liberating while enhancing the advantages of knowing women as intellectual and even spiritual equals. While I found Brites to be a beautiful young woman that probably many men might have greatly desired, I also found her as an inspiration to make myself even better. In fact, I feared my productivity may have had a codependency with her presence. She was an unconscious muse. That muse part is probably all bullshit, and I really shouldn't try to write that down anywhere in the book. Anyway, Brites was fun to be with and just good to look at. I felt alive around her, like I'd discovered a part of me I'd left in the past, even before DC and Marfa. Brites had a special quality that was hard to describe. One thing was she made me feel younger. I would sorely miss her.

I also flashed back to my army time for some reason. Other than a few bright moments as an intelligence officer in the Army, my post-college, adult life had mostly been a portrait of boredom and often traumatic challenges until I left DC to venture out to Marfa. I'd had it good in high school and pretty good in college. Great friends, some remarkable girlfriends—some good, some just plain weird—but it was always entertaining. When I got to DC everything changed for me.

During college, I'd done a six-week internship with a Senator. I thought it was the most exciting thing I'd ever done. I just couldn't wait to complete my ROTC obligations and get back to DC. I ended up staying in the Army longer than I anticipated, but I did eventually get back to DC. Service was an aspiration and I felt fulfilled, until DC.

Somehow DC just ground me down, and in all too short a time. With the hours I had to work, I got out of shape. Too much beer. Crappy diet. My skin got pasty. I got to where I'd almost forgotten how to smile, I was so cynical. Somehow, I let that go on for over three years, years I wouldn't get back. Years of stupid insecurity and some kind of strange self-importance. What a combination. I wasn't alone. It afflicted most of DC.

About a year before I left DC, it got a little better. I met a few decent friends and we occasionally traveled. One of them had a sailboat in Annapolis, so we got in a little crew work from time to time. It was hard work and a lot of fun.

That's where I met Bethany, my arrogant girlfriend. She was the daughter of a former Virginia Congressman who made gobs of money lobbying. She worked about twenty hours a week at his firm and drove a new BMW. Even if she was awful, I just couldn't let go. She was a knockout and she had a preppy way about her that to my naïve eye looked good at the time. I thought she was like a Kennedy or something. She always had rosy cheeks even without makeup. She was incredibly spoiled and clearly felt entitled. Anyway, other than that painful experience with Bethany, I really had very little romance in my life, post-army, up until Stacy. She awakened something in me that had been asleep. The sensuality of Marfa—the art, food, sun, sunsets, local culture, landscapes—had stirred in me something that had been dormant a long time. In Marfa, I started to feel alive for the first time in years. France nurtured that feeling in me. In fact, in France that feeling of being alive increased.

    I felt, maybe hoped, that I was starting to get on a roll. Stacy, a little adventure in Paris and then Pauline and even Brites. I was certain something was coming together for me. I just had to figure it out. And I had to hope the Red Angel was right, even if I didn't really believe in her.

37

Dearest Steve:

I miss you so much. I miss my "drinking buddy." I've had 2 beers since you left. I just don't want it without you. Alcohol was like a truth serum for us. It really opened us up. I just don't have anyone I want to open up with these days. Other than that, all is well.

I have news on the ranch and gallery. One, the gallery is doing pretty well. I have found an artist, believe it or not, in Fort Stockton, who seems to be getting hot. We have sold nine of her pieces and so far she is giving us almost an exclusive on her work. She's really into the whole Marfa scene. I cut her a good deal, but her stuff is fetching a premium so we can afford to. She even said she might consider becoming an artist in residence for six months if it will help increase the visibility of the gallery. I told her yes, of course.

The restaurant and the distributorship are also holding their own nicely.

On the ranch, I recently got two offers. As you remember, the weirdos—Light or whatever her name was and her friends—left the ranch about a month after you left. The Escondido Ranch next door wants to lease our ranch plus the house to serve as quarters for their foreman, but the big news is that a movie company wants it too. It was a good move for you to invest in the updates and I think they'll pay off nicely.

I think I'm going to be able to swing it so we can lease it to the Escondido folks with a proviso that they work within our habitat enhancement efforts and that movie folks can lease it as well. I just agreed to give the Escondido people 10% of whatever we get. They were good with that. The movie folks are going to agree to coordin-

ate with the foreman to avoid messing up the ranching operations. I have John reviewing it to protect us.

Steve, I want to thank you for helping me recover from a horrible, abusive relationship. Reconnecting with you was one of the best things to happen to me in years! Anyway, I just wanted to thank you for looking out for me, cuz! Again, I just feel awful about being SUCH a big jerk to you at first.

By the way, I think the gallery is going to turn a decent profit this year. We may be the only gallery in Marfa who'll be able to say that at the end of the year.

Just wanted to give you an update. How's the novel coming along?

>Love,
>Aim

Pauline picked me up for dinner that evening. She took me to a restaurant in Sommières. It was around 8:00 when we arrived. The cuisine was Moroccan. I didn't know what she ordered was, but it was delicious and it gave us a chance to just sit out front on the sidewalk and savor our food. It also gave me a chance to enjoy her beauty by candlelight again.

"Steve, I want to ask you about something."

"Please. Go right ahead."

"I mean...it is complicated, but important...how do you define wealth?'

"There was a time when I thought that was an easy question, but now I'm not so sure."

"What do you mean?"

"I mean I'm still coming to grips with the apparent wealth I inherited last year. When I was a staffer on the Hill...working in our Congress, for a Senator, I thought something like making over $125K a year was wealth."

"What do you think now?"

"I'm still working on it. It's an important question. I guess we all want to be wealthy."

"But we all define wealth differently, maybe?"

"Sure, I think a lot of Americans feel like a nice house, nice car and a little savings is wealth."

"But what do you think?"

"I think it's complicated. What do you think? Why do you ask?"

"I was curious because I see so many Americans deeply into electronics—cell phones, computers, whatever. I mean they are so connected to their view of the world and so entertained, but I sense they…at least many of them…are not connected to themselves, what's really important to them, their families and their communities." We'd chatted about some of this before, but this line of questioning seemed to have a different motivation.

"Go on…"

"I think wealth or least a part of it is knowing who you are… being comfortable in your skin is how I heard it put once. Having money and possessions is interesting, perhaps, but it does not define us. It certainly does not provide lasting contentment, does it? I suppose the big question might be: is happiness truly tied to being financially wealthy?"

She peered over at me waiting for a comment.

"Keep going, Pauline. I think you're asking the right questions."

"I believe there's a lot of money in America but not as much wealth. There are a lot of sad people who seem out of touch not only with the world perhaps, but with themselves. I mean it's bad enough that people can't relate to themselves or to each other, but they can't relate to the changes that are happening all around them, like the changes in nature…the climate, oceans, the forests, the creatures within them. Do you know what I mean?"

"Sure, I think so. Do you think our technology distracts us from what really matters?"

"Precisely. Well, in large part. Many of my American students seem so distracted by their technology they become unaware of where they are and sometimes even what day it is. They use their technology only to find information that confirms what they already think. They do not look for viewpoints or other's insights that challenge them and help them grow. How do you become truly wealthy if all you do is look for agreement only with your own perspectives? How do you find new opportunities and challenges in life? Isn't learning new things and overcoming challenges a big part of satisfaction and happiness?"

"Maybe...that's probably a good point, but I see a lot of kids in France into all the electronic toys. And, unfortunately, we're all afflicted with what we call 'confirmation bias,' aren't we?"

"Yes. Unfortunately. This 'confirmation bias,' as you call it, affects us all. It seems to be part of being human. We believe what we believe and that seems to be worsening all the time!"

"How do you define wealth, Pauline?"

"This."

"This?"

"*Mais oui*. Good friends, good food, good conversation, good wine. Right now, what we are experiencing is wealth. We are surrounded by incredible works of art...thousands of years of history and culture...we are experiencing wealth right now, this very moment. We are exploring new relationships and new insights about each other and the world around us, just as we have been since you arrived."

"I agree." Now Pauline was talking as a true French woman, maybe as a "true" European. She seemed able to think and express herself in ways few Americans consider. The sense of intimacy I felt now was striking.

She just sat there in the cooling evening, looking very comfortable, very self-assured. She was comfortable in her skin. Even though she had a modest income and lived in a small but beautiful apartment, she was truly wealthy. She really didn't have the distracted, rushed, overloaded qualities so typical in Americans. She very much reminded me of Stacy and her disdain for possessions. Both Pauline and Stacy exuded wealth even though their possessions appeared to be few. Her simpler life let her have time to read, to grow, to think. She'd get so enthused about a type of cheese from the market or the taste of some fresh raspberries. She had an incredible knowledge of local wines and French literature and history. She was on to something.

"Pauline, do you think knowledge is wealth?"

"Of course, if you mean both local and global knowledge—we must know what is around us and what is affecting others to connect to them, do we not? Connecting to each other and to our world is a big part of the knowledge we obtain."

I could only marvel at her responses.

She continued. "Knowledge may be the very best wealth, along with the language and culture to express and share it. Without it, we wouldn't have the capacity to enjoy architecture, literature, what we have built for our children. It is the foundation of wealth. And, with the most beautiful language in the world…the one we speak too little when we're together, *mon chéri*…we are among the wealthiest people in the world, right here and right now!"

I became even more aware of my growing respect and affection for this incredible French woman. She was remarkable. I'd thought maybe she was unusual in France. Over time, I realized a lot of French people were walking encyclopedias of French culture. She was the only French woman, maybe the only woman ever, with whom I had achieved this level of communication. Perhaps she was channeling the insights of the French philosophers and scientists of old that made France so great in centuries past. My heart sank a bit as I realized I would be leaving her very soon—not just Pauline, but France.

Every day however, for some inexplicable reason, I felt the growing pull of Marfa. Maybe I'd return to France after I sorted all my feelings out. Maybe not. All I knew was I had left something important behind in Texas. I was soon to perhaps leave something every bit as important behind in France. What the hell was wrong with me? I know I was worried I'd regret leaving this special woman, for even I didn't really understand this urgency to journey back to Marfa. I didn't understand what was going on in my mind. Damn Red Angel! I might as well blame her.

38

A couple of days later, I found myself sitting in the bright sunlight of southern France looking at the ruins of an ancient bridge that partially crosses the Vidourle River in Sommières. I was wrapping up my writing and editing here in the South of France. Pauline was back at work. Brites was gone. As I feared, Brites' absence bothered me, and the prospect of missing Pauline was already giving me pre-nostalgic feelings. In fact, the thought of missing Pauline was causing sleeplessness and self-doubt about failing to encourage her and more deeply explore the possibilities of a long-term relationship.

Progress on my novel slowed to a crawl so it was a good thing I'd found a way to end it and feel confident enough about it to start the final editing. My almost magical journey to southern France, and in fact France in general, was about over and I was back in a lonely *gîte* next to a cranky English couple. To escape a strong sense of loneliness, I rode into Sommières. Before, I would have been chatting things up with Brites or Pauline. I truly missed being with Pauline, though…that was far more than the infatuation I felt about Brites. The melancholy that inspired what I felt was my best writing was playing out and ending in misery; it wasn't creative misery…just plain old despair.

I suddenly felt a long way from home, wherever home was. I loved France, but something was making me restless. Pauline and I had started to connect in new ways, and I feared I was starting to grow close, maybe too close, to her. I sensed it was now or never with Pauline. One way or the other, something would have to change to maintain my confidence and avoid a repeat of what happened with Stacy. If only Pauline wasn't so smart, beautiful and French!

It was at that moment I decided to return to the U.S, as soon as I completed the first real draft of the novel. I plugged away for two straight days, tightening and tidying up. After a marathon of writing and wine consumption, I was at 80,000 words and I was feeling pretty good about where the story went. I'd incorporated much of what I'd learned from Stacy, France, Pauline, Brites and the "Sun Also Rises" gang in Paris. I felt I was becoming a new man. I was a changed man, or more simply, a whole man. The confidence was resurfacing knowing I could write something worth reading.

The metamorphosis that had begun in Marfa was coming to fruition. Sitting outside my *gîte* for what I felt was my final afternoon of pure reflection, I thought a lot about what Stacy and Pauline had shared with me about me: the good things and my shortcomings. I thought about how I'd clung to many of the experiences in Marfa to be a better person in France. I pondered how the experiences of Marfa would always stay with me. Much like Hemingway's "movable feast," Marfa had become my movable Marfa—something no one could take from me—something I would always have with me no matter where I was. Marfa was my pivot point to manhood, "humanhood." Even though Marfa would always be with me, I yearned to return to the real thing. The words of the Red Angel haunted me, "You'll be there soon enough." Wasn't she talking about Marfa? Wasn't Marfa my destiny? Was the Red Angel even real? Had I really seen her? That haunted me. It was so fantastic, too fantastic to be true.

❖ ❖ ❖

The next evening, I said goodbye to Pauline. We'd had dinner together on Thursday, but we were having such a good time, I couldn't bring myself to mention my departure. We'd grown so close. We were considerably more than affectionate friends at this point. Even though I was very attracted to her, I couldn't allow myself it to go further knowing that I had to leave. I had to speak up.

"Pauline, this has been a wonderful chapter in my life, but for now it must close. I must leave, at least for a while. I have to go back to Texas to figure some things out. I have businesses there." I knew it was a cop out, stringing all those thoughts together. I just blurted out all the things I'd rehearsed, and they all ran into each other.

She stared at me with little to say. And then I saw it. A tear began to stream down her cheek.

"*Je comprends*."

That's all she said.

After a long pause, I added, "I would like to come back, but right now, I just don't know. I love France. I've loved our time together, but this is something I have to do." I had to say something to remove the stigma of a conversation I was so dreading up till now.

"I completely understand. *Je comprends*," she repeated. No more tears. Just the one.

"Pauline, you are an extraordinary friend. I will always treasure the time we spent together. You've become so special to me. You've opened my eyes to so many things and taught me so much. Most of all, I've just really enjoyed being with you."

"When will you leave France?"

"In a few days. I leave for Paris in the morning."

Very stoically, she said, "Steve, you too are very special," she paused to study my eyes. "I will miss you, as well. I too have learned much from you. You are unlike anyone I have ever met. Very few of my American students or acquaintances are able to express themselves as you have been able to do in this short time we've known each other."

My heart was heavy. I'd grown closer to Pauline than I'd thought possible. I melted when I saw the tear. When you see a friend hurt, you learn a lot about how you truly feel about them. We'd grown from competitive acquaintances testing and trying to figure each other out to becoming good friends, intimates without the physical nature intruding. We may have been on the verge of becoming far more than friends, but the time wasn't right, at least for me. I'd grown greatly in France, but a part of me—or something else I couldn't identify yet—was missing.

We spoke of our seeing each other in the future, but down deep inside I was afraid it might be unlikely, which made the situation worse. In fact, it hurt. The emotions that swirled within me very much tempted me to delay my departure. I wanted more of Pauline, but I sensed I had to go now, or I might never leave. If I didn't go, I knew, somehow, I'd always feel a void, something missing in my life. I couldn't explain it even to myself. I knew I'd feel a similar loss upon leaving Pauline.

39

Three days later, I was on a United flight departing Charles de Gaulle on a cool and rainy, morning in late September. The flight over the Atlantic gave me a lot of time to reflect on my time in France. Of course, this adventure changed me. Maybe the metamorphoses had begun before I stepped off the plane so long ago in Paris. I reflected on what Marfa and its aftermath had done to me. I reflected on Brites, a magnificent spirit that represented the beauty of Brazil and the spirit of youth. And I fixated on Pauline, the sophisticated, lovely, demure French woman. How much would I regret leaving her? I even thought a bit more on my "Lost Generation" acquaintances of Paris who found themselves trapped in a time warp.

I also thought about my last visit to see Father Mike. I went to say goodbye to Mike on the eve of my departure. I thought I'd spend my last evening with Pauline, but she had to leave town on business. Father Mike, even though he was headed out the evening I came by, insisted I join him for a farewell glass of Bordeaux on the patio. Over the din of cicadas and the soft evening noises of a French town, he acted as though he had all the time in the world. The meeting replayed in my mind.

"So, Steve, what are you going to do in the US?" He looked me right in the eye with his own eyes filled with a sincere anticipation of my response.

"I…I'm not quite sure."

He just sat and listened, teasing out of me my innermost thoughts.

"I'm thinking about making a serious run at being a writer. I'm pretty happy with what I've been able to write the last few months."

"I see." No judgement, just another invitation to share more.

"Yeah, I think I might have it within me to write. I think I'll try to wrap things up in Marfa, establish a home base somewhere in the states, and then travel…and write. I find traveling really stimulates my writing efforts."

"Sounds very nice. Any financial issues that might present a challenge?"

"No. Uncle Clive's gift to me removed financial concerns. I'm free, I guess." I had grown to see my Uncle's gift as freedom more than money. It offered a kind of prosperity that fit more with Pauline's definition than what we Americans usually considered wealth.

"That's wonderful, Steve. Use your freedom wisely, my friend."

I paused, hoping for elaboration. He spoke no more without invitation. He just wore a kind, wise smile.

I decided that I'd held him up enough and got up to leave.

"Well, Father Mike, thank you. You've taught me a great deal. I'm grateful to you. Here's a little to help your mission," I said as I handed him an envelope full of Euros.

"Thank you, Steve. It will help a widow down the street. God bless you."

I started for the gate to the front of his house. It was awkward. I sensed there was…something more. Just as I got to the gate, I blurted out, "What do you mean?"

"What?"

"What did you mean about using freedom wisely?"

"Do you have a little more time?"

"Of course!"

"Let's walk. I'll buy you another glass of wine."

We strolled down the street to the *brasserie* where his friends waited. They greeted him warmly. He explained to them that I was leaving and that he wanted to visit with me a few more minutes. We grabbed a table just outside the bar and watched Sommières settle in for the evening as shops became illuminated with a golden glow. People closed shutters in residences atop the shops. I was a little concerned about riding my bike home in the dark, but I dismissed the worry. I wanted to know.

"I'm keeping you from your friends."

"You too are a friend...a friend who is leaving. Marcia and Claude understand."

"Using freedom wisely?" I prompted him.

"You have an opportunity few men or women ever have... to chart your own path. Don't blow it on self-indulgence. Serve people with the tremendous blessing God bestowed upon you. Make the world better. So many monetarily wealthy people blow their wealth on self-indulgent pursuits."

"How can I do that? How can I serve? I don't have any special wisdom like you."

"Then stop writing. If you don't have something to pass on, then stop wasting people's time. Of course, I speak paradoxically. You know that's not true, don't you? You realize you have much wisdom to offer in your writing, yes?"

"I didn't say I don't have the capacity to learn. Can you learn wisdom? For instance, I have strongly felt since being here in Europe that people in America don't realize what a blessing they have in wilderness, our wide-open spaces. It's a freedom that Americans so much take for granted! Maybe I can do something with that. I loved working park and wilderness projects on the Hill in Congress. I got to visit quite a few National Parks on Congressional tours. And I felt so free in Marfa. There's still time to save a lot of wide-open spaces in America and encourage new development to embrace the ideas of openness as we build new communities. I also want Americans to just start thinking in general, thinking for themselves, start caring about each other, knock off that tribal nonsense."

"Of course, you can learn wisdom. People aren't born wise. They grow their wisdom. They think. They observe. They withhold judgment of others. They open themselves up to the world. They converse with themselves and those outside those tribes you mention. They grow. You can do that. You're already well on your way. Find something you are passionate about and make a difference. Maybe it's writing, maybe it's not. You have to decide that for yourself."

I just sat there pondering what he was saying staring at the fading ochre rays of sunlight dancing on my sweating glass of rosé. It was kind of a defining moment in my life. In the cool evening breezes on that night in southern France, I learned what my life was going to be all about. I had a brief flashback to the sweat droplet coursing down my beer in Georgetown over a year before. It was like a loop had closed or something. It hit me with a clarity I'd never really felt before. I was going to grow, synthesize and share through literature. I was going to disseminate wisdom, at least wisdom as I understood it. Maybe I could do more, even, entertaining others through writing.

"Look, it's getting dark. You better ride home. I think I've given you what I can. It's now up to you, my friend, and I do mean friend."

"Thank you, padre. You've helped me enormously. Thank you for your friendship."

I got up and hugged him and started to walk back to his house to retrieve my bike. Just as I was a few feet down the street, I heard Father Mike call my name. In that "golden hour" of twilight, I looked back and saw the *brasserie*, the outside tables with dimly flickering candles and Father Mike in his horn-rimmed glasses standing there smiling—an image forever burned in my mind.

"Steve, remember how you feel right now—right now this very moment. Whether you choose to give by writing, saving wilderness or whatever. Give! Don't let it dissipate. Nurture this feeling! Stoke this fire. Don't let the world distract you from your purpose. The world will blindly extinguish your fire if you give it half a chance. Don't give it that chance!"

I smiled and waved. I hoped I'd see him again, but I also knew I'd never forget him.

40

I was drifting in and out of sleep in the darkened cabin when I heard a child nearby exclaim, "Mommy, there's the lights!"

Our plane was approaching Houston. Everyone was waking and the plane had the stale air and groggy feel of an overseas flight. Lines appeared at all the bathrooms. I was finally almost home, wherever that was in whatever time in my life this was going to be now.

After the post-flight misery of luggage retrieval and customs, I found myself alone in the too brightly lit corridors of the early dawn light in George Bush Intercontinental Airport. It was foggy and depressing outside. The air was heavy and didn't smell particularly good inside the airport, either. I wanted to get to Marfa as soon as I could, but I didn't know why. Maybe I thought I'd feel comfort in the presence of fresh air and wide-open spaces. My connecting flight to El Paso didn't leave for several hours. I had plenty of time to ponder my situation.

I felt stranded between worlds—my Pauline-Sommières-French village world and my Marfa-Stacy-heartbreak world. Part of me couldn't wait to get back to Marfa, another part of me wanted to get back on the plane to France. I didn't know where I belonged. As I walked through the airport, I noted a Houston Chronicle headline blaring about a childish Congressional partisan blow up. I hadn't missed that crap at all and didn't even follow US politics while I was in France. Right then and there I ordered myself to avoid setting foot in DC ever again, at least until the political tribes start acting like Americans first.

I was more and more thinking of myself as an American who writes in France. Even though I'd published nothing yet, it was part of how I decided to define myself. However, it was in my painful Marfa that I'd started on my personal path to maturity, to becoming a man—someone I was hoping was worth admiring, worth loving. I'd met Stacy too damned early. She saw potential, but she also saw too much immaturity and risk. Maybe I was kidding myself, maybe it was preordained. Maybe God used me to show her a true path, her destiny. I felt used by God and I wanted to let him know I resented it.

I also reflected on Pauline. I was pleased how when I thought of her, Stacy became a mild, distant annoyance. Unfortunately, my goodbye with her had been considerably less than satisfactory. Our ability to communicate eroded after I informed her of my intention to depart. A stiffness, almost formality had taken hold within our relationship.

I had that image of her sitting legs crossed in a black dress, bare footed, sipping wine from an oversized wine glass on her patio, her habitat. Pauline at her sexy, engaging best. She was a very lovely, complicated and—in some respects—frustrating creature. She'd started to let down her "Gallic" wall, but the time wasn't right for me. I hadn't dismissed the possibility down the road, however. I had to sort out in my mind what it would mean to commit to someone raised so differently and who recognized and praised a culture that was foreign to most Americans. Fortunately, Pauline had a fondness for the language and culture of the United States as well, so perhaps she could tolerate me better.

She had so much to offer and she'd captured "a corner" of my heart for sure, probably more than I would want to admit before I even got back to Marfa to see what awaited me there. Equally important, Pauline seemed willing to accept me for who I was, warts and all. At least, until I told her I had to return to Marfa.

Waiting at the airport for the El Paso flight, my mind raced between the anticipation of being back in Marfa, seeing friends there, Pauline, writing and France. I reached in my bag and pulled out a very worn copy of Saint Exupery's _Vol de Nuit._ Pauline gave it to me, as it was one of her favorites. She said it was "something to keep my French alive." I felt a pang of longing for her as I realized it still smelled of her perfume. Upon my return to Marfa, I knew I would use this sense of longing to motivate me to complete the final chapter of my novel—my first novel.

As my book was concluding, I realized the novel was about the story of a young man struggling with lost love and the need to grow up and overcome the loss. A boy really, who becomes a man—and how one can gain by losing. It was basically autobiographical, I now realized, after putting the Marfa and France experiences into context. It was set in Marfa and West Texas, but since it was kind of serious—"an epic work of literature; the Great American Novel," as the dust jacket would doubtlessly proclaim—I left out the explosive mega burritos, mephed-up Clark, finger shooting Paco, deranged Marlboro Man, the Red Angel and other bizarre elements of my life in Marfa. I definitely left out the exploding craft brewery stuff, since there was already enough about my mistakes in the book. It seemed odd to leave out the Red Angel, though. I could actually describe her as a pivotal figure in my life, even if she only existed in my mind. I briefly pondered whether other people have Red Angels. Was she real, a symptom, or what?

My parents were in New York visiting my sister, so I had no obligations at the airport in Houston. I was at the mercy of my thoughts. A condition that had become more comfortable in the last few months. I had only to wait for my flight to El Paso.

I basically just read and snoozed until the flight boarded and headed west. As the plane approached El Paso, I suddenly remembered I was about to be stuck there. Pablo had given me a lift to airport. Amy had been in Midland and I hadn't been able to reach her. Fortunately, when I got to El Paso, Amy answered on the fourth ring. She immediately agreed to drive three hours to pick me up, but it would have to be the next day. I had about 15 hours to kill while waiting so I grabbed a room at a hotel near the airport. I hated to wait another day, but it also seemed like a reprieve. It'd been an ordeal leaving France and finally getting home, or whatever Marfa was.

41

"Two questions. Were they a bunch of assholes and did you find what you were looking for in France?"

Amy picked me up in front of the hotel next to the airport around noon the next day. After a little grocery shopping and hitting my favorite wine shop in El Paso, we were in the bright West Texas sunlight travelling eighty miles an hour barreling towards Marfa. Felt a bit odd to once again see so few people after the crowded streets of Paris.

"Well for the first question, no. Not at all. Folks there are great. As for the second question, yeah, I guess I did."

"So?"

"So what?"

"What did you find?"

"I…I don't think I can put it in words yet, Aim. It's…I'm better…that's really all I know right now. Whether it stays better when I get settled back into Marfa is another question, of course, but right now I kind of feel like I'm home."

"Are you back home for good?" She just glanced at me with a half-smile. She looked good. Being a successful businesswoman obviously agreed with her. She wore a black skirt and gray sweater. She was more professional in her appearance and the way she carried herself. I saw her in a different light. Even though she was attractive, I was so glad I never let anything happen between us. We were good friends and nothing was going to screw that up.

"I don't know. I may not know until I breathe some West Texas air again."

"What do you mean?"

"I don't know. I mean I don't know if I can call myself back home because that implies that I know where home is…or where I'm even headed in life yet. I don't know that so I can't answer. I'm a little disoriented right now. Spending all that time in France…well, it altered my perspective."

"Wow, you got kind of heavy while you were over there. Where's my old flippant, easy come-easy go Steve?"

"He's in here flipping around somewhere." Even if I wasn't yet sure where home was, it did feel good to be back in West Texas. The sunshine. The wide-open spaces. I could have asked Amy to stop the car almost anywhere between El Paso and Marfa and gotten out and walked 300 hundred feet from the road and shouted as loud as I could, and no one would hear me. That couldn't happen in France.

We caught up on the gallery, the ranch and Amy's life. I was pleased to hear she had met a Border Patrol agent and appeared to have a healthy relationship growing. That greatly simplified our own relationship and helped to remove any kind of remaining tension.

The gallery was continuing to make a little money which was truly amazing. It's tough to make money in Marfa in the gallery business. About every other building is a gallery or at least seems that way. Amy was a solid businessperson, no doubt. While she lacked Stacy's eye for art, she had a colleague who was able to help us find the right artists to feature. There was a lot of great art produced in the area we specialized in, West Texas and Mexico, but you had to have an eye to recognize it.

She now had three leases on the ranch—one for ranching, one for a prospective movie and one as a hunting lease. I gave her a healthy cut on the leases and other income since she was the manager and really the force behind it all. Between the interest on Uncle Clive's money and to a lesser extent, the income from the assorted businesses, I was set. Amy had even rented out the other warehouse I owned to a local art foundation for storage. She had a real knack for seeing opportunity and making money. The three-and a-half-hour drive to Marfa flew by as Amy and I caught up. Before I knew it, she was pulling up in front of my house.

"I moved into your house for a couple of months. Now I have my own place again. You're not gonna believe this—I live in Stacy's old garage apartment."

Just the mention of her name excited me then plunged me into a mild funk. I'm not sure why I still thought anything about her, other than as a distant memory.

"Wow," I said without an ounce of enthusiasm.

"Still hung up on her?"

"I don't think so. I dunno. I'm confused. I'm hung up on something. I've been in an off and on funk since…I don't know when, really."

"She's in San Diego."

"Oh." Stacy being in San Diego bothered me a slight bit.

"You want me to help you get the stuff in? Here're your keys, including the car. That's my car parked in front."

"Nah…thanks though. I'll be fine. And, thanks so much for everything, keeping my car running, the house in good shape, running the businesses so well. I'll thank you more over dinner soon."

"Sure you're okay?" She hugged me and welcomed me back "home."

A few minutes later I found myself once again at the mercy of my own thoughts within my old house. It smelled just a little musty, but a day's worth of airing out would take care of that. It also felt nostalgic, despite feeling like I was in a stranger's house. I wasn't sure the Steve who lived here before even existed anymore. At least the old Steve had good taste in furniture, art and music. Stacy was right, I did…do have a good eye for that sort of thing. But still, looking into the bedroom mirror, it was like I was seeing myself from outside my own body somehow.

This Steve really did like Navi's taste in paint. I forgot how striking it was. Especially at night. I hoisted an old, Miller High Life beer I found in the fridge to Navajito and his choice of terracotta in my living room. I was hoping it wasn't a beer I'd left from the last time I was here. I didn't recall buying it, but who knows?

I admired the whole house as though it was the first time I'd seen it. I appreciated how good all the black and white photos in black frames looked against the terracotta paint. I had taken a couple of them and the rest I purchased from a local art dealer. They were scenes around the Trans-Pecos region—Mexican cowboys, ghost towns, military scenes in the early 20th Century and beautiful landscapes. I remembered how the terracotta paint looked at the end of the day during certain parts of the year. I remembered the brilliant rays of the sunset streaking into a corner of my living room making it look almost on fire. Navi had helped my home become a special place. I'd forgotten how much I liked it.

I'd also forgotten my Zane Grey collection of antique novels I collected from used bookstores in the region. Another world. Not a bad crib really if only the dull pain would go away. Being in Marfa felt good but had intensified that gnawing sense of loss. I was hoping that coming back, experiencing Marfa with no hope of seeing Stacy, and just being back in the US once again would somehow heal me in a way that staying in France and avoiding returning could never achieve. I was an American, and a Texan, after all. There was still a small yearning, though oddly enough, I had difficulty exactly remembering Stacy's face. Maybe it wasn't about Stacy.

❖ ❖ ❖

The first night I just sat on the front porch and drank beer. That's it. Just drank beer. I watched people on Austin Street pass by and I drank beer. I drank beer from about 6:00pm to about 11:00. That's it—just sitting and drinking highlighted by an occasional trip to the bathroom. No one waved. It was like I'd never lived here before or the whole population of Marfa had changed since I was gone. They probably thought I was a tourist.

Actually, that's pretty much how my first two days back in

Marfa went. By Saturday night, it suddenly occurred to me that I may not be "using my freedom wisely," as Father Mike had prescribed, so I decided to sober up a bit and take a walk. I walked by the house in front of Stacy's old garage apartment, now Amy's place, and felt a little emotional bomb go off within me. I then walked by the Episcopal Church and had another near-crippling emotional wave wash over me. I came back to Marfa to experience this?

I finally decided to walk over to the other side of Highway 90 to escape my little Stacy hell. Down the highway, I could see the gallery. An even larger pang of misery came over me—even bigger than the other one. An image of Pilar came to mind. That generated a very strange, almost shocking, feeling within me, and intensified the feeling of emptiness. I realized how much I missed giving her shit and getting it back from her in return. She was a beautiful and very spirited young West Texas woman. I hadn't thought much about her since leaving Marfa.

I recalled seeing Paco shoot the finger and honk her horn at the very spot where I now stood. I recalled the Red Angel, her beautiful white legs riding by me with her flowing red hair. I again questioned whether she ever really existed. Was she my invention? Did the "ghost expert" really see her?

I was overwhelmed by this nostalgic Marfa atmosphere. I was in a daze. Too much beer, almost no food and emotional overload will do that. I was about as empty as a person can be. What the fuck?

I thought I had grown. Why was I now such a wreck?

42

I guess I must have zoned out. Maybe I even passed out. I remember realizing I was hearing music. I was in a little alley. It was midnight. I figured out that the music was coming from the Liberty Theater. I groggily made my way home and went to bed. I slept about fifteen straight hours. A knocking on the door awakened me. I was starving.

"Steve! Steve, you in there?"

I fumbled my way to the door. It was Amy.

"What...hi, Amy."

"I brought you some soup. I made too much and thought you might like a little. There's some rolls from the bakery in there, too."

"Yes! I'm starving! Thank you, come in."

"Gosh Steve, you look like shit! Sorry. You do."

"I feel worse."

"You sick?"

"Yeah, you could say that."

"Stacy?"

"I don't know. All I know is, it's bad. It's worse than I thought I'd feel when I got back. What in the hell is wrong with me, Aim? I thought I was past all of this crap."

"Wanna talk?"

"Yeah...just not right now. Later. I gotta eat something and take a shower."

"You let me know when. I'm here for you. I'll help anyway I can, Steve. You turned my life around. I love you for what you did for me. You're so special to me!"

"Glad I could help. I mean it. I really am glad to help you. You and my parents are really my only family. I feel alone right now."

"I'm here for you."

"Tonight, please come back tonight, Aim."

"You bet."

◆ ◆ ◆

I ate some of Amy's soup and went back to sleep. I finally started stirring around 4:00 that afternoon. I took a long shower. I ate some more soup and bread. I was starting to feel human again. Amy showed up about 6:00.

"We sold a big piece today. We cleared about $6,000 on it."

"Really?"

"Yeah. Dallas woman saw it Saturday. She loved it but said it was too much. She got almost to Fort Stockton and turned around. She had to have it."

"Wow."

"Who's work?"

"Pizarro."

"Who?"

"Angel Pizarro. Does Matisse stuff. Very good."

"Mexican?"

"From Marfa."

"No shit?"

"Student at Sul Ross. Won some national poetry contest, but he's a great painter, too. He's hot now."

"Unreal. That's awesome."

"Yeah. We've sold four of his pieces. This was his big one. Probably our last, a big New York gallery is trying to get him."

She paused, looked away, then asked, "Is it still bad?"

I sighed then said, "Yeah, I don't get it. I haven't been this bad since I left. It's like I've never left here. Maybe even like I never went to France. It's bullshit…it's awful. Worse yet, it's pathetic. You just wouldn't believe all the interesting shit I've been through since leaving here, the people, the women, everything. Why dammit! Why?"

"What are you thinking?"

"It's over. Yet it doesn't go away. It's like I can't get it through my thick skull that it's done. Knowing how final it was doesn't seem to help. There's no purpose for this emotion."

"Are you sure it's Stacy?"

"That's the crazy thing. I don't know. It's like an emptiness that's larger than, or maybe even different than, Stacy. I can't put my finger on it! It's driving me fucking nuts!"

"Will time help? Is there anything I can do to help?"

"Exactly what you're doing now. Just listen. Just tolerate my pathetic ass a little bit. It will pass…I think."

"I know it will."

"Am I just being a self-indulgent, rich asshole?" It felt strange applying the term "rich" to myself.

"You're hurting. It doesn't matter how much or little money you have, Steve. You were dealt a big loss and there's a piece of you missing, right?"

I nodded but I didn't say anything. I just sat there. Something came over me. Thoughts of France and Pauline, Pilar and even Brites crept into my memory. It wasn't a cleansing or healing, but more like the beginning of a protective scar. The Marfa memories were still there, but the scar was forming to buffer me from the hurt. All of a sudden, I was just tired of being pathetic.

We just sat there on my porch on Austin Street and were quiet together. We just enjoyed breezes and being with someone who really gave a shit. I don't know how much time passed. Amy got up and got us both a beer and put her hand on my shoulder. She looked me in the eye and said, "Steve, I told you that you're very special to me. Please let me help. I know you're hurting. I can leave if that would help or I can stay. Just tell me."

I looked up at her then hugged her. I started to laugh and cry a little. I don't know what I was laughing at. I guess I was laughing at my miserable, self-indulgent behavior.

"What are you laughing at Steve? You don't look right. You look a little, well, crazy"

She looked at me like she was worried I was cracking up.

"I'm laughing at my ridiculous situation. Laughing feels a lot better than crying so I might as well laugh."

"Are you really okay Steve?" She was worried.

"Yeah, all of a sudden, I might just be."

"What? Just like that?"

"Yeah, maybe. I mean the hurt, well it's gone somehow. Shit, I haven't felt like this in months. I mean I was good in France, but there was always something nagging me. Shit, if that's not gone now!"

We talked until three in the morning. She wouldn't leave until she was thoroughly convinced I wasn't insane, depressed or suicidal. We actually laughed a lot.

We talked about people we knew in town. Stacy was in training in San Diego. Pillar had gone back east for graduate school. Amy said Pilar had asked for my cell number, which briefly piqued my curiosity. Breeze had been arrested on drug charges and ran off to Mexico while out on bond. Clark had been transferred to a Colorado penitentiary, but he was about to be released because of some new federal rule. Amy had been to see him a couple of times. She said he was grateful to me for trying to help his "sorry dumb ass." Amy was hopeful he was finally growing up.

Pilar's uncle was now sheriff. Deputy dud was done with law enforcement and was working at the Bud distributor in Alpine. Apparently, he had in his former role accidently shot himself—twice. Miguel was still at the Bud distributor somehow, and I had to wonder how many of his friends benefitted from the "solids" he'd done for them, passing out free or "discounted" beer.

I really was finally coming out of whatever funk had consumed me. Talking about these people sort of triggered the empty feeling again but it wasn't nearly as bad as before. I was still hurting a little, still confused, but the self-pity was for the most part beginning to wane. I always knew this might await me when I returned, but I just didn't realize how bad it would be.

I pondered whether to tell Amy about Pauline but wasn't quite ready to yet. I wanted to share some of the thoughts about our relationship with Amy, but I just couldn't decide what to say or even how to describe who she was to me.

43

I lasted about two weeks in Marfa before I got restless. Even though my writing was kind of on hold, I felt ready to get back to it and finish the damned thing. It only took a couple of days to touch it up and then I gave it to the lawyer to shop it around with one of his agent friends.

One morning while I was pulling weeds in front of the house, it dawned on me that whatever drew me back to Marfa was maybe intangible. Maybe it wasn't a thing or even a person. Maybe it was a feeling, maybe an energy. Maybe it was the launching of self-discovery. Maybe the emptiness was the fact I had to create. The thought of publishing my book seemed to ease the emptiness. Maybe it was a reluctant recognition of that need to express myself. Maybe the pain was from confronting how little I had to show for my thirty something years on the planet. Maybe that was the gift or burden that Marfa had given me. Just as I might have helped Stacy find her way, she may have helped me find mine.

I tried to get into the business of my holdings in Marfa, but I couldn't really concentrate. I liked piddling around with the beer distributorship and the art gallery, but Amy had cleaned up both operations so well there was little to do of consequence. Both were making decent profits. She had them so well managed, it felt self-indulgent to get involved. I had to practice all I'd learned about leadership in the army, step back, and just make sure Amy and her team had all they needed to do the job. Rather than be pathetic, I pulled away from being involved in them at all. I became the silent partner.

What I really wanted to do was write and thereby ease the

emptiness. I firmed up my business partnership with Amy. I sweetened the pot, so she was a full partner. She had business acumen. I didn't. All I did was inherit a bunch of money and property and that hardly qualified me to be a businessman any more than I was before the inheritance. Fortunately, for my ego, though I sometimes had little too offer, she insisted on consulting me on big moves.

I traveled around the region. I camped a few days in Big Bend Ranch State Park. I saw no one for the entire five days. It was just me, John Steinbeck, and the stars at night. The sky was so big it was overwhelming. It was beautiful and almost scary at times. I finished *East of Eden* under the big clear blue sky of West Texas while at the park.

When I returned from my five days in the wilderness, I started to have occasional beers with Maurine. She was a great woman down the street. She was sixty-five but looked about forty. She owned the inn where Emmaline lived, the little girl ghost. It had a great little bar of sorts that hosted a low key cocktail hour every evening for her guests. She was so funny and was, in a subtle way, sexy—the quintessential Texas woman. She was so damned conservative politically that I enjoyed baiting her just to watch her erupt. Her husband was always drifting about the property maintaining one thing or another and I became friends with both. But Maurine had a way of making me feel good about myself. Her flirting abilities were most impressive. I always felt good around her, even though her politics and mine could not have been more opposite, regardless of the stereotype that Pilar had plastered me with.

Between beers with Maurine at her little, informal bar or on her patio, my regional travel, a couple of trips to Mexico and my writing, I was feeling mostly healed. I'd also started to think about how the ranch could be better managed for watershed and wildlife values too. I hired a full-time wildlife biologist to make the ranch an oasis for all the local flora and fauna, not just cattle. Poor Amy supervised the biologist too, but I did poke my nose in that. That was fun and really meant something to me.

The biologist had a $50,000 budget each year to make things better.

An emptiness still arose from time to time, but I could usually push it aside. I used it at times to write. It sometimes gave my writing a hard, gritty edge that I strove for. The fact that my first novel was getting a few sniffs by a publisher made my interest in writing all the more intense. I was now working on a collection of short stories based on West Texas and Mexico. The drug thing notwithstanding, I had grown to love the Mexican culture and wanted to explore how Americans could benefit by embracing the warmth of Mexicans. The rich history of Mexico was very neglected by Americans, even Texans, as well.

No matter how much I plowed myself into writing though, I couldn't altogether escape the emptiness. I hung out with Amy and her boyfriend and Maurine when I wasn't snuggled up with my laptop or traveling. A nice-looking woman moved into the house a couple of doors down, but I couldn't bring myself to make the effort to get to know her beyond an occasional "Hi."

I finally decided one day that Marfa wasn't a town, it was an affliction, at least for me. I mean I loved it. The weather, the light, the eclectic population and businesses, even the art, but I couldn't make it work—not now. Not under these circumstances. However, it was a great town for a writer. For a very small town, it offered a lot of culture, even an NPR station. The same station Stacy and I had dealt with back in the first days of my arrival, holding off the onslaught of the Marfa Omnisexual Defense Association. But I just couldn't overcome something, and that something was a lot more than the loss of Stacy. I figured I'd find out soon what was next, but for the time being, living here was okay.

I was just looking online to book a flight to visit some friends outside DC when two very intriguing events occurred within 10 minutes of each other. I got two texts. One was in French and one was in Spanish.

44

The first text was from Pauline. My pulse raced as I read it. It basically said she wanted to see me because she felt like we had "*inachevé*," unfinished business. She wanted my address in Marfa because she was coming to Texas in two weeks! She had a ticket to El Paso!

The second one was probably from Pilar. I think it said I was an asshole and that she'd like to see me when she was in town next week.

The first text rocked my world. I quickly logged off the travel site, and started to think, how could I make myself look like I had my act together? I was shocked about Pauline's text but was thrilled. I was also surprised to find myself so intrigued by Pilar's text. I wasn't sure what was up with that. Maybe she was just wanting to catch up. That was the logical assumption. Was I quietly hoping for more? As the afternoon passed, I was surprised that I was thinking deeply about both messages and the possibilities they presented.

On one hand, I saw an embarrassment of riches as two special women had reached out to me. On the other hand, I was afraid of the choices that might face me. I thought I knew which way I'd want to choose, if that's what was really happening here. But I was also concerned I wouldn't have any real choice at all. The lack of confidence and faith was disturbing.

Thoughts of my research in Paris flooded back. I pondered that pesky topic of egos again. I noted that being back in Marfa had dented my ego a bit. Did I resent that? Having two gorgeous women reach out to me should have boosted my ego. Damn Marfa! To make myself not get too serious, I reflected that both had exquisite "stark departures" too! Even better than Monique's!

❖ ❖ ❖

The next morning, I started getting my life together by cleaning the house. There wasn't a lot to clean really since I wasn't much of a gatherer except for books and some art. I'd been restocking my wine closet and bought some art in Marfa since returning that I'd never done anything with other than set on the floor. To my domestic satisfaction, I was now hanging art on the walls. I surprised myself because 24 hours before, I was looking to bail out of town for a while. How things can change so quickly.

Along with a painting by Bill Leftwich of a western scene in my hallway, over my sofa I hung a Tomas Rodriguez I found in a rival gallery. It was kind of a Matisse meets Miro piece—very Mediterranean. It went well with my black and white pictures of West Texas and the Southwest. My favorites were some cowboys loading steers on a rail car in Kenna, NM and an image of Major Charles Young of the 10th Cavalry during the Punitive Expeditions, I think in Arizona. Being an Army guy, images of the pre-World War I Army on the southern border were fascinating. One of my favorites books on the shelf was *Intervention!: The United States and the Mexican Revolution, 1913-1917*.

I also straightened up my Zane Grey novels, all hardback and most first editions. I felt a pang of sadness when I picked up and examined a special book, *Chihuahua Crossing*, by Bill Leftwich as well. Bill was my renaissance cowboy friend who passed away while I was overseas. Missing out on seeing him one last time was one of the few things I regretted about my adventure. The great thing about Bill, a former tank commander in Vietnam, was that he'd say that he was proud I got off my ass and finally did something worth a damn; he would've said it with an endearing grin, of course. I loved that man.

Okay. Once I got my place in shape it was time to build a

stocked gourmet kitchen and further enhance the wine rack. That'd require a road trip to El Paso and a little time online. I wasn't going to have Pauline eat substandard fare. I was also hoping we would do a road trip to get some real New Mexico chiles; after all, Hatch wasn't that far away! I was getting into this. Nesting and getting ready for Pauline, and in some kind of strange way, Pilar as well. I hadn't sorted out what this all meant. Both were very special women. Time to think about that later.

After I got the house in order, I started trying to learn more about what was new in Marfa—galleries, music venues, and so on. I wanted Pauline to be impressed. Turns out most of the galleries were still in town except there was a new western art gallery I wanted to explore. Up to this time, in my first weeks back in Marfa, I was basically just hanging out with Amy and Maurine, so it was time to explore Marfa, Alpine and Fort Davis to see how they might stack up against the South of France.

Pauline was in for a treat. A couple of new restaurants were open. Sadly, my little brewpub or tavern or whatever it was had closed. Amy had moved what was left of the brewing equipment after my little self-induced "incident" to my distributor. The guys had started playing with it and talked Amy into investing in repairing and replacing enough stuff so that "Marfa Lights" beer was now being periodically brewed at the distributor. The Paisano and another restaurant were both offering it when available as a local brew. The chef returned to Fort Davis, so I hoped all would be forgiven with them! I guess success is all in how you define it, after all.

Within a week, I had my terracotta house completely decorated and the kitchen well stocked. The wine collection was less robust than I'd like, but that was okay. Some of my wine was local: "Alta Marfa." I thought that'd really impress Pauline. Their rosé was becoming quite serviceable. A little landscaping outside the house also helped. Amy, my hero, had managed to employ some soaker hoses to keep most of my flowerbeds alive. My basil kept coming in every year, so I had a bumper crop this season, along with my pecans. Pecan pesto would definitely be on the menu for Pauline, and maybe Pilar, who knows? My specialty of pecan pesto and grilled chicken was always one of my favorites.

I took Amy and Maurine out to dinner a few times to size up the restaurant community and I visited a couple of the music venues just to appreciate the current scene. I checked out the exhibit at the Marfa Ballroom knowing it would still be on display the next month. It struck me as funny that Pauline and I had never much discussed art even though she knew I had a gallery. She did make a point of the two of us going to the Salvador Dali museum in Figueres, Spain while we were in *Llançà*. It was remarkable, for sure.

Incredibly, while awaiting the arrival of Pilar, I was notified by my agent that my self-published book had received enough attention that a medium-sized publisher wanted to do an exploratory run of it if I would agree to ridiculously generous terms and to a robust promotion schedule. I jumped at it except I curtailed the promotion schedule somewhat. I refused to go anywhere but Texas, New Mexico, Arizona and Europe with one trip to New York and one to New Orleans. Embracing an eccentricity I always wanted to indulge, I wanted to stop flying. Except for Europe, I knew I could get to these places via short road trips or a relaxing train ride. I know, kind of weird and demanding, but I cut them a great deal. Money really wasn't the goal. I really wasn't into traveling unless it was for pleasure or to write!

Knowing my book was going to be published made me want to write even more. I decided to go visit the grave of my friend Bill and let him know I was going to be published but he was, as I found out, resting in a National Cemetery in Dallas. That sojourn would have to come later. I tried to squeeze in some writing before Pilar arrived. I didn't know if I'd see her 20 minutes or perhaps a great deal more. Again, I don't know why I was so excited. She might hate me, probably did. But why'd she want to see me?

45

The Thursday before Pilar's arrival in Marfa, she called to ask if there was any way I could pick her up at the airport. Her sister, now a freshman at Sul Ross, had an exam she couldn't miss. I said I'd be happy to come and get her.

Saturday morning my mind kind of raced as I made the three-hour drive to the airport. As I'd just recently experienced, there's very little between Marfa and El Paso except beautiful scenery. It's good thinking space for sure. For some reason, I was in a country music frame of mind as I raced through bright mountain scenery. I'm normally not a big fan, but sometimes some Dwight Yoakum, Waggoneers, and Marty Stuart can do a soul good. I only like a narrow niche of the genre.

Okay, here's the deal, I reflected. Why was Pilar reaching out to me and why was I excited to hear from her? Especially with Pauline's arrival imminent? I kept asking myself what the hell was going on. Of course, I had money, but I sincerely doubted that'd mean much to Pilar and practically nothing to Pauline, based on what I knew about them. I mean it's a thing, but surely not a big thing. I was confident of that.

I kept asking myself if I was really attracted to Pilar. The answer was hell yes! She was stunning, beautiful, feisty, smart, multicultural, and could make me laugh, even though she was probably too young. I kept checking myself. I kept telling myself that she's probably just being friendly. But why'd she tell Amy she wanted to see me? I tried to adjust what I was thinking about so I wouldn't be so nervous when I first saw her.

It was just me, the landscape, bright sun, a cloudless sky and a couple of freight trains rolling along the highway between

Pilar and me. I was a new person. Amazingly, I hadn't thought of Stacy in a very long time. Damn! I was finally healing. Since getting that call from mom about Uncle Clive's passing, my whole world had shifted, and I'd changed my whole outlook on life. I'd grown to know a few amazing women, including Amy, and acquired a second language for real, unlike my scant proficiency in Spanish. I'd also experienced another world, published a book and generally just grown up…well, mostly.

I had great moments in the Army, but the Army isn't designed to make you complete, at least as a junior officer. On reflection, after the Army, I'd really felt only like a partial man, a bit of a stunted person. That had stayed with me, I think, up until only recently. I knew there was more growing ahead of me, no matter what. Maybe that was also a sign of becoming more complete. I had no idea what the future held, but that didn't bother me. I just wanted to see what happened over the next couple of weeks. I really couldn't wait to see Pauline either. I had had a feeling of joy and excitement since receiving her text. I felt like my France was coming to see me in my Marfa.

❖ ❖ ❖

"Hey Gringo!"

I turned to see a very beautiful woman. Pilar had blossomed even more. I smiled and walked toward her. She gave me a big West Texas grin and set her bags down and hugged me like a lover. I was shocked. We'd never hugged before. It felt so right, so amazing.

"Pilar, you look awesome! Seems like New York agrees with you. Honestly, you look like a movie star."

"It does. I love my school. The winter is dreadful, but the school is great."

A few minutes later we were heading down I-10 barreling back to her beloved Marfa. She didn't want to stop anywhere. She just wanted to be back in Marfa as soon as possible.

"Steve, thanks so much for picking me up. My mom and dad

are getting on up there and it's hard on them. We all appreciate it."

"Of course. It's so great to see you. What's it been? Almost a year, right?"

"I think that's about right. I left for grad school before you went to Europe."

It felt good but weird to have a normal discussion with Pilar. Behind her sunglasses, I could see her absorbing the beauty of West Texas as we hopped off I-10 to head toward Marfa.

As we were heading out of Van Horne, Pilar remarked, "I miss hearing about the burro lady. You ever see her?"

"Nope. Heard of her. She was gone well before I got here."

"Of course, I was just a kid when I would see her. She was so interesting. Everyone knew about her, but no one actually knew her. She was a mystery, for sure. People would see her between here and Presidio just riding her burro. I understand back in the 60s she got a big ole Cadillac. She let her burro ride in the trunk! She took the trunk lid off for the burro. Only around here!"

"Tell me, Pilar, what are you studying?"

"I'm in Ithaca College's Physical Therapy graduate program. I got a free ride. Believe that shit? I accepted it thinking I was going to be the token "Mexican girl," there just to feed a quota. Turns out, the school is amazing, and they really want me in the program. I'm very comfortable there. The faculty is great."

"You don't feel out of place living in New York?"

"Some ways, but at no fault of the school or my classmates. I love my classmates. They're mostly from New York and New Jersey. Been great getting to know folks from other parts of America. And I have to tell you, Ithaca is no less eclectic than Marfa, it's just bigger. There's no problem with being diverse there! I feel very welcome."

We traveled in a relaxed silence for quite a while. This country almost demands that. You must be a little in awe if you're human. I hope it never changes.

As we passed through Valentine, I finally couldn't hold back any longer, "Pilar, why'd you reach out to me? I mean I'm glad, for sure. Just curious. I kind of thought you might hate me."

"You asshole, couldn't you tell I was jealous of you and Stacy? I liked you but I was mad in a silly way about your liking her over me. I thought you were cute ever since I saw you come into town. You were kind of awkward and off balance and endearing. I never pushed it. You were head over heels crazy about Stacy. Plus, some white dudes aren't into Mexican girls. I mean around here, it's not a thing, but, you know, you were from Houston, whatever. I'm cool now. I got a boyfriend back in Ithaca. I just thought it'd be neat to know you better, since I heard you were back in Marfa. According to Amy, you've had such an interesting life since you lived here and I left. Frankly, I was surprised you were back here at all after living in a place like Paris."

"Okay. Cool. I'm way cool with it. I'm enjoying getting to know you without that funky tension that was there. I also thought you were pretty dang hot. I was just so into Stacy, I never made a move. I'd sometimes go out of my way to come by the gallery to see you. I enjoyed our banter. I always wondered if there wasn't more than met the eye in the way we went on. I was worried about the age difference too, of course, but it didn't seem to matter since Stacy was in the picture anyway."

"You got a girlfriend now? Probably some beautiful French woman, huh?"

"I have some French friends, but I'm definitely not in a committed relationship." I felt a little sheepish answering like that, but it was technically true.

We talked about life in France, the book, her studies and other odds and ends on the rest of the trip. The chatter was comfortable, relaxed. I struggled a bit to know if there was still any sexual tension between us. I felt something. We agreed to have dinner Tuesday.

❖ ❖ ❖

I took a close examination of my latest "new life." My house was in great shape and Amy was running the businesses like clockwork. She'd opened an office in what was a truly run-down store in the heart of town on North Highland near the county courthouse. Amy had also set up a more robust business management enterprise, even including a receptionist. I had her name the business after her dad and my uncle: Clive-Miles Enterprises. Uncle Clive got first billing since none of this would have happened without him. We didn't really need an office, but it made us more a part of the community and it kept Amy from working out of her tiny place.

With my concurrence, we'd also become part owners of a local Mexican food restaurant. It created some neat partner opportunities for the beer and art businesses. She also had bought an adjoining ranch, so Clive's old spread was becoming an even bigger outfit. Given our heavy emphasis on wildlife habitat, our hunting leases were fetching great prices. The ranch had plants coming back that no one had seen in decades. A local professor was also running very successful birding trips onto the place. It seemed everything Amy touched turned to gold.

With Amy in control, and the house in order, I really didn't have anything to do but write and think about what I wanted to do with Pauline, and maybe Pilar. I convinced Pauline to extend her trip to two weeks. I'd finished two short stories for the new book, but I was struggling a little with the next one. It was based on a chat with a friend of mine, Nick Dutchover. Nick was riding out to check on his cows in a pasture that was a good distance from the ranch headquarters. The road he'd used to trailer the cows to this remote pasture had recently suffered a bridge washout, so he was on the lookout for alternative paths or even other pastures for grazing. Nick dreaded driving them to the next pasture in a few weeks, but at least he could keep tabs on them on horseback for now. He told me he was out on his favorite herding horse. I was trying to picture the different settings to describe them in the story, including maybe adding a rebellious steer or a marauding coyote.

Anyway, as Nick was riding back to the ranch headquarters

around sunset, he saw in the fading light a lone rider on the horizon. He was surprised. It was on land he'd leased for years and no one had any business being out there. As he carefully approached the rider, the man gave him a weak waving motion, kind of like the old West Texas "hi sign" with just his forefinger. The mysterious rider called out to Nick and started to approach him, his hands well away from his saddle or belt, showing he was safe, I guess. Nick was on guard, though. Something was strange about this guy. The guy on horseback wanted to know if my friend had seen anyone riding around out there. Of course, Nick hadn't. Nick hadn't seen anyone else out there in a long time. He'd certainly never come across any strangers in this very remote corner of his ranch. The nearest paved road was over five miles away.

Goosebumps surfaced when he described the rider. He fit my "Marlboro Man" perfectly, even as to his mannerisms. The "Marlboro Man" was looking for a ranch hand who'd mysteriously disappeared recently from an adjacent ranch. He was clearly worried about the missing wrangler. Nick said he hadn't seen anyone like that, or anyone else for that matter. Nick told the strange rider that his neighbor was a jerk, hard to work for and paid shit. He had ranch hands haul ass all the time. The "Marlboro Man" didn't buy that and told my friend, "Look, I know things, things I can't talk about, but I bet the government or the law knows about," as he looked up at the darkening sky. With that, the mysterious rider just drifted on into the darkness. He didn't look back at Nick. That was it. Nick never saw him again and that was about six months ago. Nick said he had goosebumps from that, too.

That did indeed sound chilling, given my own encounter with the strange cowboy. I half expected Nick to tell me he encountered the Red Angel on the way back. It seemed like a great story, with maybe just a little embellishment as needed. Not sure why I was struggling with writing the tale for the current generation of my "sophisticated" readers. But I'd keep working on it. It was those kinds of tales that captured the mystique of

West Texas in any age. And, after all, how many "Marlboro Men" were still around these parts?

46

I had butterflies as I waited for Pilar in her living room while she finished getting ready. Her parents lived in a very modest stucco house east of town near the old stock pens on the railroad track. It was small but very well maintained. We chit-chatted about France for a few minutes until Pilar made her entrance. Their house was simply furnished but I liked it. It looked like Mexican furniture. Road trips to Ojinaga to buy things like furniture were once common before the border got more restrictive.

I'd never thought about where Pilar lived. She and her sister still shared a small bedroom. Where a person lived was not a big deal in Marfa. People just knew each other. Not much judging. I guess that was another thing I liked. For the most part, people just tried to live and let live. Unlike now, the Texas I grew up in was pretty much like that everywhere back in the old days. People kind of minded their own business. A lot less judging went on. Marfa had a lot of "kooky" people who were mostly just accepted, not ostracized unless they hurt someone. Marfa hadn't changed a whole lot on that front.

Pilar came out of her room wearing a dark blue Ithaca College t-shirt and cutoffs. I was a bit crest fallen. I was hoping she was going to dress up. I was in kakis and a sports shirt. I felt overdressed. She was wearing lipstick and looked great. I told myself she did say she had a boyfriend.

"Hey, Steve!" I think that may have been the first time she ever greeted me by my name.

"Hey, Pilar. You doing okay tonight?" We said goodnight to her parents and headed out to the car.

As I opened the door to let her in, she asked me if everything was okay. She looked at me funny. Maybe I was showing some disappointment.

"No, everything's great, "I answered, "Really good seeing you again."

"Yeah, well, okay."

"I have reservations at Otay's."

"Oh, shit. I'll be right back." She bolted out of the car and went back in the house. My mind raced wondering what the hell was going on.

Five minutes passed and she emerged in the little yellow dress she'd worn on the plane and heels.

"What just happened here Pilar? You look great by the way. I mean you looked great before too."

"I dunno. I just don't know, Steve. Is this a date? I'm confused."

"Me too. Let's just roll with it." I smiled and put my sunglasses on and shifted the car into drive. We chatted about her school and classes on the way to the restaurant.

The food was great, the conversation interesting and the earlier funkiness was gone. We caught up on all her family and we talked more about her physical therapy courses and what she might do when she graduated. She promised to examine my achy shoulder. I cursed myself for slacking on my exercises. Pilar would see that the abs were a little soft if I had to take my shirt off. I thought lots of silly things like that. To my chagrin, we discussed her boyfriend as well. Somehow, maybe defensively, I ended up mentioning Pauline as well but stopped short of discussing her approaching visit. I couldn't help but wonder why I was disappointed that Pilar was in a relationship. Maybe it was a little jealousy or maybe it was one more sign the Marfa of a year ago really was fading into the past.

To say I was filled with mixed emotions would be an understatement. Pilar compounded that feeling by the mixed signals I felt she was sending. Sometimes she'd send off a vibe of romantic interest when she'd talk again about how she was jealous of

Stacy. Other times, romance, if there was any, wasn't in the conversation at all, particularly when she talked about Ithaca and her friends. Maybe she was as confused as I was? I mean this was sudden for both of us.

When it was time for the check, she called out to the waitress and said something in Spanish. Within moments, she appeared with a bottle of red wine and a sack.

"Guess what Steve? We're going to go to your place and drink this wine. We need to talk something out."

Crap. I didn't know if I was ready for any serious discussions. I was torn. Pauline and I had great chemistry in France, but we hadn't really gone all that far with our relationship. We did have those French-American issues that both spiced and at times complicated the relationship. The cultural complexity was far less with Pilar. We connected in ways I hadn't with Pauline. I wasn't completely sure how big of a thing that would become. Plus, I didn't know how things between us would feel with Pauline in America. Was I really into her or was I into her only in France? I was afraid the old waffling Steve might be making a comeback here, and I didn't like it all. Worse, I wasn't sure what to do.

We entered my house at the bewitching hour for me. It was the time the sun was just doing its lightshow on the terracotta paint in the living room. Pilar was blown away by how nice my place was, especially the effect of the sunset entering into the living room from the side of the house. I could tell she was impressed. She was also impressed I had a picture of Colonel Young on the punitive expedition. He was the first African American to achieve the rank of colonel. While she hardly a fan of the punitive expedition, she was impressed I commemorated a person of color. She talked about my taste in art.

"Not bad, Steve. I like it. You aren't exactly who I pegged you for. Pictures of that colonel and even Mexican Cowboys. Lots of books too. Okay. New data to process. Get glasses now. I'm ready to do this while I have the courage to sort this out…," she peered over at me with raised eyebrows, "… in case there is something that needs to be sorted out."

We sat in my living room as the sun dropped off the horizon. After a little while, I turned on a small stained-glass lamp that filled the room with a yellow-reddish glow. She looked spectacular sitting in my living room. She made herself at home with her knees tucked under and legs kind of sprawled out on the couch. I had forgotten how tall she was. She was definitely comfortable in her skin.

After a few diversions about the house and what I, or Navi and the gang, had done with it, she finally blurted it out, "Okay Steve, was this a date? I don't know how to feel about this. I don't even know at this point how I want to feel about it. That make sense?"

"Yes. Complete sense. I guess that summarizes my situation too." I stared at the floor as I decided what next to say. We both then spoke at the same time and both effectively said something like, "Let's kind of sort of explore this, and be careful."

"Yes, Pilar, I do want to be careful. Look, I'm going to put my cards on the table. I was always attracted to you, but I was under the spell of Stacy. I was obsessed. I really couldn't even give you an honest assessment. And you seemed younger then somehow. I'd be lying if I said that I wasn't very intrigued when you reached out to me. As I said, even though I was under Stacy's spell, I had a little bit of a thing for you, as well. Crap, that sounds bad. I don't want it to sound like that."

She was just looking at me. She wasn't going to let me off the hook yet. Clearly she wanted me to have the floor.

"Okay, Pilar, why'd you reach out?"

"I told you. I just thought you'd be interesting to talk to given you've been abroad, writing and stuff." She almost said something else and then suddenly stopped. My time to be quiet.

Unlike me, she didn't take the bait—I was just so easy, I thought. She got up and went over to look at the bookshelf.

After a couple of minutes of silence, I gave in. "Look Pilar, I'm sorry if I misread anything. I want to be your friend. I don't want this misunderstanding to screw that up."

She sat down next to me and looked me in the eye and with a very serious expression said, "Don't you have some fucking music around here?" and burst out laughing. I guess it was her way of loosening us up.

Within a few minutes, I had some soft jazz in the background.

"More wine, Pilar?"

"Of course."

We just sat there and listened to the music and sipped our wine. It was surprisingly comfortable. Very different dynamic than I felt with Pauline, more relaxed somehow.

Finally, Pilar said in a low voice, "Really Steve, I'm not sure why I reached out. I meant what I said, but there might have been more. I mean I had a pretty strong crush on you. I kind of almost hated you for not noticing me as a woman. I'm over that. I guess…I guess I maybe just wanted to see if I was over the crush before I got into any kind of serious relationship back at school. I honestly don't know for sure, you know?"

"Are you over me?" I kind of joked, still confusingly hopeful.

"I don't know. There's still something there. This is happening pretty fast, I just…"

"No need to say more. It's complicated for me too. When you reached out, it rekindled something in me, too. Again, not sure what it is for me."

We took the bottle outside and sat on the front porch. The evening was cooling nicely. Cicadas and the soft lights of the neighborhood were pleasant accompaniments.

"Look Pilar, its 11:00. I need to stop drinking if I'm going to take you home."

"I texted my mom, I told her I'll be in late. No rush. We need to talk this out. I won't be in town long, you know."

We talked, really talked about our childhood and college and I bored her with a few military stories and political tales from my time on the Hill. We were so caught up in learning about each other that we didn't talk about a potential romantic relationship. I guess we were too busy building a friendly relationship to get to that. I didn't talk about Pauline or southern

France. I was still disappointed in myself about that. Why was I holding that back?

As I dropped her off that night, I sensed we were both confused. I think for both of us, there was a sense that something great could evolve between us, but neither of us were sure we wanted to go there. We decided to see each other, a semi-date, we called it, Thursday night.

47

Even in jeans and a tee-shirt, she looked memorable.

"You don't look disgusting to me," I said with a smile.

Pilar's mom had slipped and broken her leg the day before, so we had to cancel our "semi-date" and I had to drive her over to visit her mom at the hospital in Alpine.

"Yuck, let's go. I hate hospitals. I haven't been in a hospital since they took my tonsils out."

"What's the latest on your mom?"

"Good. Just a hairline fracture but we were worried why her blood pressure was low. All the tests came back fine, and her blood pressure is good now."

I waited in their living room. Pilar's sister was home too, getting ready to go to an evening class after working a shift at a restaurant. Their home was clean even with all the turmoil from the emergency trip to the hospital.

Twenty minutes passed.

"Finally! Feels great to get a shower. I have mom's things. I'm ready."

"Need to grab some food or anything?"

"No, I'm good. Mom may get released tonight but we're betting tomorrow."

"What's your dad do, Pilar?"

"He owns a plumbing contract company."

"Good to know."

"Did you grow up in this house?"

"Well, my parents have three houses. They have the other two leased out; they're bigger. Once my brothers moved out, we downsized. Leasing the other houses out is kind of my dad's retirement program."

"That's smart."

"Especially with what houses in Marfa rent for the last decade or so. He needs to retire. He can do it. I think he just enjoys serving his customers."

"I get that."

"Let's go. My mom's waiting on this stuff."

When we pulled up to the hospital, Pilar jumped out and said she'd be back in a few minutes. She was back in less than five minutes. She hopped back in my car, smiled and said, "My parents say hi and thank you."

I sat there waiting on Pilar to tell me what to do next.

"Okay, let's pull over closer to that building. A little more out of sight."

"I like the sound of that!"

"Don't get any ideas lover boy. I just have a little surprise for you, us."

Once we pulled a little more out of sight, Pilar opened her bag and pulled out a bottle of wine and a couple of plastic cups.

"How's this for class, muchacho? Even a screw top!"

"I like it!"

"Look, I only have about half-an-hour or so, but I told mom I'd be back for her doctor's evening visit. I just wanted you to know I care. This kind of sucks, but I just wanted you to know I really enjoyed us seeing each other."

After a few sips of wine, I asked her, "So, did you do any more thinking about what we discussed?"

"Of course, a lot."

"Pilar, I'd really hoped to treat tonight as a real date to give us a chance to find out what we are." After a short pause I asked, "When will you be back?"

"This spring. Sadly, I'm scheduled to be overseas over the Christmas holidays, it's kind of related to my degree. It's important. It sucks but I need to do it. You could come see me in Ithaca."

"Hmm. Let me ask you. I know you have a boyfriend. And, as

I indicated, I have a friend out in the world, too. I just don't want us to look back and think about what might have been. Does that make any sense?'

"Shut up and drink a little! You make more sense when I'm drunk," she smiled.

"Okay."

"Look, Steve, I don't know. I'm still attracted to you, but this may just be too complicated. It's one of those things where if I flipped the switch, I could probably be into you big-time. I just don't know. And, I do really care about my boyfriend. He's a sweetheart. I honestly see a future with him."

"Crap! I don't know what to say. I could probably melt right into a great relationship with you, too. You're beautiful. I love your feisty, smart personality. You make me laugh. And, you are super honest. Plus, your legs are almost more than I can endure," I said with wink. It was true.

"So, what are we supposed to do?"

"Look, we go on about our lives and see if we feel an ache. My only hope is that if one of us aches, we both ache. We both have a lot to think about."

"Yes. We. Do."

We just sat there staring into each other's eyes. Finally, she said, "I gotta go."

"I know."

"Whatever happens Steve, know I care about you. You don't suck nearly as bad as I thought you did!"

"Hey, thanks for that, anyway. It kind of sounds like you're shutting the door on this."

She had a very serious look on her face. She was beautiful in the last moments of daylight.

"No. I'm not. Just being real in case this is it."

"I hope it isn't."

"Me too."

She got out of the car. I hopped out to hug her. She looked me right in the eye like few people ever had. As I was hugging her, she pulled me into the shadows and kissed me passionately. I felt like I was on fire. It might have been the best kiss ever.

Again, staring into my soul she said, "Sorry. I needed to know."

"No need to apologize. I understand, kiddo."

"Damn! There is chemistry for me, in case that matters. That was good. I probably got lipstick all over your face!"

"No worries...the lipstick will be a good memory when I get home. I can assure you the chemistry is there for me too."

She gave me a beautiful smile and then she was gone. She was gone. What the hell was I supposed to do with this? Shit, I wish she hadn't kissed me. Talk about complicating things. What a mess!

Of course, I wasn't able to focus exclusively on that moment too long because as I eased out of the parking lot, I saw none other than the decrepit posture of Clark standing near a cab in the shadows, grinning at me and showing me his feeble version of a two thumbs up. I was so shocked in seeing him, I didn't even think to stop and talk to him, not that I really wanted to.

48

I called Amy on my way back to Marfa. No answer. My mind raced exploring the implications of Clark reentering the scene. That turd-bird was supposed to be locked up for a while yet.

I tried to push that out of my mind as I admired the purple and orange sky as the sun eased lower beyond the horizon until the orange only appeared as a thin halo to the western horizon. Pauline was going to love these sunsets.

I drove back to the house quickly and realized how tired I was. I decided to just prepare for bed and hit the hay early.

Right before I turned my light out, Amy called.

"What's up Steve?"

"Hey, is Clark out?"

"Oh, I forgot to tell you, he's on probation. They busted someone else for two of the counts against him! I'm so happy for him!"

"Oh."

"Don't worry Steve. He's a new man. They helped him this time. Federal prison is so much better than Texas jails. They helped him get his mind straight, I think."

"Oh, okay."

"Steve! Give him a chance. I know he wants to come thank you. He has to keep a job as part of his probation. He's just been busy. He's driving a cab. Seriously, he's grateful to you. Don't worry about him. I mean he could still screw this up. He is Clark, but I'm optimistic."

"Oh, okay."

"I'm sure he'll drop by soon, Steve."

"Okay. Hey Amy, on second thought, I need a favor. It's real important. I need him to stay away a few weeks. A special friend from France is visiting. I don't want him screwing this up. It's so important. I know this sounds bad, but can you keep him away from me? Just 'til she leaves town?"

"Sure, Steve. I'm on it."

 "I mean, I'm not sure how…Clark would be perceived by someone from Europe, you know?"

"Got it! Clark is your biggest fan Steve. He'll get it. He seems smarter now."

"Thanks Amy!"

Somehow her assurance didn't allay my concerns. I feared another late-night knock. I had just a couple of days to get ready for Pauline. I was growing concerned because she wasn't replying to my texts. She was supposed to have been in the States for a few days, but I hadn't heard from her since she left France. I was supposed to head to El Paso to pick her up in less than forty-eight hours and no word. Not good.

Throughout the next day, no word. My mind raced. Maybe she got cold feet. Maybe something happened. Maybe her phone crashed. Ugh! I cursed myself for not getting the travel details before she left France, but I didn't want to pry.

I was starting to get super-worried. I had no clue until Monday night, when I got a text from a number I didn't recognize.

"Yo bro, did you a real solid, man! Leest I could do! I owe you big time, cuz, and real glad I got to start paying it off, man!" I texted back right away asking who this was. I feared the worst.

After I finally reached "my bro" the next morning, AKA Clark, I found Pauline had been in town since Sunday! Her cab from the airport only could take her to Van Horne. Clark was dispatched out of Alpine to get her to Marfa. Lucky Pauline and me! Clark dropped her at the Paisano. He started to tell me more as I hung up on him. I immediately called the Paisano. My heart dropped when I found out "the beautiful French woman" checked out the very next day. No indication of where she was headed next, but she was asking the desk clerk about tours of Big Bend National

Park. Out of desperation I decided to text her again.

Just as I was about to call it a night, I got a text from Pilar. She was on the way back to Ithaca and she just wanted to let me know how much she enjoyed hanging out. "Hanging out" was what we did. I deserved that and I understood. I'm glad we both agreed. My desperation to see Pauline quickly put in context my brief Pilar affair.

❖ ❖ ❖

Wednesday evening, she finally replied. Her text read: "So sorry to inconvenience you. Leaving tomorrow."

Pauline answered on the fifth ring. She was in Marathon. I got her to agree to stay put there, or at least that was my hope. I raced on Highway 90 to the tiny town about an hour east of Marfa. It's about twice as far from Marfa as Alpine, which I drove through on the way. Night was falling fast. It was pitch dark on these moonless nights! The ride was agonizingly slow but uneventful. I think I pulled into Marathon in record time, however.

Built in 1927, the Gage Hotel is a relic of another era. It's an impressive tan brick historic structure sitting in the middle of almost nowhere. I shouldn't say nowhere. Marathon is a neat little, and I do mean little, town of 400. You can see mountains in most directions and Big Bend National Park sits an hour and a half or so south of town, down US 385. Marathon rightly bills itself as a gateway to the park.

The hotel has a great restaurant, the elk is fabulous, and swimming pool is huge. It's a very nice place where I'd thought Pauline and I might enjoy a little romantic rendezvous, but not this! Whatever this was going to end up being.

I immediately saw her as I pulled in to park. She was sitting in a dimly lit rocking chair up on a porch near the entrance. I melted the moment I saw her. My pulse was racing. She was the most beautiful woman I'd ever seen. I cursed myself for ever leaving her.

I quickly approached her, "Pauline. You are so beautiful, and I've missed you terribly! Where the hell have you been?"

She didn't smile. "I didn't want to be a pest." Her look was one of disdain. It made me heartsick.

"What are you talking about! You had me worried sick!"

"That person, that *plouc*, told me about her and all of your lady friends!"

"Pauline, what are you talking about!"

"That girl from Mexico!"

"What did this person tell you exactly?"

"He said you are a man of ladies! He said he saw that girl from Mexico kissing all over you just a few nights ago."

I started laughing. Pauline's disdain only increased. It was clear she didn't like me seeing humor in any of this.

"*Ce n'est pas grave.* I leave soon. Laugh all you want." She stood up to walk away when I gently grabbed her and tried to hold her closer to me. She felt so good. She melted for a few seconds then started to pull back away from me.

"Please sit down with me a minute and let me explain, Pauline," I pleaded. She just stared at me. She quickly wiped away a tear and looked off to the open dark horizon in front of the hotel.

I finally got Pauline to walk with me to a quiet corner of the courtyard surrounding the pool. We were underneath a large oak tree. The blue-green light from the illuminated pool danced in her eyes. I noted her cheeks were a little rosy from being in the sun of West Texas.

I lost focus a second when I glanced a pair of white legs across the pool. I couldn't see the Red Angel's body in the shadows, only her legs. I snuck a second look as I told myself to focus, damn it. She was gone, but I could feel the warmth of a smile coming from the other side of the pool. I looked squarely at Pauline and smiled myself.

"Pauline, I am so, so, so happy I found you. I was really afraid I'd lost you. I must explain something important. I almost screwed up royally. Well, not really. I was just confused after I left France. The woman the cab driver described was an old friend. Someone I knew a long time ago. She was kissing me goodbye the other night. We used to know each other, and she just wanted to know if there was something there between us. At least I think that's what we were doing. The more I explain it the worse it sounds, and I never, ever want to mislead you or tell you anything but the full truth."

The glare persisted but was softening some. Man, she was so beautiful when she was angry.

"Look, Pauline, I guess there was a trace of doubt about us when Pilar, that's her name, asked to see me. We used to have a crush on each other."

"Crush?"

"We kind of thought we might like each other, romantically, I guess you'd say, *bequin*? We never dated or anything, because I was seeing the woman I told you about, Stacy, and because I thought Pilar was too young, anyway."

"Why were you making out!"

"Good question. It was one kiss, Pauline. Look, I think maybe we were just trying to see if there was chemistry. She kissed me. I didn't mind it. She's gorgeous and I care for her, but that was it. One kiss."

"That…huck…*péquenaud,* said you were making out."

"Hick? *Comme un plouc?*"

"*Oui*, yes!"

"Sorry. That's my cousin. I have to apologize. He's not all there. Let's just say he has abused drugs for a long time."

"He's a junkie?"

"He was."

"He's offensive."

"Yes, I'm afraid so."

"He said you have women all over you! You are a man of ladies!"

"Ladies man?"

"Yes, ladies man."

"Well, I'm not. I don't know why he said those things. He is truly what we called in the Army a knucklehead."

She was thawing a bit more. "Yes, we have those in France, too. And, they are almost always men."

"Look, I haven't dated or been with any other woman except the one kiss Clark described."

"That knucklehead, as you say, his name is Clark?"

"Yes. Pilar and I went out to dinner one night and then her mom had to go to the hospital. I helped her by giving her a lift. She's a friend! We ended up kissing once, before she went back to college in New York. She has a boyfriend there."

'You love this woman from Mexico, this Pilar?"

"I care for her. I don't love her. I like her, not like you. I love…" I froze. "And she's from Marfa. Not Mexico."

She was confused.

"You don't like me?"

"Pauline, I like you and I'm just now realizing, after all this craziness, that I love you. I love you, Pauline!"

She pierced me with her eyes, and then threw herself at me.

I think we must have kissed like teenagers for 10 minutes. I was so aroused. I wanted her so much.

"Do you have a room here?"

"Yes."

"Can we go to it?'

She got an alarmed look on her face for just a minute.

"How do I know?"

"Know what?"

"How do I know you are telling the truth? How do I know you really love me?"

"I'd like to prove it right now, in your room!"

"Steve. Let's take this slow. I am still sorting out all this craziness you described."

"Okay. Look Pauline, I'm just so happy you're here! We can wait as long as it takes, but you must know how much I love you. I want you completely, know that. I want us to be together the rest of our lives."

"*Moi aussi.*"

"You will believe me. I'll do whatever I need to make that happen. I'm just so wonderfully happy you're here."

"You said that."

"I'd like to show you how happy I am, now, in your room."

"You said that already, too," she said with a smirk.

With that smirk I knew I'd broken through. We were both in love.

49

About three AM, in Marathon, Texas of all places, our passion was consummated.

"You *were* very happy! I think you showed me very deliciously that you loved me."

"I told you I was. Tell me, were you really going to leave me?"

"Yes. I had it all planned. When my phone stopped working in the US, I thought I'd surprise you and arranged for a cab. I had to take two! I even had a super sexy dress on to catch your eye when you opened your door and then your hick cousin showed up."

"Wait, how'd your phone start working?"

"I got it fixed in the town between here and Marfa, Alpine is it?"

"You weren't going to even call me?"

"I was going to call your wretched soul from the airport as I was leaving."

"Wow, scorched earth!"

"Scorched earth?"

"Yes, you were extremely mad!"

"Yes, I was. Still kind of mad at you, Steve."

"You didn't seem so mad a few minutes ago."

"*Ouais*, I tried not to reflect on it." She gave me the cutest, playful smile. She was so beautiful. She sighed and rested her head on my chest.

"Back mad again, though? Did you experience jealousy, perhaps?"

"I was mad with jealousy, *cheri*. But…you have a lifetime to make it up to me if you so choose."

"I do so choose, my love. Do you love me, too?"

"Well, if you can't figure that out from what we just shared, you must be a knucklehead, too, no?"

- The End -

A Moveable Marfa is a labor of love of over 13 years by a Texan who grew up in Houston and has served largely in public service all over the United States and Europe, including in his beloved West Texas. In his travels, CE Hunt has taken close note of how people seek and find fulfillment in their respective cultures.

A Moveable Marfa is his first novel length work in fiction.

CE Hunt would like to thank his brother, Carl, for his valuable editing and wonderful content suggestions. He helped make this book much better and it would likely not have come to completion without his generous help.

❖ ❖ ❖

Other published works by C.E. Hunt--

Big Thicket People: Larry Jene Fisher's Photographs of the Last Southern Frontier (University of Texas Press, 2008) *Houston Atlas of Biodiversity,* selected chapters (Texas A&M University Press, 2007)

Cover credit - Brise de Nuit by CE Hunt, 2005. All rights reserved.

Printed in Great Britain
by Amazon